Lieutenant Hotshot

The Story of an Invisible Child

Lieutenant Hotshot

The Story of an Invisible Child

Julia North

**LODESTONE
BOOKS**

Winchester, UK
Washington, USA

First published by Lodestone Books, 2016
Lodestone Books is an imprint of John Hunt Publishing Ltd., Laurel House, Station Approach,
Alresford, Hants, SO24 9JH, UK
office1@jhpbooks.net
www.johnhuntpublishing.com

For distributor details and how to order please visit the 'Ordering' section on our website.

Text copyright: Julia North 2015

ISBN: 978 1 78535 127 3
Library of Congress Control Number: 2015939703

A CIP catalogue record for this book is available from the British Library.

Design: Stuart Davies

Printed and bound by CPI Group (UK) Ltd, Croydon, CR0 4YY, UK

We operate a distinctive and ethical publishing philosophy in all
areas of our business, from our global network of authors to
production and worldwide distribution.

This story is dedicated to all the "Invisible Children" of the Joseph Kony's Lord's Resistance Army who have not been lucky enough to escape to tell their own story.

Chapter 1

My mind leaves the world of dreams with heaviness inside. It is many moons since I have dreamed of Thandi and that time. She was standing on the rubbish like a meerkat calling, "Modestse, my brother, where are you? Where are you?"

I shake the sadness from my head and try to open my eyes in the darkness. Aiee, what is this? Why can't I open them? I rush my hands up to my face. It feels fat and there is a wide bandage across my eyes. I try to pull it with my fingers but it's stuck fast. My heart beats hard against my ears and my breath comes quickly in and out. What has happened to me? I must see. I must. I tear at the bandage with both hands but it stays stuck. A sharp smell hits my nostrils and catches in my throat. I know that smell. It is the antiseptic we use to clean the wounds. I grunt and try to sit up but a strong pain burns like fire through my back. Who has done this? I shake my head and try to remember but my mind is mud.

"Mobuto...David..." I shout.

The air stays silent. What's happened to them? Why are they not here? My heart jumps. I have to find them. If Mobuto and David can't come I must escape by myself. They must be held prisoner somewhere else.

There are voices...footsteps. People are running. They shout something. They are coming to get me. I cry with pain as I roll to the side. I touch cold metal. Hands grip my shoulders. They push me back down. I scream and hit out with my fists but the hands are too strong. They hold me tight. I can't get away.

"It's okay; it's okay, son. Calm down," says a man's voice.

"Who's this?" I scream. "Where am I? What's happened?"

Cloud pictures rise in my mind. The government pigs attacked us. There were helicopters, too many helicopters. I see again the gunships with their dark bug eyes...they were shooting, killing; burning us with their flames. I groan. My ears fill again with their noise. My throat closes with the iron smell of blood. There was too much blood. Blood like a river flowing...

"Steady, son. It's okay," says the man's voice, "it's okay. Don't scream."

His voice pulls my mind away from these pain pictures. I feel his hand tight around my arm and then I feel a sharp prick. I try to pull my arm away but it grows heavy. My head begins to spin. My spirit is falling far away into blackness...

Chapter 2

I remember the bitter taste of the glue the first time Umama pushed it by my face. Aiee, I did not like it. I pulled back my head and screamed as its fumes ate at my throat and nostrils, but Umama she laughed and said, "There's no food, Modetse. You must sniff the glue." She knew that soon I would relax and let the glue fill my empty belly with its tricks. Thandi was still like a little frog on Umama's back and drank her milk for food and did not yet need the glue. Then Umama was no more. The glue had eaten her up and she joined the stars of the black African sky.

I opened my eyes as the pink rays of the morning sun peeped into our sewer pipe house. I pushed myself up and put my hands to my head. A big hide drum was beating inside. I needed my glue. I found the yellow glue bottle by the blanket and pushed it hard against my mouth and nose. I breathed deep. The glue did its trick quick and the drumming grew better. I tried to lick my lips but my tongue was dry like the stone.

I looked around for the water bucket and crawled past Thandi's sleeping cat body to fetch it. She snored softly with Enoch next to her and her little arm stretched over him. Enoch gave a snort and made a sucking noise with his lips. I smiled. He must be dreaming of the glue

I picked up the water bucket from the far end of the pipe and crawled back past them to the opening. I took big breaths of the cool air and sighed. The smell was okay and the rubbish trucks had not yet come. The dump was sleeping except for the roosters who crowed their many "Good mornings" to the dawn.

I pulled the bucket behind as I kicked through the rubbish to the big green water container that the Council brought every week. I kept my eyes alive in case any big boys or men were around. Some women stood near the container with their buckets on their heads. They chattered loud like chickens.

3

I waited until they left with their big backsides and then ran to the container. I put my fat tongue under the tap and drank from the cool water like a dog until my mouth was better. I put the bucket under the tap and waited while the singing water went plop, plop into it.

"Hey, you! Leave the water!"

I turned with big eyes and saw a man running at me from the side of the rubbish. He was waving a stick, which squealed through the air. "That is not for you, shithead," he shouted. "The Council only gives one tank. You leave it or I'll kill you."

I leaped up and pulled the bucket with its full water fast back up the rubbish away from the man. Many strong voices shouted now across the dump. Their glued throats were awake and crying for water and they did not want to share with boys. I clenched my jaw. I should have come before the sun had woken. I ran faster and faster through the squelching rubbish. The water splashed out with my big steps and I cursed myself for being a stupid.

"Give me that water, shithead!" shouted the man. "Give it now!"

My heart was hurting my ears; my chest was tight. Why would the man not leave me? His feet crunched through the rubbish behind me. I clenched my teeth and ran harder, closing my ears to his shouting. My heart was happy when I saw our cement pipe house. I held the bucket in front with both arms and ran fast with big steps down into its mouth. I dropped the bucket on the cold floor. My chest was too sore and I had to take the big breaths of air like a fish.

"Modetse," said Thandi, sitting up and wiping her eyes. "What's matter?"

She looked at me with big eyes while I waited for my breath to slow.

"Shh, have water," I said. "Your head will be crying for it."

Thandi frowned. I put the bucket by her and she put her head deep inside to lap at the water like a cat. She drank lots and then looked up and wiped her mouth with her little hand. I smiled down at her.

"Where you been?"

"To get the water for you, silly. Lie back down; the sun is just waking.

"Why you breathing fast?"

"Because a man was chasing me.

Thandi looked at me with worried eyes. "Did he beat you?"

I shook my head. "No, it's okay. Rest. When the sun is full up we'll go into the city."

"No dance," said Thandi pushing out her bottom lip, "my feet, they are still sore."

I pulled a sad face at her. "I know, Thandi, but we need the money for food and glue. I will beg too from the cars. We can do that first then maybe you just dance a bit. Okay."

Thandi kept her bottom lip pushed out but said nothing. She bent over to take some more water and then lay back down on the cardboard next to Enoch and pulled the grey blanket with its red cross over them. She looked at me with slit eyes and then closed them and pretended to be asleep quick. I smiled at her stubbornness. I got the drum and strings of red and yellow beads and seedpods ready in the supermarket packet and then lay down by her.

When we woke the sun was strong in the sky like the big copper coin. It beat hard on our hot heads as we climbed through the rubbish.

"Here, Enoch, you carry the packet," I said as I took Thandi's hand. "Hold your noses, the rubbish is strong now."

They pulled their noses up and pinched them with their fingers.

"Can I stay tonight again," said Enoch as we went with big steps through the stinking rubbish. He made his eyes like stars at me. "I want you to tell more story for me."

I laughed. "Okay; you try beg some money and then I'll make

sure I get glue for us."

"I will beg too good," said Enoch.

The rubbish was hot now and squelched in our toes like dirty mud. I looked at it with hawk eyes in case there was glass to cut us, or people's shit to hurt us with its germs. The sun made the smell very bad and my stomach jumped. I climbed faster, pulling Thandi with me. Loud rap music boom, boomed over the whole dump.

"Enoch, watch for the big boys. They could be drunk already," I said as my eyes walked fast across the rubbish.

"*Ndiyo*, Modetse," said Enoch. He made his eyes slits to hide the sun and looked from side to side across the dump as we climbed.

"Hey, Modetse, this side."

We stopped. My body went tight. I turned my head to see who was calling. A thin body with a front head like the blunt horn of the rhino was standing far from me. The tight left my body. Sipho, only one boy on the dump had a head like that.

"Hey, you going begging?" he said as he ran up to us. "Can I come?"

I nodded. "*Ndiyo*, come. You can help Enoch."

Enoch smiled at Sipho and gave him a high five.

"Where you sleep?" I said as Sipho walked along next to me.

"In the rubbish; I sniff too much glue," said Sipho, lifting his eyebrows and pulling a face.

I gave him a hard look and shook my head. "You are lucky the big boys didn't stab you. Why didn't you come sniff by our house? Enoch stayed by us."

He looked down and shrugged his shoulders.

"You were the stupid," I said.

He nodded but kept his eyes down. "*Najua*. There was fighting so I hid in the bush and then the glue made the sleep come fast."

"You must stay by us."

Sipho looked up at me. "Thank you, my brother. That will make me Mr. Happy."

"*Ndiyo*, no more bush sleep."

Sipho showed me his gap teeth and we walked fast to the main road by the shops. Two big boys were already by the cars. "Hey," they shouted as we got close. "You kids, fuck off. These are our lights. You come here and we'll beat you."

"Okay," I said. "We can go to the far lights."

We turned and ran towards the next big road down. There were some boys, maybe seven years old, by the lights. They looked at us with big eyes but said nothing. We came close and they moved away down the side of the wide road. Sipho lifted his eyebrows at me and smiled. They were too scared of us. There were many cars and white minibus taxis huffing and puffing like the angry bulls at the lights. I looked around.

"Okay," I said. "It's safe to beg. There's no police to beat us. You go that side, Sipho, and take Enoch. Thandi and me will stay here. Enoch, give me."

Enoch gave me my packet. Sipho took his arm and they ran towards the stopped cars on the other side.

"Please, sah, I'm hungry," I heard him shout. "Please, God bless you, sah. Please help us."

The driver looked sideways at him and then made down the window a small bit. He dropped some copper coins into Sipho's hands.

"Thank you, sah. God bless you," said Sipho, showing his gap teeth.

Enoch gave a big smile and then they ran to the next car.

I saw the silver BMW at the lights and ran to the driver. "Please, madam, can you help us?" I begged. "My sister she is so small and I must feed her. We have no food. Please, madam, help us."

I made my eyes big and sad and poked Thandi so that she made small crying noises. She looked up at the lady with honey eyes but the rich lady inside just stared hard front through her big brown sunglasses like there was no one there. I tapped on the window and saw her lips grow fat. When the light turned green she shot away from us like the bullet.

"Bitch," I shouted after her, showing my fist.

"Horrible bitch lady," shouted Thandi, pulling a face after her.

"Okay, we'll try another, my sister," I said, taking her small hand and waiting for the next car.

The light was red and a big white Chevrolet with a man and woman in it stopped next to us.

"Please, sah, we're too hungry," I said, cupping my hands together like a prayer. "We've no mother to help and no food. Please, sah, help us."

The man looked at Thandi who made her eyes big and her bottom lip shiver. He opened the window small and dropped the two silver shillings into my open hands. I smiled down at the silver and bowed my head to the man.

"Thank you, sah. Thank you, madam. God bless you."

The man and woman nodded but shot off with a 'vroom' as soon the light went green.

"Come, we must work quick and try some more cars, Thandi," I said. "Soon the police will come."

I pulled her up to a white taxi filled with many Africans and loud rap music that beat through my heart. The driver put his head from the window and shouted, "Move, you kids, before I beat you. We're sick of you begging by the lights."

Thandi made a cross face at the man and went to kick the tire with her foot. I pulled her back before the man could hit her and we ran to the Ford F20 behind.

"Careful." I frowned at her. "You can't fight the big men."

"Horrible bitch man," said Thandi.

I shook my head at her and smiled. "Ay, you are too naughty."

Thandi giggled.

"Please, sah, can you help us," I said to the African man

driving the Ford F20. He made like he was deaf and put his window up by our faces. We went to three cars behind the F20 but all the people made like they could not see us.

"We will make more if you dance," I said to Thandi after five more cars also made like we were the ghosts.

Thandi pulled a face and stamped the ground with her foot. I looked down. Her feet were still red from yesterday.

"I said no more dance," she said, and pulled a cross face.

My stomach felt bad. "I know, but we can go to the soft sand by the river, Thandi. That will be better for your feet."

Thandi kept her cross face but said nothing. I took her hand and went over the road.

"Hey, Sipho, Enoch," I called, "we're going riverside. See you later by the dump."

"Okay, go safe," shouted Sipho.

Enoch gave us a thumbs up sign as him and Sipho ran towards another car.

I put the red and yellow beads around Thandi's neck and tied the dried seedpods with their green and brown beads around her ankles. They made a good jingle, jingle as we walked towards the big lake of the city. Soon the water smell came to our noses and I saw the brown waves of the big water lake.

"It'll be better by the water, Thandi."

"I'm tired. Carry me," she said with a cross pout.

"You're five years now, Thandi. I can't always carry you anymore. Come, take my hand. We'll run and be there quick."

She stuck out her bottom lip but gave me her hand. I closed mine around hers and soon our feet touched the good wet sand by the fishing boats. The air was full with the fish and salt and it made my stomach hungry. The water made the small, slap, slap waves on the sand. I smiled at the nice sound. The fishermen looked at us with hard eyes and held tight to their nets. We kept away from the boats and walked with slow steps on the wet sand.

"See that feels better. The soft sand won't hurt your feet."

"I only dance a bit," said Thandi looking up at me with a firm face.

"*Ndiyo*," I said. Thandi pushed her feet in the soft sand. The pieces of sand stuck to them and made many diamonds in the sun. She gave a small giggle and I looked down at her and smiled.

"You stand here. I will beat the drum on this side," I said, patting her head, as soon as we found a good place near where the people walked. Lots of tourists were around today and many held big white ice-cream cones. They caught the falling ice cream with long, pink tongues. I walked my eyes across the crowd. There were some white faces and two well-dressed African women that were coming for us.

"There are rich ones coming," I said to Thandi. I began to beat the drum loud. Thandi moved forward with her hands on her hips and her head high.

"Good girl, Thandi. Dance your magic for the rich mothers."

The two African mothers walked towards us with their big pink and white tongues. They had on the smart blue and red dresses and the bright yellow and green headdresses. The talked loudly like hens. I pushed Thandi forward some more so that she was in their way and beat the drum harder and harder while her little feet danced fast to the rhythm, and the seedpods made the jangle, jangle song. Thandi looked up at them with big brown eyes like the honey and smiled. The red and yellow beads swung around her neck in time to the beats.

"Please, mothers, help us to buy the food," she said, holding out her hands.

One of the mothers stopped and gave her a sad look. She gave her ice cream to her friend to hold and pulled out a red leather purse from her black bag.

"Here have this," she said, giving Thandi a shilling.

The other mother handed the two ice cream cones to her and

then took her black purse to also put a shilling into Thandi's hands.

"Thank you, mothers," said Thandi in her sweetest voice giving them a smile like the angel.

I smiled inside at my clever sister. She knew just how to play these mothers. I winked at her when she turned to look at me. She winked back and then started her dance again as I beat away at the drums.

"The white girls will also be good pickings, Thandi," I said as her feet jumped again to the beat.

"Oh she's so cute," said one, as Thandi held up her smiling face and moved her little feet too fast, "but she should be in school, not dancing."

Thandi stretched out her arms and showed her palms to the women. They both pulled a sad face and put a shilling each in her upturned hands.

"God bless you, mams," said Thandi with a smile.

The girls looked over at me with a frown and then gave her another shilling. I made hate eyes at them.

"Why they looking bad at you?" said Thandi.

I shrugged. "Because you are not in the school; they are so stupid. Don't they know my dream is for the school?"

"Bitches," said Thandi, pulling a face.

"Yes, horrible bitches." I laughed and gave her a hug. "One day when I'm big I'll have lots of money and send you to the school."

"Yes, I want lots of money and I want to go the smart school," said Thandi with bright eyes. "I want the nice uniform."

"Okay. I will try hard," I said. "Now dance." I straightened my back and hit the drum with strong arms. "One more and then we can go. It is a good day today," I said, "we will eat well tonight."

Thandi nodded and then her feet drummed as she danced for more mothers and a fat man coming along by the water. The seedpods flew up and down and jangle, jangled through the air. The fat man looked at us over his pot stomach but pulled a face like we were dirt and kept walking. I stared with slit eyes at his back but kept hitting the drum as the mothers came past. They looked at Thandi with her big eyes and smiled and each gave her a shilling.

"Okay. It's enough. You are tired," I said. "Come, let me count the shillings."

We ran down towards the river and sat like frogs on the wet sand. Thandi pushed her sore feet into its cool wet as I counted our silver.

"We have nine shillings. Ay, this is too good," I said with a big smile. "I think we can even buy the KFC today."

"Yay," said Thandi clapping her hands together. "I love the KFC."

We ran through the hot dirt streets of the city to a side alley in the Arula district where I knew there was a KFC place. It was full of many people shouting and shoving to buy the chicken. I held tight to Thandi's hand and pushed past them to the counter.

"Two pieces chicken and chips," I shouted loud at the man.

He looked at me with narrow eyes. "Six shillings."

I put the shillings loud on the counter. He looked at them and then at me like I was the thief. I looked hard back. He turned and shouted our order and soon we were back outside the shop stuffing the spicy chicken and fat chips into our mouths.

The sun had fallen fast and the street was full of shadows. We moved to the door of the next door shop and squatted down in front of its grey steel door to eat.

"This is too good," I said smiling with a big chicken mouth at Thandi.

Thandi nodded and stuffed another fat chip into her mouth. She put up a shiny hand and gave me a high five. My stomach grew warm inside. It was good that she had a brother like me to feed her.

Sideways I saw some soldiers in camouflage standing across from us, looking hard at me. My heart jumped. Why were they looking at me like that? I put another chip in my mouth and chewed slower, keeping watch from the side of my eyes. Then one of the soldiers moved for us. He was very tall with strong arms and legs like the buffalo.

"Hey you," he shouted. "Come here."

He took a big step across the road. "I said, come here," he shouted.

My mind went round and round. Why was his voice so full of hate? Why?

"You," he shouted again, showing me to come with his fat finger. He took big soldier steps towards us. My heart jumped to my mouth.

"Modetse, what they want?" Thandi's eyes grew very big.

"I don't know. Just run," I said, dropping my KFC and grabbing her hand.

I pulled Thandi past the people on the pavement with the soldiers' hard boots coming, "doff, doff, doff" behind us. What did they want? Why did they look with such hate?

My heart blocked my ears with heavy beats. My chest grew tight as we ran and ran through the many people in the street.

"I'm scared…Modetse…I'm scared."

"Just run, Thandi, run. Don't stop," I panted. "We mustn't stop."

"Hey, you kids. What you doing?" said an old man as we pushed past him. "You're thiefs," he said. He tried to catch us.

"Leave us you fool. The soldiers are trying to take us."

"You're thiefs, that's why," he said. "You must catch them, sahs. You must beat them. They're dirty thiefs."

Other people on the pavement started shouting and tried to snatch at us. I went fast in and out by them and pulled Thandi screaming behind me. A strong hand grabbed my arm so hard that I thought it had said goodbye to my shoulder. Thandi's hand slipped away and I fell with a thud, thud, onto the road. The hand pushed me down by my chest. It was the fat soldier. I pushed against his big hand but it was no good. The fear ate my mind. My breath was stuck in my throat. Thandi stood frozen, looking with big eyes.

"Run, my sister, run," I shouted.

The soldier made a horrible smile. "Knock him out," he said.

Another soldier with coffee skin and a nose like an Arab bent over me and took out a cloth and brown bottle from his top pocket. I fought against the fat soldier's iron hands but it was no good. I heard the cork pop in my ear.

"Hmmm..." I screamed against his hand, which he clamped across my mouth. I kicked my feet and tried to hit him with my free arm. The fat soldier pushed my arm hard onto the pavement and a pain shot up my shoulder. I groaned. The Arab nose soldier put something from the bottle onto the cloth and pressed it hard against my nose and mouth. A fuzzy feeling like the glue came over me and a bitter smell blacked out my brain.

Chapter 3

My mind was still fuzzy as the fat soldier and the Arab one carried me away from Thandi. I could hear her screams following me. They threw me in the air and I landed hard with a clunk on cold metal. I could smell diesel. Then the roar of an engine started and the fat soldier climbed in next to me. The smell of his sweat was so strong in my nose that my stomach shot into my mouth. What truck was this? Who were these men who had caught me? Why?

"Aargh!" My back hit hard against the iron floor of the truck as it bounced along the road. The engine roared louder. I could smell the oil of the guns and my body prickled. Where were they taking me? Aiee, what would happen now to Thandi? Had they caught her also? My heart beat so loud that I had to gasp for air.

The truck hit a pothole and my teeth bit into my tongue. The iron taste of blood filled my mouth. I swallowed it down. It was good I was hurt. I wanted to taste my own blood. I was a stupid. I had let the catch me and I'd failed Thandi. If Umama were alive she would be cross that her only son had failed so bad. A sob grew up from deep in my belly and came out my mouth.

The fat soldier looked down at me with an ugly mouth. His round face was so close to mine that I could smell the stink of old beer on his breath. I looked away, scared by the hate I saw in his eyes. He snorted and shifted on his backside. I stared at his side by his thick arm. The long barrel of an AK47 gun lay across it. The silver of a machete smiled ugly from the other side of his belt. I shivered.

The soldier must have smelt my fear. His nostrils went wide and his lip went to the side.

"Ha, you are crying. We do not like crybabies," he said. "You must be a soldier boy now. If you cry we will cut you so that all your blood runs out. Here, drink," he commanded as he pushed a dirty water bottle to my mouth.

I tried to sit up to drink it but my arms were too weak. He yanked me up by my shoulder and I grasped the bottle and tried to hold it still enough to get a drink. He laughed and pressed it hard against my mouth, pulling my head back with one hand and pouring the water down my throat so I gulped and spluttered. I took big breaths through my nose and let the cool water wash away some of the hurting from my brain.

"Where's my sister, sah?" I whispered as soon as he took the bottle away.

"You have no sister," said the soldier. "She was too young for us. She'll find a new brother."

I let out a shaky sigh. At least they had not taken Thandi or chopped her with their evil machetes. But she was all alone on the rubbish. How would she live? I scrunched up my eyes to stop the tears. I must stay strong and get away. I must get back to her.

I looked around the truck. There was a boy with a blindfold and hair like a scarecrow sitting at the side. He wore ragged clothes and had many open sores on his legs, which stuck out from under his shorts like sticks. He sat tense and still with his fists clenched at his side. Another dark boy lay with his body curled like a question mark in front of him. He looked older than me and had muscles in his arms and legs. I wondered where they had caught him. He did not look like someone from the streets. His arms were curled around his head and I couldn't see his face. I turned as I heard a small cry from the other side. I saw the fat soldier grab a small boy from the corner and heard a crack as he hit the boy across the head.

"Stop sniveling," he shouted, as he threw him across the back of the truck. "We've not time for crying brats."

Enoch's face, full of fear, passed in front of me as he fell in a heap on the side. My heart dropped. It was very bad they had caught him. He was not strong enough. Enoch's thin face crumpled with the tears and I frowned at him.

"Enough," shouted the soldier.

Enoch curled himself into a ball to get away from his hate. The soldier kicked him hard in the stomach and he screamed.

I held my breath in my body and hoped he would not throw him onto the road, which bumped beneath us. There was a knock from the cab window and the fat soldier turned to look.

"Hey, Bilole, take a beer," said the Arab nose soldier as he slid open the window and gave the fat soldier a big can of Tusker.

I leaned forward and looked around the truck. Sipho was in the corner with his arms around his bent up legs. My stomach dropped some more. Now there was no one back with Thandi. Sipho looked at me. His eyes were full with the tears. Aiee, fear ate at me inside like a tiger. I needed glue to take it away. I began to shake and stared in front, trying to chase the fright thoughts from my head.

The boy with the funny hair groaned as the truck swung round the corner. I saw now that there were also girls in the truck. Three had blindfolds on but one stared forward with eyes like a scared buck. She had on a dirty torn pink dress with small flowers. They must also come from the streets.

The truck turned off the road and began bumping through the bush. The grass was high and yellow on each side of us and the air was thick with the sweet smell of the bush. My back bounced harder as we went down the small dongas and ditches. I clenched my teeth so that I would not cry out. Sipho gave a cry as his head hit the side and the fat soldier laughed. The soldiers talked loud and joked in Swahili.

Then the truck went onto a dirt road with tall wattle trees with white spotted trunks and many dark green leaves on each side. They blurred past and made me feel dizzy but their shade was cool. My head still throbbed from the poison they had given me which felt like bad glue in my brain. I closed my eyes to try and stop the vomit coming up.

All of a sudden the fat soldier stood up. He shot his AK47

high into the air. The thunder from his killer bullet made my ears dead. He turned and shouted something at us. I nodded at him with bug eyes and looked to see if the other boys could hear. Then my ears popped and the truck's tires squealed off the road and across into the veld. A big bump threw me forward so hard that my head hit the side of the truck. Then the tires screeched to a stop and I was flung back up.

We stopped in the veld with high yellow grass all around. I sat still and breathed hard. The fat soldier was talking to the Arab one through the cab window. I stared around. Far at the side of the veld stood many tall breadfruit trees full with deep green leaves and bunches of big yellow fruit that looked like the rugby balls. In front there were many long dark wood buildings. Soldiers stood around them. All wore the camouflage and carried AK 47s. One tall soldier with afro hair took some steps closer and aimed his AK47 at us. I held my breath and heard Sipho make a small cry. The soldier made to shoot us but no sound came out. I gave a big sigh and shivered inside. The soldier laughed at our fear then moved to join more groups of soldiers who were playing cards near the trees. They also had AK47s and had strings of bullets around their front. At their side sat sharp machetes.

I looked away from them to the far side. There was a high guard hut with an iron pole next to it and a dirt track. It lifted as a jeep full with soldiers came through. All around was a high wire fence with barbed wire on top. I followed it with my eyes until it disappeared behind the rows of breadfruit trees. It would tear to pieces anyone who tried to climb it.

My heart beat heavy in my head and my nostrils burned. How would I ever escape? How would I ever get back to Thandi? I felt empty without her; like someone had cut my arms from my body, but these soldiers would shoot me with their devil bullets if I tried to run. I would have to think and be clever before I could find a way to get back.

The boy with the wild hair had his blindfold off now and the other dark boy was sitting up straight. They both looked out with eyes like trapped nyala and sour faces.

I heard a soldier shout to the side of us. I looked over and saw many young boys like us with a soldier in front of them. The boys were trying to stand like spears but the big grey stones in their hands were pulling them down. The soldier man walked up to one and hit him across the head so hard that the boy fell down and the sound cracked across the air. The soldier kicked him. My stomach felt sick and I looked away.

On the other side of the field sat more wooden towers with soldiers on top and more of the fence with its evil teeth. Fear ate into me. I held my mouth tight so that I would not scream. I would never get out of this place. All over, like a thousand hungry lions, eyes were watching, just waiting for me to try so that they could pounce and kill me.

I began to shake and big drops of sweat covered my face. I would never see Thandi again. I had failed to take care of her. I began to shake as the truth of her alone on the dump grew real in my mind. "No, I must not think like that," I told myself in my head. "I must stay strong and try and find a way back to her."

Suddenly the fat soldier stood up and threw open the back of the truck with a loud clank. My body jerked as he pulled me up and pushed me out onto the hard ground. I stumbled to the side of the truck as the soldiers outside turned to look at me with the cold eyes. My legs shook under me and my brain screamed. I wished Umama could come back to help me.

Someone was pushed into me and I turned to see Enoch. He looked up at me with fear eyes full with the tears. His bottom lip shook. I frowned at him and pulled a face.

"Stay strong, Enoch," I whispered.

Another boy was pushed out from the back. I had not seen him before in the truck. He was more big than me and his skin was like coffee; his eyes were wise and big with long cow lashes.

He saw me staring and whispered, "I am David; keep your eyes front."

"I am Modetse," I whispered back. His voice was low and had kindness in it. It helped my fear.

The boy David nodded and gave Enoch a small smile while he looked at him with sad eyes. Enoch's mouth was trembling and he just dribbled. He was too lost in his fear to even smile back.

"Be strong," I whispered to him. "Stay by me." I looked at him and inside my stomach felt sick. How could I protect him here?

Shh," said David. "They are coming."

I saw the fat solider move towards us. He had Sipho in front and was sticking his back with the AK47. Sipho kept his head looking down and walked forward with quick steps. His legs were shaking too much.

"Get into a line now," he shouted at all of us as he pushed Sipho into me. I moved up and so did the boy David so Sipho could join in the line. "Go. Line up by those trees near the bush. Move!"

The Arab one jumped from the cab of the truck and marched up to the fat solider as we began to move. He held his AK47 high in the air and his machete glinted at his side. He had the frightened girls in front of him. I looked at the machete. I'd heard many bad stories about them and I shivered. There was an expensive gold watch on his arm. He took some sunglasses with gold frames from his top pocket and put them on. He walked like he was a film star. I could see from his proud walk that he would feel nothing to kill.

"Move faster to the trees fast you fucking pieces of shit," he shouted at all of us. "You lot. Move to that side," he shouted as he pushed the girls to the side of us. "I want you on that side of the trees, now!"

The girls made squeaking sounds with their eyes full of tears and ran towards the side of the breadfruit trees.

The Arab soldier watched them go and then turned and

pointed his AK47 at us. We broke into a run. I ran behind the boy David with Enoch in front. Sipho panted behind me. The air grew thick with my panic.

"Stand to attention," shouted the Arab solider as we reached the trees.

We turned to face him and made a long line with straight backs. The air was hot and heavy and I could smell the damp bush around us mixed with the sweet smell of our sweat.

I don't know how for long we stood like that by the trees. My spirit felt like it was out of my body and I think time had stopped to move. I kept my eyes hard to the front but had to blink often because they were too dry. Then a tall man came out of one of the wood huts, which had soldiers in front. He came towards us with big steps like a giraffe. On his head was a green beret with five gold stars and his eyes were covered with mirror sunglasses with gold frames. He was very big with smooth brown skin. He looked like power. I could see his muscles under his uniform as he walked. It was not like that of the other soldiers. It was light brown and very smart with no creases. I thought he must be the main man because all the soldiers jumped and gave him the salute. Even our fat soldier looked frightened of this man.

"You've been quick," said the man.

"Thank you, General," said the fat soldier holding his hand to his head. "We've six boys and four girls."

The General looked at us with his mirror eyes. His wore a smart moustache above his fat lips and smelt of rich polish and strong spice. He looked at the fat solider who flinched and stood straighter in his salute. I was happy to see him feeling fear but it made me even more afraid of this General.

The General walked with strong steps in front of us. I kept my eyes down but my body shook as he stared at us with his mirror eyes. Aiee, this man had too much power. It stayed in the air around him and made me shiver bad inside. I wished I could see his eyes so I could know what he was thinking.

He looked over at the girls who stood shivering with their heads down in front of the trees. "Take the girls to the training camp," he shouted at the fat soldier.

"Yes, General," said the fat soldier with a big salute.

I watched as he marched the girls away. They ran with shaking bodies before him back across the field.

The General turned back to us. He came closer with his big steps and stopped in front of us. He took off his glinting sunglasses and looked close at us. His eyes were cold like the shark. I kept my breath inside. My heart fought against my ears. The General moved up our line and looked us up and down. I shivered and wished he had kept the glasses on. My eyes fell to the ground as his shiny black boots stopped in front of me and my hands grew wet. Aiee, I could feel his eyes eating into me. He was so close I could smell the peppermint on his breath. My heart was stuck in my throat. I stared so hard at the ground my eyes burned. I must not look at him. It would be rude and he would surely kill me. I kept my breath inside until he moved away. He had a very bad heart this man. I could feel it. I did not know if he would tell the soldiers to kill us or beat us for fun.

I would not care if I died. I had seen many dead people on the dump. They were happy in their sleep with no worries for food or drugs. It would not be so bad. But if you had a sister who needed you then you could not die. Pictures of Thandi screaming and crying for me hurt my mind. I had to stay strong. I had to get back to her.

"Nkunda, get them to the blockhouse," said the General to the Arab soldier.

I let out a small sigh. He was not going to kill us yet. Nkunda pushed us into a line with his AK47. The sharp, cold steel of its bayonet stung my back. He pressed it harder so that it made me jump and then he laughed low. The boy David was in front of me and I hoped Sipho and Enoch were behind me. My stomach was sick and I breathed in a big gulp of air so that I would not be sick,

We came to a long wooden building and Nkunda stopped and shouted, "Get inside!"

We rushed inside. It was dark inside after the sharp sun and smelt of creosote. I stood still for a while until I could see better. There were many beds. I followed David to the end of the hut. He stopped by the one bed and I stopped by the other. I looked at the bed. There was a camouflage uniform lying on top of the grey blanket. There was a pillow with an old white cover. Then I heard a noise and turned to look back at the door. A great man with a round stomach and stubble beard was standing in the doorway. He wore polished brown army boots and had a smart dark green camouflage uniform with the pants tucked into the boots. The sleeves of his shirt were rolled and I could see his strong arms. On his head was a dark green beret, which sat sideways with a three silver stars in front, showing he was an officer man.

He narrowed his eyes and come towards us with heavy steps on the wood floor. I could see the muscles in his arms and legs move. He was too strong this one. In his hand was a thick brown stick. He hit the stick on the iron end of one of the beds and laughed low as we all jumped at the big clang, clang noise.

"New recruits, Nkunda. I hope they are good ones and not like the last."

His voice was like the thunder and my stomach jumped.

Nkunda laughed like he knew a secret and said, "We shall see."

"So, you are soldier boys now," he said as he marched up and down between the iron beds and hit them some more with his stick. "Well, are you happy? All little boys want to be soldiers don't they? Come, smile at me and say "Yes, sah" otherwise I will hit you," he suddenly roared.

My shoulders jumped at his voice and I shouted out, "Yes, sah," with the others.

"Yes, sah." He copied our voices and then shouted, "Fucking

pieces of shit; now salute. Like this! Click your heels together. Now!"

My breath stayed in my throat as I copied his salute. Enoch's eyes were so wide I thought they would pop from his face but he touched his heels together and hit his forehead with his hand.

The soldier man gave a deep belly laugh. "Hmm, not bad," he said. "Maybe I will keep you. I am your Commander and you will do whatever I tell you. My name is Commander Mobuto. I'll train you well but if you let me down I will kill you. Do you hear?"

"Yes, sah," we shouted, and my voice shook.

Commander Mobuto looked down at us and sneered. "Soon you will be good little killers who'll do good work for the L.R.A. Do you know how lucky you are to be in the God Army; hey, do you? Do you?

"Yes, sah," we shouted again.

A shivering snake moved up my spine as I saw the teeth around his neck. They were not the teeth of the animals. He gave a smile and I saw a flash of gold in his dark mouth. He was a trophy man this one with a bad spirit. I must be careful. He would be a hungry crocodile who would eat me up with one snap of his jaws. I was glad they had not caught Thandi. He would have felt nothing to kill a little girl. It was better that it was just me they had caught, but how would I ever escape this man?

"Now, get on these uniforms but go wash first in the showers out back. You are dirty street children who stink and steal. You are stupid thiefs and drug addicts. We will beat you until you are men. You will learn to kill and taste the blood and fire. You are soldiers now. It is time to grow up. Move! I want you clean and in those uniforms in ten minutes. If you're late I will beat you until you scream.

I ran behind the other boys to the showers. They were cold like knives but the water helped to clear the poison from my head. Nobody talked or looked at each other. I threw my head back and let the cold water fall into my throat and rubbed myself clean with the rough red soap until my body stung.

Then I ran behind David with Sipho, and Enoch behind, back to the hut. The boy with the hair like a scarecrow was already inside and putting on his uniform. The dark one pushed past me and grabbed his. I went to the bed I had stood in front of and took the folded uniform and quickly put it on. It was too big but it felt stiff and strong and I liked the feel on my skin. There were rubber sandals on the floor made from the old tires. I tied them tight on my feet. They felt soft like air and made me taller. The clothes made me feel funny inside. They did not look like me.

I looked over to Enoch. His uniform was so big it looked like he was falling out of it.

"Roll up the legs and arms, Enoch," I said.

He looked at me with frightened eyes and rolled up the ends. Then he put on the big rubber sandals. He looked stupid but the boy David was tall and the uniform fitted him good. He gave me a smile but I could see the fear in his eyes. I nodded and looked at Sipho.

He had also rolled up his trousers like Enoch. I showed him a thumbs up sign.

"Hey," said David to the other two boys. "I am David. This is Modetse and Sipho."

"And Enoch," I said.

The boy with the mad hair looked at us. "I am Richard," he said.

"Jabu," said the dark boy without a smile.

"Where you from?" asked David but before they could answer heavy footsteps came to the door and we all jumped to attention and showed the salute.

Commander Mobuto was back with a bad smile on his face.

Chapter 4

"Don't tear the bandage. It's okay. You're safe," says a woman's voice. "My name is Nurse Sophie. Don't be scared."

"My eyes," I wail. "My eyes!"

"It's okay. It's not serious they're just badly swollen. You're not blind."

I let out a big sigh. My arms go soft and fall back by my side.

"You are a lucky boy," goes on the woman. "We removed a bullet from your back but you're going to be okay."

Who is she? Why is she helping me? I can feel that my back is numb and sore. I've seen the people with the broken backs. They can't walk or move. I can't sit up with the pain; fear jumps through my body. I can't move! I push down on my toes and feel them twitch. I try again and sigh with relief. No, it's okay. My back must not be broken.

"Where's my AK? Who are you?" I shout against my blindfold. "Take this thing off me. I need to see."

"Shh, it's okay," she says, and takes my hand. I yank it away and hear footsteps approach. "Here's Dr. Zuma."

I hear a deep man's voice. "You don't need a weapon here. Just relax. Lie back down, it's okay," he says, and I feel strong hands against my chest. I tense but do as he says. I'm too weak to fight right now.

"You're in a Mission hospital. We're going to help you."

"You've made me a prisoner. You are enemy," I shout.

"No, you're not a prisoner and there's no enemy here. It's okay. Can you remember your name?"

"I am Lieutenant Hotshot."

"I see. Can you not remember your other name?" says Dr. Zuma. "The one your family gave you?

I feel a deep pain stab through my belly. He has made David march into my mind. I catch my breath and pull away. I throw

26

back my head with an open mouth and groan. I can smell the soil of the camp again. I can smell the blood in its red dirt. David is dead. The bullets ate his chest and sprayed his heart blood across the camp. David my brother is dead. He cannot be here now. He will never come again.

I moan and retch and retch as the picture of his broken body fills my head and then

I remember Mobuto. He was on his side like a wounded hippo...his stomach was falling out...long pink snakes of his stomach were lying on the ground. Everywhere was blood, so much blood...blood covering me, drowning me...

A thousand ants have walked across my body. My forehead is wet and I feel sick. "No..." I say. "No...this cannot be true. Not my father too. Not my Commander."

But my mind shows me Mobuto trying to put his stomach back inside...he was screaming...his fat face was full of fear and then he was gone. Bilole had come panting up to me, his big stomach heaving and his eyes wide. His fear had hit into me and I'd screamed, "They have killed our Commander, Bilole. They have killed him."

"We are finished, Hotshot," he said. His arms lay limp by his side. His AK had fallen to the dirt.

I looked up at him with water eyes. "Why have the spirits failed us, Bilole? Why?"

Bilole shrugged his shoulders and his bottom lip trembled. His eyes filled with water. I stared at him as my heart hit hard against my ears. My chest grew tight. There was a deep pain in my belly. What was this? Bilole did not cry. I had never seen him cry. He was a tough soldier, a Captain; how could he cry? If he was crying then we were dead meat. I swallowed the bitter liquid, which had come into my mouth, and gazed around our camp. Fierce orange flames and black smoke were everywhere. The flames crackled high into the air and ate through our buildings; they snaked around the fences, they turned our guard towers black and burned our soldiers like the firewood. The smoke came for me. It stung my eyes with red tears and tried to choke the breath from my body.

"No..." I shout, squirming in the bed. "No, I have no family...they are dead, my L.R.A. family is dead! They are dead."

Before I can stop them the sobs come over me and I cry out, "I want David; I want Mobuto...please bring them back to me; bring them back. I need their help to find my sister. I am an officer. They would help me, please..."

As my body sobs up and down with my loss, the anger rises in my belly. I hate this doctor. He has made me remember. He has made me cry and made me be weak.

"Fuck you," I shout. "Who are you? Fuck you."

"It's okay," says Dr. Zuma holding me down. "We'll help you. Nurse get me a sedative."

He takes hold of my arm and I try and pull away but then feel something sharp and my mind slowly calms. The doctor pulls the cover up under my chin. I take a deep breath as my sobs stop like the car with no petrol. I don't know where I am or who has caught me. If it's the enemy doctor he's being too nice to me. Why's he doing this? Maybe they want to keep me alive so they can try and make me talk? I'll never betray the L.R.A. Never. I must survive this and get back and find Thandi. I must not let them defeat me. I am Lieutenant Hotshot. I must get out. My eyelids are beginning to grow heavy as these thoughts run through my mind.

"It is best to sleep now," says Dr. Zuma. "We'll remove the bandages tomorrow and then you'll feel better. I know it's not nice when you can't see."

His voice is deep and calming. It's a long time since I've heard a voice with such kindness. I'm confused. If he's the enemy doctor he won't sound like this. Who is he?

"It's not your fault, my child," he goes on. "Just rest now. It'll be better tomorrow."

I jerk awake at his words. "I am not a child; I am fourteen years," I shout. "What the fuck are you talking about? What fault? Of course being shot isn't my fault. It's the dirty enemy pig's fault. How stupid are you?"

I sink down deeper into the bed. I just want to be back at our camp. I want to be back with David and Mobuto and my AK47 and make my plans to find Thandi. I am Lieutenant Hotshot. I will not be weak. "I'll take revenge for you," I silently swear to the spirits of Mobuto and David. "Don't worry, my brother and my father. I'll get them back and then I will find my Thandi."

My spirit grows hard with hate. I'll rest now like this doctor says. I'll use him to help me get better and then soon I'll make the enemy bleed like he's never done before. I'll make rivers and rivers of their blood; so much that the whole land will be red and stinking. I'm not finished yet! I'll get revenge for you, my family.

Chapter 5

Fierce rivers of blood filled with thousands and thousands of hands and feet flow towards me. The hands rise up from the red waves and chase after me like the devil crabs. I scream and run and run but they are too fast and keep coming closer and closer. They hold machetes now and are cutting me and screaming out their hate. The feet rise up and kick me in my head until my head becomes soft with my brains and my blood. They want revenge. They won't stop until I am dead.

"No, leave me alone! You are the hands that help the enemy pig. You are the feet who work for the enemy. I am Lieutenant Hotshot. You can't kill me!"

I scream and scream but still they keep on cutting and kicking until my broken body begins to crack open allowing my spirit to flee down into the darkness.

"It's okay. Wake up, wake up. It's okay."

The voice breaks through my screams and I shudder awake. It is the nurse's voice and she's shaking me. I smell the antiseptic smell. I blindly feel around myself. I'm wet with sweat.

"You've had a nightmare," she says, and I feel stupid now for my weakness. "We're taking off the bandages this morning. That'll make it much better for you."

I feel her hands on my eyes. The bandage moves against my eyes. I can feel the light on my eyelids, but they are too fat to open properly.

"Dab them," says a deep male voice.

That doctor is back. I feel soft fingers on my lids. I push them slow open. Small light sneaks into my eyes. Everything is like it is underwater. I think there are hands over me. Water washes through my eyes. I can see the white cloth of the nurse and doctor now. I blink. The doctor is leaning over me. He is tall and thin and wears a long white coat, which is open. I see some lines of blood on the side of the coat and glare up at him. I don't know whose blood that is but if he tries to touch my blood I will kill him. He has brown trousers and a blue shirt, which is open by his throat. There is no blood on them but they look crumpled like he has slept in them. There is no sign belonging to the enemy army on him. A silver thing with two black rubber straps hangs around his neck. I stare hard at it. There are no sharp ends; he cannot hurt me with it. He fiddles with a small torch and I look at his hands. They are smooth and one finger has a gold ring on. He puts the light on the torch and bends closer over me. I look through my sore eyes at his face. It is brown like coffee with the milk in. He has wrinkles across his forehead so is not a young one and wears smart glasses with silver frames. His brown eyes behind the glasses look big at me. His hair has bits of grey mixed with the black like peppercorns. He must be at least forty years.

"I'm just going to shine this in your eyes to see how they react. Ah good, they're working well. You're lucky. There's a bit of swelling but no real damage. We need to roll you over now," he says, and gives me a wide smile showing good teeth. He turns to the nurse and nods.

"Okay, we're going to roll you now. Don't worry it shouldn't hurt too much," says Nurse Sophie.

I turn and look at her. She is darker than the doctor and is small and skinny with a straight body and small head with a pointy nose and round eyes like an owl. She looks like she is old like thirty years and wears a smart white uniform with a red cross in front. She hides her hair with a white scarf over her head. I don't want her to touch me with her thin hands but she suddenly grabs my side and says, "One, two, three."

I feel cold air rush in behind me as they push my body over. I clench my jaw as the pain shoots through my back. I wish I could stop them touching me but I'm too weak and my legs feel funny. I grunt and fill my mind with hate to take away the pain. I know that I'll have to let them make me better. Then I'll kill them. I'll find the camp and my squadron and be the new leader now that Mobuto's dead. A small fire deep inside me still burns with the hope that Thandi will not be dead. I close my eyes and see again her small face with her bottom lip out. She is strong my sister. I will not believe she is dead until I see her body. I must get better and look for her. I will be Commander Hotshot. I will not need to ask to leave the camp for a short while. I can take my squadron and find her. I will go back to the dump. Soon I will do this.

"Aargh..." I cry as the pain grows worse and shoots across my back like the fierce bush fire.

"Sorry, I just need Nurse to take off the dressing," says the doctor. "I'm going to have to press down a bit. It may hurt."

I feel his hands on my back and cry again as the pain grows fiercer.

"Sorry, son. It's nearly over." He pushes my back some more and then turns the nurse.

"It's healing well," he says. "Put on a new bandage and we'll check it again in a week. I think you must try and get him to take a few assisted steps later."

"Yes, Doctor."

"Good. Now, who's next?"

They roll me back down and I turn my head and see there are other beds with bodies in the room. I watch as they move to the next bed. A boy is lying there with a blood soaked bandage around his chest. I hear the doctor mumble and see him shake his head.

"We'll need to get him back to theatre. It doesn't look good. Wheel him down there and I'll be along as soon as we finish here."

The nurse nods and makes quick steps to fetch a trolley. The doctor and she put the boy on the trolley and the nurse wheels him back past me to some doors at the end of the ward. I look to the other side. There are more beds with humped bodies like white ant hills. They are silent. Maybe they are all dead and it's only me that's alive? Maybe this doctor and nurse have killed them and it's my turn next? I shiver. Why are they still here if they are dead? They must be our boys. What have they done to them? Aiee, I must get out of here before they kill me.

I try to sit up against the pain and then I see the sheets move on the bed near the window. I hear a moan. Who is it? Maybe it is the boys from my squadron?

"Joshua...Bongi...?" I say. There is no answer, only a moan. Whoever it is they are in big pain.

The nurse comes back in. She goes over to him.

"It's okay," she says. "We're going to give you a painkiller. It'll be okay."

I see her take out a long needle and push it into the boy's arm. He moans and jerks and then soon is still again. I lie frozen. They can kill us all with their drugs and there is nothing we can do. I have to keep my mind clear. I have to stay alert. I can't show my pain and let them put this needle in my arm.

I narrow my eyes and watch them close through my puffy lids. The doctor is visiting the other beds. The nurse joins him and they and whisper to each other as they stop by each bed. I see two more boys get the needle while two more get put onto trolleys where they lie waiting with their faces covered. I think they must be dead already. The doctor and nurse finish looking at the last bed and then go back and wheel the trolleys out by the same doors. I hear the doors swing closed behind them. Everything is quiet except for a soft whooshing sound. I look up. The blades of a fan on the ceiling spin round sending cool air onto us. I lie and watch them go round and round. My mind too is spinning. Who are these people? Why are they helping me? What will they do with me when I'm better? I close my heavy lids. My body wants to sleep but I'm too scared the bloody hands will be back to attack me. I wish I was back at our camp.

Chapter 6

Commander Mobuto stood in front of us with his arms on his hips and his legs apart. He stared at us in silence and tapped his leg with his thick stick. I kept my eyes down and prayed he would not get angry with me.

"Outside – March," he shouted. "The General will inspect you."

My skin prickled at the name. We marched to the door and Mobuto kicked us with his shiny boots as we went out. We tried to march like soldiers, lifting our knees high in the air like gazelles. I saw the boy Richard trying to keep his back straight and look brave but I could see the fear in his eyes. His fear helped me feel stronger.

I pushed my head back and kept my eyes stiff to the front. My body was shivering inside. I knew I needed the glue. I turned to see Sipho and Enoch. Their legs were shaking. My stomach grew tight. Aiee, how would we survive in this place?

We followed Commander Mobuto to the end of the field and stopped. He shoved us into a line with his AK.

"Attention!" he shouted.

I kept my eyes staring to the front and wide open so they wouldn't betray my fear. Enoch was next to me and I could feel his body trembling. I turned to him and frowned but he didn't look back. My heart dropped. These soldiers were like dogs with sharp teeth that would attack when they smelt our fear. We must hide it.

"Right, now move there in a straight line; one behind the other. Go!" shouted Commander Mobuto. We shuffled into a straight line and we marched to the row of breadfruit trees along the side of the field where he pointed. The copper sun was high in the sky now and the hot rays beat onto my head. My body was wet under the new uniform. I gave a sigh when we got to the shade of the trees. At least he hadn't made us stand in the fierce sun.

"I said a straight line!" shouted Commander Mobuto. "That is not straight."

He walked in front of us and hit our legs with his brown stick until we were all very stiff next to each other.

He looked at us with narrow eyes and gave a snort. "You stay like that and don't move. You hear me!" he shouted.

We saluted and he snorted again and went over to join some other soldiers who were sitting on big logs among the trees. We stood like sticks, all looking straight in front. I could see that the soldiers playing the cards. I heard the slap of the card onto the tree trunk table they had made. It reminded me of the dump and the big men who sat by the cars with their rap music and played cards, shouting and fighting for the money. I felt a pain in my chest. Thandi was still at the dump. Please God, let her be all right. I clenched my jaw. I had to stay strong for her. I must not look weak before these men. I looked back over at the soldiers. They looked like they had forgotten us standing there. Mobuto sat on one of the logs and tapped the ground with his big boot to the rap music. He slapped down his cards and then laughed loud, hitting his leg with his hand.

"I've won," he said. "Pay, you fuckers, pay."

"Shit," said one of the other soldiers while the rest pulled faces. They all pulled out some notes and put them on the tree trunk. Mobuto grabbed them and stuffed them in his pocket. The soldier dealt some more cards.

"So, Commander Mobuto, you have found some new boys for us," he said, looking over at us with narrow eyes.

"Of course," said Mobuto. He pushed out his big chest like a giant rooster.

"You sure you haven't caught little goat boys," said the soldier.

Mobuto pulled a face. "They're city boys, not villagers. We

can train them good."

"Good. We don't want the fucking goat boys. City boys, they are like hyenas. They know how to be bad."

Mobuto grinned showing his gold tooth. "Yes, my friend, but the goat boys are good hunting."

All four of the soldiers laughed with big mouths and yellow teeth. They sounded like the hyena they talked of and I shivered inside. Enoch's lip had started to shake. Sipho had bug eyes and so did the boy Richard. We all stood straight trying to hide our fear in our silence.

Suddenly the General came from across the field with big strides. Mobuto and the soldiers jumped up from their cards and stood stiff in the salute. One of the soldiers jumped over to the radio and switched off the rap. Their laughs were gone. They marched into a line next to us with their AK47s on their shoulders.

My heart beat hard in my ears and my hands grew wet as the General and his power smell came closer.

"Attention," shouted Commander Mobuto. "Salute, you fucking pieces of shit, or the General will cut off your balls and tie them round your necks. The General will see if you are good enough to join the L.R.A."

My mind showed me a horrible picture of my balls being tied around my neck. My stomach jumped and I swallowed hard. I threw my hand up to my head and stood stiff as a spear.

"At ease, Commander," said the General with a sideways smile.

Mobuto dropped his hand and followed behind the General as he walked in front of us. He stopped and stood proud with his head high and his power legs apart and then looked at us one by one with his mirror eyes. My breath stuck in my throat.

"So, these are the new recruits?"

"Yes, General. I have these six. They look strong."

"Where did you get them?"

"In the city, General."

"Hmm," said the General. "Stand straight and keep your eyes to the front," he shouted suddenly to us.

We pushed our backs straighter and my heart jumped. My whole body was stretched to the sky and my eyes stared so hard in front they hurt. Inside my mind jumped around with the fear. My eyes blurred and I blinked them quick and swallowed hard.

The General marched up and down our line with slow steps. He stopped in front of each of us and took off his mirror glasses. He looked hard with his shark eyes. I held my breath. I knew he must be testing us. He wanted to see if we would break. I had to look strong otherwise he would kill me. "I am strong, I am strong," I said over and over in my head so that he would not read my fear.

He stopped in front of Enoch and stared at his shaking body. Enoch gave a small cry and I saw from the side of my eyes that he was crying.

"We have a mouse," said the General. "Kill him."

Enoch screamed and my stomach dropped. I could smell his fear as Mobuto grabbed his arms and pulled him away. His thin legs dragged kicking behind him.

"Help...help me," he screamed. "Modetse, help me..."

I shook as I heard him shout my name and kept my eyes down and my face firm. His scream stayed like a knife in my brain. I swallowed hard. Aiee, Enoch was dead meat but I could not help him. Poor Enoch! My spirit felt like it had left my body. I could not believe they were going to kill Enoch. Aiee, why was this happening? Enoch's screams grew louder. I stared straight as I tried to block them from my ears.

I jerked. The General was looking at me now. What was he thinking? Was he reading my fear? Had he heard Enoch shout my name? Did he want to kill me next? I held my breath and my heart hurt my ears with its beats. I could not die. I had to stay strong for Thandi. I was Umama's only son. I could not die. I had to look after Thandi. I promised Umama I would. I must not let the General see me weak so he could kill me. I lifted my head and made my back like the spear. I pushed back my knees more so they were stiff to hide the shaking inside my legs. The General still stared hard at me.

Then he gave a loud sniff and turned as the "Dada-dada-dada" of the AK47 bullets shouted at us from the trees. I pushed the picture of the bullets tearing into Enoch from my brain. I did not want to see his broken, bloody body and his brains out from his head. I'd heard of these AK47 bullets and how they tear you like a pack of hungry wild dogs. The soldiers laughed at the sound and then looked back at us with evil smiles.

Commander Mobuto came back from the trees with a big grin. His gold tooth glinted at us. The General gave him a nod.

"He broke well, General. The vultures will eat good tonight."

"Make sure these five hold," said the General looking back at us. "If not kill them too. Take them to the training ground."

Mobuto saluted and turned to us. "Follow me, you pieces of shit, and keep up. I've had some blood, but I want more. Any failure and I will drink your blood too."

Chapter 7

Commander Mobuto led us to another field. "See those grey stones," he shouted. "Pick them up and run around the field. Now! Go! One two, one two, lift your knees."

We ran over to some big grey rocks lying on the field. I bent over and snatched one of them and grunted as I lifted it. My arms pained and my knees bent. I took a big breath and held it in.

"Right, run. Drop the stones and you're dead," said Mobuto.

He stood tall with his legs apart and hit the side of his big leg with his stick. David began to run and I ran behind him. Sipho grunted behind me. As we went round the field I looked back and saw Richard and Jabu running with fierce faces and open mouths behind Sipho.

"Faster, you stupid soldier boys. How will you crawl through the bush and kill our enemy at the village if you're so slow? Huh? Faster! Faster!" shouted Commander Mobuto.

Bilole had come to the field with another small boy. He pushed him towards the stones and the boy picked one up and nearly fell over.

I looked to the front and breathed hard. The stone was digging into my shoulders now and the ground was moving in front of my eyes. I swallowed hard. My arms ached too much but I knew I mustn't let them drop. I must not be dead like the cold grey stones. I must get back to Thandi. I focused my mind and counted in my head. "One two, one two, one two," I chased the other thoughts from my head. "One, two, one two." The stone felt better as my spirit became lost in the counting.

I heard a crash behind me. My stomach turned. I prayed it was not David or Sipho. I looked back as I went around the curve of the field. Richard was bent over and making slow steps forward but he still had his stone by his stomach. Jabu looked stronger. His face was firm and his small eyes looked fierce to the front with his knuckles white around the stone. It was the new boy that Bilole had brought. I looked more closely at him. He looked like only ten years and was small and dark with a round face and fearful white eyes. He must be a weak country boy and the stones were too heavy for him. He had dropped his and was quivering with big eyes. Aiee, he looked too scared. Mobuto would not be happy. I kept running and moved my eyes to the front, but from the side I saw Mobuto grin. His big crocodile teeth with their glinting gold were ready to eat and I swallowed down the sick that came into my throat. He was going for the kill and wanted us to drop the stones so he could crush us with his fat fists.

I heard a loud crack and the new boy screamed. I could see the picture in my head of him lying down with blood coming from his head like Enoch. I kept my face firm to the front and swallowed again. I ran harder and harder, holding my stone so tight I thought my hands would break.

"Boys who drop my stones are dead boys," shouted Mobuto, hitting his trouser leg with his stick. He moved around in the middle watching each of us. "You must be tough in the L.R.A. We want only the boys who are strong like the ox. We don't want the fucking weak shit."

He began to jog behind us as we ran. I felt a stinging pain across my legs. Aiee, it was too sore but I didn't cry out as Mobuto came past me with his stick. He moved over to David and whacked him hard across the back of his legs. I kept my eyes looking straight in front and bit down on my lip. David kept running and did not cry out. I was glad. He must be strong inside too.

Mobuto marched back to the middle of the field. Bilole joined him and they watched us as we ran around.

"You must be good killer soldiers otherwise we'll use you for our targets" shouted Mobuto pointing his AK at us.

"Yes, ha, ha, ha. Good targets, you fucking weak pieces of shit," said Bilole.

Mobuto turned to him and gave the big sneer. "Maybe we'll blow their brains out of their stupid dumb heads, hey, Bilole? Come drop some more," he said, turning back to us. "I want more blood. Drop some more. Ha, ha, ha. Run, you fucking rubbish boys. Run until you are good soldiers."

The sweat ran down my arms and the stone became slippery. My stomach went round fast with the fear. I made my arms hard and pressed my fingers deep into the ridges of the stones so they hurt. I must keep going. "One two, one two. I must not drop the stones. I must not drop the stones."

"Stop!" said Mobuto. "Put down the stones."

We stopped and panted as he marched over to us. I dropped my stone onto the yellow grass and it landed with a crunch. My beating heart was happy but my arms were so weak they floated. I heard the thud of Sipho's stone behind me. The boys Richard and Jabu had also dropped theirs. The stones were so big that they've made a deep cut in the red ground beneath the short yellow grass. My chest heaved up and down so much it hurt to breathe and my whole body was wet.

"So, soldier boys. You've made it. You're the toughies who can carry the heavy stones. That is good. You will be able to carry the weapons for us in the bush. We can't have soldiers who are too weak to carry their own weapons, huh? Bilole take away the feeble insect. I'm tired of seeing his bloody body on my ground."

Bilole picked up the broken body of the new boy. His head fell back and was so red with thick blood that I couldn't see his face properly. His arms hung funny and his hands were dead. His spirit had flown far away into the jungle. I bet he was glad that he was gone from this place. He was too weak. It was better for him not to be here anymore.

Chapter 8

Bilole took us back to the hut and let us have water and bread and then told us to sleep. I chewed the hard bread, took big gulps of the water and then lay on the bed. I had not had a bed since I was little in the squatter camp with Umama, but the pain in my heart was too great for me to even like it. I closed my eyes and squeezed back the tears. My breath shuddered inside me.

I heard a small sob and turned to see Sipho. He lay with his eyes closed and his arm across his big forehead. His stomach moved up and down and the tears came from under his eyelids. How had this happened? I shook my head and wished I could just pretend this was not real. Aiee, how would I survive in this place? Enoch was already dead and so was that other new boy. These men felt nothing to kill. They wanted to drink our blood. Tomorrow maybe we would all be dead. My mind turned black and I groaned. I covered my eyes with my hands. We were all too tired to speak and soon I heard the others snoring and let myself also fall into the sleep.

Next I knew I was waking and there was weak pink light outside. Inside I wanted to cry. Bits of my dream came back. I'd been with Thandi eating KFC in our pipe house and me telling her the favorite story of the sly jackal who stole the farmer's butter until the farmer tricked him by making him sleep in front of the fire so it melted out of his bottom. I squeezed back the tears. If only I could really be back there. Why had this thing happened to us? Why did we go to that KFC? I felt so empty with only the fear in my head. I wished I could just run away, but how would I ever do that? I was trapped and had no idea what this day would bring.

"Bilole's here," whispered David. "We better get up."

I pushed back the tears, which had come into my eyes, and jumped to my feet. I scrambled for my uniform as Bilole's heavy steps came in the door.

"Wake up. Here have this water and bread. I want you dressed and out of the hut in ten minutes. Is that clear!" he shouted.

"Yes, sah," we shouted.

Sipho jumped up and grabbed his uniform. David picked up the steel basin of bread Bilole had thrown on the floor. He gave a piece to each of us. I went over to the jug of water and helped him to pour some cups. I gave to Sipho first and then to the boys Richard and Jabu. They just grunted when they took them and I glared at them.

"Dress first and then eat," I said to Sipho.

He nodded and pulled on his uniform and sandals before crunching on the piece of bread.

I did the same and we rushed outside before Bilole could shout at us or beat us. He marched us to a field at the back of the hut. At the end stood a long row of wooden poles with fat sacks on them.

"Make a line here," said Bilole, stabbing the ground with his hard boot.

We obeyed and shuffled into a line next to him. I looked down at the big wood box beside him. Inside was a pile of wooden AK guns with sharpened wooden bayonets carved underneath. One by one he gave us a gun. My hands were wet and I held it tight so it would not slip out. At least it was not heavy like the stone.

Commander Mobuto came to the field. "Run across the field and stab those sacks," he shouted. "Do it fast otherwise I will beat you with them."

David raised his eyebrows at me as I panted next to him. Sipho was behind grunting as he ran.

"Stab the bodies. Kill the enemy who have harmed your family," shouted Mobuto.

I saw David stab the sack with the bayonet of his wooden AK. His muscles were tense and he frowned hard as he ran again and again at the sack. I grunted and also hit the sack as hard as I could again and again. The sand was packed tight like the mountain and the wooden gun made my hands tingle but I kept hitting it.

"Break, you stupid sack, break," I panted. I hit and hit as I pulled back my arm and ran again at the sack.

Richard hit his sack with scrawny arms and I lifted my eyebrows as red sand poured from his hole onto the dry grass. He did not look so strong. He turned and lifted his eyebrows at me like Mr. Proud Boy.

I glared at him and stabbed harder. David's broke next to me and so did Jabu's. I stabbed again. My heart beat hard as Mobuto looked at me and took a step towards me. I took a deep breath, pulled back my arm, and then ran and threw myself at the sack. "Thwack, thwack, thwack." I stabbed with all my strength and then let out a big sigh as at last the red sand dribbled to the grass like blood tears.

"Well done," said David, and smiled.

I smiled back at him and wiped the sweat from my head with my arm.

"So, you are lucky today," said Mobuto as Sipho gave one more stab and his sack broke just in time. "Maybe next time you will not be so lucky."

Chapter 9

The smell of the hospital antiseptic is strong in my nose as I open my eyes. The early orange light of the morning has painted the window. I stare at it until the sky turns dark pink and the rooster cock-a-doodles hello to the new morning. Its crowing makes the memories of Mobuto and David jump back into my mind and I squeeze my eyes tight to chase away their broken bodies.

I shake my head and look around at the white humps of boys in the silent ward. Some of them are snoring. I squint into the pale light of the room. One boy at the end has messy brown hair. My body tingles; Richard! I smile and let out a big sigh. At least I am not alone.

The strong pink sky turns to blue and soon the nurse comes with a trolley filled with bowls of steaming yellow maize meal porridge.

"Good morning," she says, like she's happy. "Time to eat. You feeling better?"

I nod but say nothing. What is there to be so happy about?

She picks up some more pillows. "Come, I'll help you sit up and put these behind you," she says.

"Aaargh." I grit my teeth and then hold my breath as I push myself up while she plops the pillows in.

"Think you can feed yourself?" she says, giving me a warm bowl and plastic spoon.

I grunt and begin to spoon the steaming mixture into my mouth. It's so hot that it numbs my tongue but I swallow and clench my jaw so she can't see.

A boy moves on the far side and the nurse also helps him sit up. I stare at his square head and dark skin. He turns his head and I see slit eyes and the long scar down his cheek. I smile. It's Trigger, from Nkunda's squadron. He's covered in a big bandage across his chest and moans as the nurse moves him but she helps him to sit up for his porridge. He stuffs a big spoon into his mouth.

Richard's got a plastic bag on a silver pole next to his bed with a thin tube going into the top of his hand. The nurse fiddles with the tube and turns something. She doesn't give Richard any porridge. I stare at his thin scarecrow body. He hasn't moved much and his eyes are still closed which is not good.

"Trigger, Richard," I call as soon as the nurse leaves.

"Hotshot?" says Trigger. He turns and looks across the room. His eyes find me and he gives a big smile. "Hey, that you?"

"It's me. You okay?

He nods. "The bullet nearly got me but the doctor says I'm okay it didn't go inside. I thought you were dead, my brother."

"Me too. They nearly got me."

Trigger stares at me.

"David's dead; so is Mobuto!" I say and my voice croaks.

"No!" gasps Trigger, and then groans with pain as he tries to sit up further. "Bilole was shot and Jabu, then Bloodneverdry too. I saw the bullets rip them and ducked to the side. I think the bullet went through Shithead in front and into me. If it hadn't hit him first I'd be dead," he says.

"Lucky shit," I say with a heavy spirit. I'm glad he's survived but I want David here. Why did he have to die instead?

"What happened to Nkunda and the others?"

Trigger shrugs his shoulders. "There was so much fire and smoke. All the boys were going mad. I don't know if they survived. I didn't want to die that day." His eyes cloud over and he looks down. "How you escape, Hotshot?"

I shake my head. "My mind cannot remember. I started running into the bush with Bilole when the rebels came on the ground. All I can remember is running and running through the forest and then falling with a fire in my back. I don't know how I came to be here."

"Me too," says Trigger with dark eyes. "We are lucky. They

must have left us for dead and then Dr. Zuma must have found us."

I nod. "Richard's that side," I say, pointing to his bed.

Trigger brightens and looks over and calls, "Hey, Richard. Wake up."

Richard stays silent and doesn't move at all.

"He's not good," I say. "The nurse didn't give him food. Maybe he's dying?"

Trigger stays quiet for a bit and then says, "We must let them help us."

I nod and turn away. I'm so empty inside. There's been so much death. I wish I could just run away from it all. I wish all of this was not true. I wish I was back in our camp with David and my AK.

"How could the juju fail us? How could the great witchdoctor not protect us?"

Trigger shrugs and shakes his head. "I don't know, Hotshot. I don't know."

"I think the spirits have turned against us. They have cursed us," I say.

Trigger turns to me with wide eyes but says nothing. I sink back into my bed. What will I do now? How will I find Thandi if I have no power? I feel like the hollow person. Tears prick by my eyes and I push the thoughts away and tense my body. My fists lie clenched by my side. I must not be weak.

* * *

"You can go to the dorm this afternoon. I think your back is strong enough now," says Dr. Zuma as he prods and presses his big hands across my back.

It hurts a little and I give a small cry but time has passed and I'm feeling better now and want to be out of this place with all its sickness and blood.

"Yes, that looks good. Put him in Dorm two, Nurse. You'll have a short exercise regime to follow every morning before breakfast and we'll start doing some crafts too. We have a strict routine for you here. There'll be church on Sunday morning."

His eyes shine at me behind his silver glasses and he gives a big smile.

I don't smile back and then look away. I won't answer him. I like routine; I'm a soldier but what's this church shit? All I'll do is the exercise.

The doctor stands still next to me, pats me strong on the shoulder and moves off.

"Right, you get some rest I'll check on you again after supper," he says.

I say nothing but watch as he moves over to Richard and begins to examine his bandage. Trigger's already gone from the hospital two days, but Richard's still not ready.

That afternoon Nurse Sophie comes to fetch me.

"We've given you some new clothes and shoes to wear." She smiles, bustling up to me with her straight back and turning down my sheet. She puts some clothes on the bed and then turns to draw the curtains around my bed.

"Come, you get dressed now and then I'll take you to the dorm. You can use this walking stick to help you for a bit."

She tries to help me sit up but I push her away and grunt. I get up and slowly put on the clothes. My legs still feel weak and my back is stiff and paining but it feels good to be out of the bed. I pull the curtain back hard and give Richard the thumbs up as I take the stick and limp behind the stupid Nurse Sophie from the ward. Richard smiles at me and shows his thumb.

"Go well, Hotshot," he says.

"Stay strong," I say.

Nurse Sophie is waiting at the door with a stupid grin on her face.

"You have done well," she says. "You are a lucky boy."

I glare at her and want to hit her with my stick but she turns and goes to like fast rabbit down the step and I follow slow and sore behind. I'll be glad when Richard is out and we are all strong again. He's still very thin but is eating on his own now so maybe it won't be too long for him to be better. Then we can train again and soon we will escape back to find the L.R.A.

"Hey, Hotshot." Trigger smiles, with his slit eyes shining as I shuffle into the dorm. "We're together, my brother!"

I give him a double handshake and a small smile and look around the dorm. It is a big rondavel with cool mud walls and a fresh thatch roof. There are three beds inside and two big chests of drawers. There is a small table with a big jug and washbasin on. I see Nurse Sophie go to a bed next to where Trigger is lying. She puts a pile with two white folded shirts and a pair of khaki shorts onto it.

"These are yours to keep," she says. "There's a chest of drawers over there. The bottom one is yours and has some more things in as well as a toothbrush and paste for you. Okay. You rest now and I'll come fetch you both for supper."

She stands with a stupid smile on her face at the end of my bed like she's waiting for me to say something. I stare at the bed. It's covered with a soft grey blanket covered with a big red cross. Suddenly Thandi stands strong in my mind and a deep pain attacks my belly. The dump feels so long ago now I can't even remember how she sounds. She must have grown lots now. How will she look? I push down the sob that wants to climb out of my mouth and shake my head.

"You'll be comfortable here," says Nurse Sophie, pulling my mind back to the bed. I glare at her and push past to throw myself on the bed. She gives me a sad smile and then goes from the hut. I lie with my arms behind my head and stare at the ceiling.

"I don't want to talk," I say as Trigger opens his mouth to speak. He glares at me and then shrugs and turns on to his side away from me. My stomach clenches. I don't care if he's cross. I feel so empty inside. I just want to be left alone.

Chapter 10

As the days go past I force myself to walk even though it's still sore and I have to use the stick.

"Hey, Hotshot," says Richard as I limp over to where him and Trigger are sitting under a big acacia tree. "Come sit here."

"Hey, Richard. When they let you out?"

"This morning," says Richard and grins. "I'm also in your Dorm."

"Good," I say as I collapse on the grass next to them.

"See my scars," he says, and shows me his arm and then lifts up his shirt.

I stare at the jagged dent all the way up his arm and a long one across his stomach. "You are lucky you made it," I say.

"It was a bad day," he says. "I'm glad you also made it," he says, after a while.

I nod and lean back against the trunk of the acacia. I close my eyes and feel my stomach jump. My muscles have been jumping too much and inside I've such panic that I want to run screaming into the bush. I frown. What is this panic? Why does it suddenly come in the waves and make my whole body to go hot with the sweat? I feel weak inside and silently curse myself and stiffen my face so that Richard and Trigger can't see.

"My body's crying for the brown-brown," I say, opening my eyes and looking to see if they've been watching me. I give a small sigh. Richard is staring to the front and so is Trigger. They also look like they are not good inside. Maybe they have the same panic?

"Mine too," says Richard when he feels my eyes on him. "We've all been in the hospital too long, that's why our bodies are crying."

"It is too long." I say and nod. "We've got to get some."

I turn my head and look away. Inside I am dead. I don't even know how long I've been here. Nothing makes sense anymore. I hate this. I feel like a weak dog. I clench my fist and hit the ground. I need to feel like a soldier again.

Trigger looks over at me. "Hey, I've heard there are the good tablets in the surgery. Maybe we can have those?" he says.

"That stupid doctor won't give us any," says Richard, spitting onto the ground. "He says our bodies will stop craving soon. He never even gave me the pain tablets when I came out today."

"I hate him," I say." When I'm better we'll break into the surgery and steal the drugs."

"We must watch Nurse Sophie," says Richard. "She always locks the cabinet"

"No problem. We can break it easily."

"Yes, when your back's better we'll do that," says Richard.

I look sideways as he says it. He still needs me to lead and just wants to follow like he did in the camp. He feels my gaze and looks away.

Trigger takes out a crumpled packet of Lucky Strike. "Here," he says.

I take the smoke and matches and strike up, glad that at least they let us have the cigarettes even though they say it is just until we are better. I pull the smoke deep into my lungs pretending it is good jamba. "Soon we'll go back to the L.R.A. I must find the General," I say.

"I hope he is not dead too," says Richard. "There were too many dead that day."

I nod and turn my head away. I don't want to think about that day. I just want to get out, find the L.R.A. and take revenge.

"I need my AK and my machete," I say, stabbing the earth with my fingers.

Richard and Trigger laugh. "They'll never give us that," says Trigger. "They even lock the forks away because they're frightened we'll stab them."

"I want to stab that stupid Nurse Sophie," I say. I can see her bustling over towards us with her big owl eyes. "I'm going," I say. I push with pain from the ground. "See you later."

"Okay," says Richard, while Trigger laughs and gives me the thumbs up. He knows I want to get away from the stupid bitch.

"Richard's coming with me to do some crafts later," says Trigger. "Maybe you want to come?"

"What crafts?" I say pulling a face.

"We draw things. I like the art. I can draw well," he says, and puffs up like the rooster.

I frown at him. "Maybe," I say, but all I want to play with is an AK.

I see the nurse coming closer with her small fast steps and I hobble away as fast as I can. I don't want her talking to me in front of them. I'm only a little way away when she catches up behind me and asks with her owl eyes,

"You okay, Pumpkin?"

I turn and try and hit her but she ducks away from my arm and I miss.

"Call me fucking Pumpkin again and I'll kill you, bitch," I shout with a face filled with hate.

She steps back from me but calls out after me,

"You need to see Dr. Zuma today and let him help you with your nightmares. He's asked especially to see you and you must try and come to the church this Sunday."

"I don't want to see him and I don't want the stupid church," I turn and hiss in a low voice glaring at her with narrow eyes, but inside my mind is jumping. How does she know of my nightmares?

"You must. He'll help you to feel better in your mind and so will church," she says.

I step towards her again. "Fuck off! There's nothing wrong with my mind."

"Okay" she says. She stands straight, puts her head to one side and gives me a big smile. I feel like my blood will explode in my head. "I'll send him to find you," she says.

"Get the fuck away from me," I shout. I can feel the veins standing strong in my neck. I can't take this woman anymore. She will drive me mad. I turn sharply and shuffle off as fast as my legs and back will let me, down towards the river. There are tall breadfruit trees there, which remind me of the camp. I will hide away behind their wide green leaves.

I fall on the grass beneath one of them and lean my back against the rough bark. My chest is heaving with my panting breaths. I'm so angry I just want to scream. I close my eyes. My back is paining bad from the walking. I press it hard against the trunk. I take in a deep breath of the damp bush air. It helps a little for the anger inside.

"Here you are."

What the fuck! That Nurse Sophie's found me again. I try to get up and make to hit her but Dr. Zuma is with her; he pushes her away and comes towards me smiling. He stops and looks with kind brown eyes behind silver-framed glasses.

"Leave me alone. I don't want to talk to you!"

If I had a knife on me I would stab both of them. I am like the exploding grenade inside. I look around for a sharp stick or stone I can use. The doctor sees my movement and backs away. I snort.

He stands and looks and then asks, "May I just sit here for a while?"

He turns to the stupid Nurse Sophie. "It's okay, Nurse, I'll find you later."

"Okay, doctor," she says, giving me a smile and going away with quick steps.

I stare hard out in front as he lowers himself down next to me. He pushes his back against the tree and bends his legs in front. I stare at them. They are strong with big muscles. He wears brown sandals on his feet. I see a flash of silver as his watch shows under the sleeve of his white coat. He must have money. What is he doing here? Why is he helping us? Somebody must be paying him to do it. The anger rises up in my belly. Why can't he leave me alone? I close my eyes but I can hear his breathing going in and out. I try to shut my ears to the sound.

He says nothing and we sit like this for a long time. I look at him with a corner eye. Maybe he's asleep? But he's not; he's playing with a piece of grass between his big hands and has another hanging out of his mouth like a cow.

He feels my eyes and takes the grass out of his mouth. He clears his throat and looks at me. "Can you tell me your proper name?" he says. "I'm sure you don't like being called Pumpkin. If you give me your proper name then I'll get Nurse Sophie to use it."

"It's Lieutenant Hotshot. I've told her that," I say, and glare at him.

"Lieutenant Hotshot. That's a long name. Maybe it's too long for her to say," he says. "You know these women; they're not good with names. Maybe your old name's shorter? Can you remember it?"

"Of course I can remember it but only my friends can call me that. She's not my friend."

He's made me remember David. Only David and Sipho called me Modetse. I've had enough. I push myself up and bite my teeth from the shooting pain in my back. I walk with my stick deep into the green forest of fern trees. Their hanging green leaf fingers touch me as I move through them. I turn left where there are thick palm leaves and tall reeds. I want to hide in them like a cave. I want to be alone. I don't want to talk to this man.

"Leave me alone! Just leave me alone," I shout as he comes after me through the forest. "You are driving me mad."

"If I do that you'll never get better. You need to talk it out and realize it's not your fault. It'll make you feel better."

"I don't need you," I shout. "I just need my back and legs to be strong again so that I can go back to the L.R.A. They are my family; only them!"

My body is so full with anger that I go dizzy. I steady myself and take in a deep breath. The doctor stops and stares at me with worried eyes behind his silver glasses.

"Okay. I'll call on you tomorrow," he says in a soft voice." My wife and daughter are coming back tomorrow and maybe you'll come and eat some of my wife's delicious stew."

I shake my head in disbelief and pull my lip in disgust. Why would I want to eat with his stupid family? What's wrong with this mad man? Doesn't he understand that the only other people I want to see are L.R.A. boys? I glare at him as he stands staring at me and then he smiles and my blood boils up inside my head and I bite my lip to stop myself lunging forwards and tearing out his eyes.

"Fuck off!" I shout. "Just fuck off before I kill you."

He gives me a sad look with his head on one side but obeys and turns back into the forest leaving me so full with the anger that I think I'll explode. I stare after him, clench my fists and stay standing there until the pain in my back forces me to go back to the dorm.

* * *

The next day I'm sitting in the dining hall drinking my Coke and listening to Bob Marley singing 'Jammin' and tapping my foot to the beat when the doctor comes in. He sits his big body down next to me on the wooden bench without asking. I glare at him and shift down to the end.

"Hello," he says. "Don't you want to be at the football with the others?"

I pull a face and turn away without answering. Stupid question! If I wanted to play I'd be there! Can't he see that my back isn't strong enough yet? What kind of doctor is he?

"If you've time we could talk a bit now," he says.

What's the matter with this idiot? He's too stupid to see I don't want him here. I slam off the button and Bob Marley stops. He's spoiled my fun and I hate him. I push myself up as fast as I can and move from the bench.

"Wait, Modetse..." he says touching my arm as I try to shuffle past him.

I yank away my arm and freeze. I turn on him and shout. "How do you know my name?"

"I heard one of the other boys say it," says Dr. Zuma.

"Who?" I shout. "Who told you my name?"

Richard starts to enter the dining hut but stops in the doorway, his face pale and his eyes big.

My eyes dart over to him. "You," I shout. "You told him. Didn't you?"

Richard hurries out and I hobble as fast as I can after him and catch him just as he tries to head for the field. I yank him hard by his shirt so he loses his balance and falls backwards. I jerk him again, his shirt rips and I lunge forward to grab his hair and pull. I bring my free arm around and with my clenched fist smash him in the face so that his head goes sideways and bright blood spurts out from his lip.

"You fucking scarecrow," I shout. "Why did you tell them? No one must call me that."

"It is just a name," says Richard.

"Bastard," I shriek as I hit him again. I feel more of his hot blood on my hand.

Dr. Zuma pulls me away with strong arms, but I push away and grab out again at Richard's shirt and rip it some more.

"Calm down," says Dr. Zuma holding my fighting arms and pressing his fingers into them. "Calm down! You okay, Richard?"

Richard nods. He doesn't want to look me in the eye. I pull and scream against the doctor's grip but he's too strong.

"We need to call you by your proper name," says Dr. Zuma. "It's important."

"No, you don't," I shout. "I told you. You are not my family."

"We'd like to be," says a woman's voice and I turn to see a fat woman in a bright red and black zigzag pattern dress and headscarf. She has the same coffee skin like the doctor and is pretty with a round face with a fat nose and lips and big honey eyes. She is holding out a square silver tin towards me.

"I'm Mama Zuma. Here, I've made these for you."

I stare wide-eyed at the tin and my stomach gets butterflies and my cheeks grow hot. What is she talking about? She doesn't even know me. She takes a small round cake from the tin and holds it out to me. The doctor lets me go and I hit her hand so that the cake with its chocolate icing and red cherry goes flying in the air, then I turn and hobble away to the forest before I can see how she looks.

My chest heaves up and down with my breath. It's a long time since I've seen an African mother like her and she makes my stomach strange. I feel like I'm in a mad place. I must get away before they break me. They are trying to break my mind. They want to make me mad so they can defeat me. I must stay strong. I must get back to the L.R.A.

Chapter 11

"This is your lucky day," said Mobuto as we marched to a line of trees he had shown us. "The General has given you a fortunate order. He has no time for wasters. You've tried the wood AKs, now is the time to touch the real AK, the gun of Mother Africa. You'll taste her strong bullets and feel her power. I am Mr. AK. If you do not fire my AKs properly I will make the bullets eat you like a hungry lion."

"Yes, the General he does not like the soldier boys who can't shoot," said Bilole.

"You will love this gun and polish it like the sun. It is now your mother. If you damage my AK, you are dead boys. Do you hear me?"

We nodded at him with big eyes. I stood straight and full of fear inside as I watched Mobuto and his AK.

He grunted and turned to Bilole. "Bring the AKs."

Bilole saluted and marched over to a hut behind us. Soon he was back with Nkunda carrying five AKs between them. I stared at the fierce guns. They were blue steel with a case underneath like a banana arm where the bullets lived. It must have many bullets in it. Under the barrel lay a glinting bayonet. My heart jumped. I had to be good with this AK or Mobuto would kill me with those bullets.

Mobuto looked at the AK with happy eyes. He took a white cloth from his pocket and rubbed it up and down the gun with soft strokes. The AK shone like it was new from a shop. He wiped it up and down some more and then shoved it up high onto his shoulder. He turned and pointed it and yanked down the lever and then let it jump back. I heard a loud "kadock" and my body prickled.

"Now, the bullet is in the chamber," said Mobuto. "Are you watching, you stupid boys? If you get this wrong I will send the

AK bullets into your fucking brains. Do you hear! Now it is ready for firing."

We nodded our heads and I swallowed hard. We all looked with big eyes at the gun. How would I shoot this gun? What if I could not hold it properly? What if I dropped it? I bet the General was doing this because he wanted Mobuto to shoot us. He wanted more blood.

I heard the kadock of the bullet in another AK. Bilole was loading them one by one. His face was hard and Nkunda watched us with narrow eyes. I watched Mobuto's hand on the gun barrel with the killer bullet inside. He turned and gave us a horrible smile and then pointed the gun at the sky. Fire jumped out in a big spurt and my ears went dead from its thunder.

Mobuto did not move. I looked at his ears and saw that he wore plugs in them. He handed the AK to Bilole and picked up a big metal box. He opened it. Rows and rows of AK bullets stared up at me. They were big with sharp pointed ends and looked like shiny brass teeth full of power that could eat me. I swallowed and my breath caught in my throat.

"This is an AK bullet," said Mobuto as he rubbed one of the bullet teeth between his fingers. "This will be your best friend. It will tear your enemy to pieces. Now, you must hold the gun like this. See," he shouted, and pushed the one end of the AK into his shoulder. He held the long piece in front with his hand. His other hand was by the trigger.

"Here, catch," he said suddenly, and threw the AK at me.

I jumped forward and let out a whistle as I caught it. My hands were wet and I rubbed them one by one on my pants. I lifted my eyebrows. The AK was not too heavy. It felt strong in my hands. I stood up straight and held the gun like I had seen Mobuto do. Its hardness fitted into my shoulder. I held it tight, feeling its power in my hands. I gripped the long piece with one hand like Mobuto had done and pushed the other end back harder into my shoulder so that it was stiff and kept my breath in.

"You are lucky to have caught my AK," barked Mobuto. "Now you will learn to fire her bullets. What's your name?"

"Modetse, sah."

"You are going to make love to your AK Modetse. Have you made love before?"

"N-no s-sah," I said and my cheeks grew hot.

Mobuto gave an ugly smile. I heard Bilole and Nkunda give a horrible laugh behind me.

"So now you will learn to make good love. Is that right? Will you make love to your AK?" shouted Mobuto. He put his fat face close to mine and I could smell the stale beer on his breath.

"Y-yes, s-sah I will," I said.

"Yes, sah, I will make love to my AK," shouted Mobuto.

"Yes, sah, I will make love to my AK," I said. My cheeks were hot and my hands turned wet.

Mobuto glared at me and then poked me hard in the stomach with his fat finger. I bent over and nearly dropped the AK. I coughed and tried to stand up straight. I put the gun back in my shoulder.

Mobuto stared hard at me. "Now, hold it tight. I will show you how to shoot the magic bullet. You will do it on a single shot and later you can do automatic. Watch!"

Mobuto took the AK back. He took out the bullet and then showed us how to put the bullets in the banana case.

"Load it," he said, and gave me some of the bullets.

They were hard and cold in my hand. I kept my mind strong and put them in the case like Mobuto had done. When they were all in I tilted the case and it slid back under the AK. Then I pulled back the lever and heard the loud "kadock."

"The bullet is in the barrel now," said Mobuto with narrow eyes. "You keep that pointed forward, you fucking piece of shit, you hear."

I swallowed hard and nodded.

"Now you look through that hole. It is the sight. You need to line up that mark."

I watched him with strong eyes and nodded.

"See those steel plates?" he said. "You are going to shoot in the middle of them. Shoot plate number one."

I stared at the shining metal plates standing at the bottom of the trees. I could count ten of them.

"Stand there," said Mobuto.

I walked over to where he pointed with the AK buzzing in my hands. I pushed the living AK into my shoulder. I narrowed my eyes and stared hard at the number one plate. My ears stayed alive to what Mobuto had told me. Inside my heart beat hard and my stomach felt sick. I took in a big breath and kept it tight inside.

"This is a good gun," said Mobuto. "It will rattle not jam and will not kick you like an ostrich. Now squeeze the trigger like it is your ladylove; slowly, slowly."

I touched the trigger with my finger. It was alive. My body shook and I took more breath to make it stiff. I must do this for Thandi. I must not fail. Please, God, I must not fail.

I looked at the steel plate in the sunlight. It was calling my bullet. I held my eyes on the number one plate and put one eye to the sight like Mobuto had shown me. I kept the AK straight. I saw the middle of the plate in my sight and clenched my teeth. Then my finger touched the trigger. The AK was full of energy. The bullet wanted to be free. I could feel its power in my hand. I let myself be one with the gun and squeezed the trigger. "Thwaka." The AK jumped and spat out the fire bullet so fast that I could not see it. I staggered back. My head hummed and my body felt wet.

"Take the gun, Bilole. I will check the target," said Mobuto.

I watched with big eyes as he moved to the tree line. I stared for the plate number one. My eyes blurred and my heart was in my mouth.

Mobuto marched to the tree. He turned and nodded.

My body grew weak. My knees shook but inside my mind smiled. I had hit the plate. I had never shot a bullet before, but first shot and I had hit the plate. I grew warm inside. I turned around and saw Sipho and David smile at me. I smiled back. Maybe it was not so bad. Maybe I would be able to escape back to Thandi if I was such a good shot.

Mobuto marched back with the metal plate hanging in his big hand. I stared at the plate. It had a small hole near the top. Mobuto turned it over and I saw big broken pieces at the back where the bullet had gone through.

Mobuto grunted. "You are lucky. The spirits must like you. You've made it," he said. "Let's see if the next one will be so fortunate." He gave a bad smile and his gold tooth glinted at us.

Chapter 12

The doctor's wife doesn't try and give me cake again but she keeps smiling at me. She is doing the cooking for us, which is good because the stew she makes is too good.

I'm eating my stiff yellow maize porridge in the breakfast hut when she comes in.

"Good morning, boys. Now that I'm back you're all going to start the school today," she says.

A murmur rushes through the hut. I look at Trigger and Richard with my spoon of porridge halfway to my mouth. My stomach tenses with excitement. I didn't think they had the school here. My heart beats hard. With the school I really can be a Commander one day soon and find Thandi. I smile inside. It will be good. I must let this woman help me.

"Eat up," says Mama Zuma with a big smile which lights up her round face.

I scrape out the last of my porridge and follow Richard and Trigger to put our plates in the washing up bowls outside. Richard washes his carefully but Trigger and me just splash water on them and then throw them on the drying rack. Washing up is not men's work!

Mama Zuma waddles outside and shouts, "Come on. We are going to the school now."

We follow her fat behind towards a long white washed prefab hut on the far side of the Mission. It has lots small square windows along the side and inside are rows of wood desks with brown chairs. In front is a big blackboard and white pieces of chalk and a big desk with a pile of red books. I have to keep my face strong to stop showing everybody how happy I am. So this is a school. Ay, I never thought I would go to the school now.

"Modetse, you sit here," says Mama Zuma.

I tense inside as she says my name but walk proud to the desk where she is pointing. "Richard, you sit here, Bernard, you here."

Trigger and Richard obey. Trigger doesn't seem to mind being called Bernard, his real name and I look at him like he's weak.

A tall boy with light brown skin enters and stands with Mama Zuma at the front. He smiles at us and then whispers something to her.

"Who is this idiot?" I say loudly to Richard. "He's too young to be a teacher."

"I've seen him before," replies Trigger. "I think he's an aid worker."

"Fuck the aid workers," I say loudly. "We don't need them here. We can help ourselves."

I hope that my words hurt and I see him close his fists, but he doesn't look at us.

"Boys, this is Bengu. He's from Kinshasa and is here to help me today."

The boy looks full of himself. I look at his clothes. He has nice jeans and a blue Nike T-shirt. I look at them with jealous eyes. He must have the money. I hate him. What does he know of pain?

"Good morning," says Bengu.

We stay quiet. Who does he think he is? I glare at him and he looks embarrassed, which makes me feel good. He looks sideways at Mama Zuma. She gives a small smile and then comes in front of us.

"Now, we're going to start learning the Arithmetic," she says. "We're going to do the times tables. We'll start with number one and before long you'll be able to do right up to twelve."

Mama Zuma takes out a piece of white chalk and draws big figures on the board. She shows us how to do one times one all the way up to twelve. I take out my book and write it down. It is easy and doesn't take me long because I remember some counting from Umama.

Bengu comes down the aisle to check our work. He thinks he's such a main man. I see Trigger put out his foot when he comes near and Bengu nearly trips. We laugh and he looks angrily at us.

"Stop being silly," says Mama Zuma. She bustles over to look at my work.

"Well done. Twelve out of twelve," she says. "You've got a head for figures, well done."

She ticks her way through my sums with her red pen and my chest swells and grows warm. I look at Bengu with a proud smile, but he doesn't smile back. Good, he must know he is not the only clever one.

Mama Zuma breaks my thoughts. "You keep going like this and in the not too distant future you could do the big exams for university entrance you know," she says.

I just look at her. What's this university business?

"I'm not going there. I'm going be Commander of the L.R.A.," I say frowning at her.

"I hope not, Modetse. I hope you can do better than that."

My mouth drops. Better than that? What does this stupid woman mean? There's no better than that. I glare at her. She's not L.R.A. She can't understand. I'll just use her and then I'll escape.

"Hey, some girls are coming past," whispers Trigger.

I turn and look as the group of girls come down the path. A girl wearing tight blue jeans and a red T-shirt with white letters reading "Coca-Cola" is leading them. She has light brown skin with a straight nose, big brown eyes, which slant like almonds, and full lips. She's talking to one of the Pineapple girls and laughing with her. She gets closer and looks up at our window and straight at me.

"She looked at you," sniggers Richard.

"Shut up," I hiss. But I hope he's right. I glance up at Bengu. I can see him watching her. She sees him and smiles. He smiles back. I want to smash his face in. How come he knows her?

"That Bengu likes her," whispers Richard.

"I'll fucking kill him," I say.

The girl looks away from us and talks again to the Pineapple girl. They move down the path.

"Come, join us, girls," shouts Trigger, banging on the window.

"Yes, come here," shouts Richard.

"Leave them. We don't want them here," I say.

"Yes we do. You want the pretty one."

Mama Zuma hits the desk with her wooden stick. "Boys, leave the girls now, they're going to swim. You need to get on with the Arithmetic," she says.

We ignore her. She's not in charge of us. Stupid teacher! Trigger and Richard keep banging on the window as the girls move away down the path.

"Why can't we swim with the girls?" says Trigger.

"Yes, why not?" we all shout.

"I think you boys know the answer to that," says Mama Zuma lifting her eyebrows at us and pulling a face.

The girls wiggle their bums as they walk away. That pretty one did look right at me. Where's she from and why is she here?

"We must find that pretty one and take her to the bush," says Trigger. "Then you can have her."

"Don't being stupid. I don't want her," I say, but my stomach jumps. I see Bengu watching us. He knows I like her. I bet he'll try and stop me.

* * *

"Hey, Hotshot," says Richard running up to me a few days later. "I saw that girl with Mama Zuma. It's her daughter."

"You sure?" I say as my heart sinks. The doctor won't let his daughter be friends with us.

"She's called Tula. She goes to the school in Kampala but now her mother says she must come here. I heard her shouting at Mama Zuma."

"What'd she say?"

"She wants to go back to the city and not be on the stupid Mission."

"Fuck her, the only thing stupid is her! Let her go back," I say with clenched fists.

The roar of an F20 truck starting up makes me jump. I turn around and catch my breath. It's that Tula, sitting in the front with Bengu laughing. Her head's thrown back and I'm sure they're sharing some secret joke. Maybe they're laughing about us?

"Where're they going?" says Richard.

I try to hide the anger in my eyes and just shrug as if I don't care.

"Bitch – she's probably happy because they are going," I say, and pull up my top lip.

"I've seen that Bengu go in the truck before," says Richard. "He always comes back."

I stand up angrily and walk inside. Bengu's older and handsome and can drive. How can I compete with him?

Richard follows me inside and pokes me playfully in the ribs. "Don't worry, Hotshot. She fancies you better."

"Fuck off."

I lie down on my bed, put my arm across my eyes and pretend to sleep. Inside I'm boiling with anger and dream about cutting Bengu into little pieces. My nighttime dreams jump back into my head. Last night it was children's hands chasing me. It was horrible. My whole head filled with their screams and I had to get up to walk in the cool night air to breath. I wish that I could just paint out these memories. They are killing me.

"You okay?" says Richard. He sits on the end of my bed and looks strange. After a while he mumbles, "I can't sleep."

I see he has a worried frown on his face and looks pale. "Is it bad dreams?"

Richard nods and moves his finger around the red cross on my grey blanket. He looks like he wants to cry. I sit up.

"I have them too; every night."

He looks up at me and smiles. "Really?"

"Yes. I think we all do."

"Trigger's better," he says.

"I'm sure Trigger's a traitor," I spit. "That's why he doesn't have bad dreams."

"I think it is because he spoke to Dr. Zuma," says Richard.

"Fuck Dr. Zuma, Richard. All we need is drugs. I'll tell Nurse Sophie I'm in pain and then we can get painkillers."

"That'll be good. You must limp more then. You're walking too straight now."

I smile. "I know. My back is feeling strong. Soon I can escape."

"Do you really want to go back?" says Richard with a funny look in his eyes.

I narrow my eyes and look at him. Is he also turning traitor? What's the matter with these boys and this camp?

"Of course," I say. "Don't you?"

"Of course." He nods, but I can see in his eyes he doesn't mean it and inside I feel sick. Richard's changing. I'm losing all my friends. My mind fills with hatred for the doctor and these people. They're destroying our love for the L.R.A. We must get out.

Chapter 13

Richard and Jabu's AK bullets hit their plates, but they both hit near the side and were not good like me. Mobuto grunted at them and didn't smile. He showed for Sipho to fire next. I held my breath as he loaded the AK. He walked with shaking legs to the place and squeezed the trigger. The bullet jumped from the gun and the plate moved.

"Get it, Bilole," said Mobuto.

Bilole marched over and I saw there was a small hole on the end of the plate when he came back. My heart cheered. I looked at Sipho and raised my eyebrows with a smile.

David was next. He stood stiff and pushed his AK firm back into his shoulder. He squeezed the trigger. "Thwack," the bullet flew out and the metal plate fell over. David's shoulders relaxed. Bilole went over and showed a thumbs up to Mobuto.

Mobuto grunted and looked at us with hard eyes. "You've done better than I thought," he said. "Now you can go back to the hut. March, quick."

We marched behind Bilole's fat body back to the wooden hut. Inside I felt warm. I was glad I was the number one shot. We had all hit the plates but no one had done as good as me.

"Commander Mobuto will see you at supper in two hours," said Bilole. "You've been here three days and passed the tests. You can eat in the hall now and have new clothes. There's a pack next to each bed. You must unpack and meet me outside in thirty minutes. Move!"

We saluted Bilole and went to our beds. My body had started to shake again for the glue but I tried to just think about my good shot.

"You did well," said David, patting me on the back.

I tried not to look like the rooster too much. "Thanks," I said.

"Are you from the city?"

"From the East side by the rubbish dump," I said, and my voice cracked. Thandi was back in my mind. I shivered. Pray to God she was okay and that she'd been able to find some food. I cleared my throat and asked, "Where you from?"

"Not too far from you. I was at the squatter camp on the West side. Did they catch you on the dump?"

I shook my head. "I was in the city. We had just bought the KFC and they chased me." I pulled a face and looked down. Thandi's frozen cry was alive in my ears. I shook my head to try to chase it away. The pain inside from her was too deep.

David stared hard at me and asked. "How old are you?"

"Twelve. You?"

"Thirteen."

I nodded. "Sipho's only eleven. Enoch who they killed was also with us. He was only nine years." I looked away for a bit and shuffled my feet.

"It is bad," said David, biting his bottom lip.

"Hey," said Sipho. He came over to my bed and sat on the end. "You shot well, my brother," he said.

I nodded. His face was pale and his voice was small.

"I'm glad you hit the plate, Sipho," said David.

"Me too." Sipho nodded. His eyes clouded over and he looked at the floor. "I hate this place, Modetse," he whispered.

I nodded. I think he was thinking of Enoch and I understood his pain. My mind filled with Enoch's screams and I shivered. These men did not play games. We had to do as they said or they would feel nothing to kill us.

Richard and Jabu talked in the corner and did not look at us. They were not friendly boys these two and my mind grew hard as I looked sideways at them. I would not talk to them either. At least I had Sipho and David wanted to be my friend.

"We had better unpack," said David. "Bilole will be back soon."

I lifted up my brown rug sack at the foot of the bed and took out some underpants and two camouflage T-shirts. There were a pair of khaki shorts, a toothbrush and two pairs of brown socks. I put them folded on my bed and looked at them with wide eyes. I had never had clothes like this with no holes in them. There was a water bottle with mesh around it and a wire basket under the bed to keep the things in. I pulled it out and packed mine good.

"It's best to think like a soldier," said David as he packed his basket next to me. "That's the only way to survive. You must hide your thoughts and feelings."

I looked at him with raised eyebrows. He was a clever one with an old spirit and I was lucky he was my friend.

"You are right," I said.

I finished my packing so that I was ready for Bilole.

"These are good clothes, hey," said Sipho as he packed his basket. He watched how I did it and then did it the same. Good, he knows I liked things neat like in our pipe house. Umama had always taught me that. I looked over at Richard and Jabu and pulled my lip. They had thrown their clothes in the basket so it was all messy. Their bed covers were not even straight.

"I need the glue," said Sipho in my ear.

I turned and saw his hands were shaking. "Me too," I said. "But there is no hope. You must try not think."

"It is hard," said Sipho, and his eyes filled with tears. "I am too scared."

"Stop it," I said. "Don't cry or they will kill you like Enoch."

We jerked as footsteps came to the doorway. Bilole appeared and shouted, "Outside!"

We marched behind him across the waving yellow grass towards tall green pine trees. The fresh smell of the pinecones cleared my head and I took in a deep breath. Bilole took us past many rows of long wooded barracks on the side of the camp where big soldiers stood in front. They jeered as we went past but I kept my eyes forward. Fear prickled over me like a porcupine when one soldier pretended to shoot me with his AK. He laughed at me and kicked the dirt after us.

Bilole led us around the back on one long building, past some chickens and roosters and to a big veranda. We went inside the hut. There were many long grey steel tables inside with rows of rough benches in front.

"Go sit on the benches there," commanded Bilole.

We obeyed and all moved to the benches in a bunch. I ended up next to Richard and Jabu and frowned. David and Sipho were the other end.

Richard looked at me. "You shot well," he said.

"Thanks," I said, surprised that he was now being my friend. "I'm glad you also hit the plate."

He nodded and asked. "Where did they get you?"

"By the KFC in Arula," I said. "You?"

"In the bush on the west side of the dump," said Richard. "Jabu was near there too."

I nodded and clenched my jaw. I did not want to remember how they got me. It made me pain too much to think of Thandi. Jabu grunted and said nothing. I looked over at his muscles. He was not thin like Richard with his sores.

"Did you live on the streets?" I asked.

Jabu looked at me with his deep eyes and shook his head. "The squatter camp with my father and brothers. They caught me when I went into the town."

"Oh," I said, and smiled inside because I was right. He wasn't from the streets. His eyes went sad when he said this so he must miss his family. I stared at him and he felt my gaze and glared so I quickly looked away. He shifted in his seat. I saw his fist had clenched. Maybe he was also angry at this place.

Bilole came in front with a big iron pot. He put a big spoon of chicken stew on the steel plates in front of us. Nkunda came behind him with a dish filled with big pieces of brown bread. He threw a piece on each plate.

Richard stuffed the stew into his mouth like a hungry

mongrel dog and then looked up at me and grinned.

I spooned the stew into my mouth and grinned back. It was good to taste the hot food.

"There are more boys over there," said Richard through his full mouth, and pointed with his finger to the other side of the long hut.

I followed his eyes. There were four boys who looked like they were thirteen or fourteen laughing with each other. "They look like they've been here long time," I said.

Jabu looked over at them and nodded. "They don't look feared."

Nkunda had joined them and all of them laughed like they were sharing a joke.

"That one is bad," said Jabu showing one boy with his eyes, "I know these things."

I looked at the boy soldier. He was tall and had braided hair and dark skin that shone like ebony. Jabu was right; his eyes were empty and hard like they had no feeling. I think his spirit inside must be dead. We stared at him and then Nkunda shouted, "Badboy – take the bread over that side."

Richard, Jabu and me looked at each other and lifted our eyebrows. He had the right name that one. Maybe Jabu was also clever like David.

Bilole came over and glared at us with his hands on his fat hips. He banged his stick on the steel table and shouted, "Eat faster. It's time for the movie."

We obeyed and I took big spoons of the stew and big bites of the bread. It felt so good in my mouth. It was a long time since I had food like this and it helped to stop my body crying for the glue. I wiped the last of the stew from my plate with the bread, stuffed it in my mouth and then jumped up from the bench. I pushed past Richard and Jabu so that I could be with David and Sipho. Sipho gave me a small smile.

Bilole was waiting by the steps. We lined up behind him and

marched with stiff bodies to another long wood building. We went through big doors into a large room with one small white light.

"Sit on the floor there," said Bilole, shoving us over.

I shuffled behind David with Sipho behind me and sat on some grass reed mats. Richard and Jabu sat next to us. In front was a big white wall. There was a buzzing sound as Bilole fiddled with something on a machine behind us. I heard heavy steps and then Commander Mobuto marched in. He stood in front of us with his legs apart.

"So, soldier boys," said Commander Mobuto, "tonight you are going to see the Rambo movie. You are lucky, soldier boys, hey?"

"Yes, sah," we said.

I'd never heard about this Rambo but my stomach was excited because I'd never seen a proper movie before. Mobuto grunted and pulled his pants over his fat pot stomach. He went to a machine by Bilole, picked up a black plastic square and pushed it into the machine. The machine whirred, loud music started and a picture came up across the wall. I stared at it with wide eyes.

"It is called *First Blood*," said David. "It's about a solider."

"Oh," I said, looking at him with raised eyebrows. "Have you seen the movie before?"

"No, but my brother he told me about this movie. He works in the city. I think this man Rambo is too clever."

I nodded thinking David was clever too. Even though I hated these men, my head buzzed waiting for this movie.

A big white soldier came on the screen. His arms were filled with muscles and his face was stern with long black hair across his head. I stared at him with big eyes and leaned forward. I had never seen anyone like him. "He is too good," I whispered to David as he fought all the men. No one could beat him. He was like magic.

David leaned forward to the movie and Sipho's eyes were like the owl. We turned to each other and smiled. Jabu and Richard too were smiling. I forgot where we were as we watched the movie. It was like I was there with this man Rambo. He won all the battles because he was such a good shot and so good with the knife. We all shouted and cheered every time. I wished Thandi could see this. She would love to see the movie and be proud that I also was a good shot. Then the music started and the writing came across the wall. We sat quiet. I wanted to see more of this man but then Commander Mobuto came in front. He had a big smile on his face and his tooth shone at us.

"So, soldier boys," he said. "Now you see what it is to be a soldier. You want to train and be like Rambo, hey? Do you?"

"Yes, sah," we all shouted.

"Well, you better train hard. We don't have failures here. You must all be like Rambo if you want to live. Do you hear?"

"We hear, sah," we said.

"Good. Stand and salute. Now!"

We scrambled to our feet like the crabs and gave Mobuto the salute. He saluted back and then marched from the hut. We stayed stiff until Bilole shouted at us to follow him.

As I got back in my bed my spirit felt confused. The bed was hard and the grey blanket was itchy but I had the pillow and I was warm and had eaten well. Inside I ached for Thandi and my stomach felt sick when I thought of her. I didn't know how I could escape this place. I didn't know what to even think. These men were cruel and Enoch was dead but then they were nice, gave us food and showed us the movie. My mind was still full of the Rambo pictures. I would become like Rambo and then I would get Thandi back. This thought made me smile and I closed my eyes and pretended I was with Rambo, fighting all these men to get back to my sister.

It seemed like I had just gone to sleep when someone banged on the door. I jerked awake and sat up so did the others. Bilole's big body came in the door.

"Get up," he shouted. "It's five a.m. you are to run around the field. Move. I want you lined up in two minutes."

We scrambled into our clothes in the weak yellow light and ran out to form a line behind Bilole. We jogged behind his fat backside, which moved like the bull elephant's as the sky started to turn dark pink. Soon we were on the field and panting our way around while Bilole stood in the middle.

"Again. You must do it ten times. Faster or I will beat you," he shouted.

I counted "one two, one two," as I ran and my heart beat hard. I pushed my teeth together and breathed through my nose. My legs hurt but I kept going. "One two, one two." The ground was coming up to me but I must not fail, I must not fail.

"Stop. Get to breakfast," shouted Bilole at last. "You eat in the dining hall all the time now."

I gave a big sigh, bent over and panted until my heart slowed. The sun was a yellow ball now, low in the sky, which had turned to blue. We marched behind Bilole to the same hut with the long tables. They gave us stiff white maize meal and water. I put big spoons in my mouth. It was sweet and stuck inside my mouth. My stomach was happy to be there even if my mind was not.

Commander Mobuto came just as we finished.

"You will shoot again today," he said. "Make quick."

"Line up and salute your commander," shouted Bilole.

We scrabbled to our feet and gave the salute and then we marched behind Bilole to the far field with a row of breadfruit trees behind. Through the trees I could see silver grey metal plates hanging between the wide green leaves and the yellow breadfruit. I felt the wind on my cheek and saw the plates dance. My stomach grew tight. These would not be so easy to hit. I heard David catch his breath next to me. Sipho stared at me with big eyes.

"You, come here," said Mobuto, pointing at me with his fat

finger.

I marched over with a tight stomach. My legs were weak but I pushed back my knees to keep them stiff and saluted. "Yes, sah."

"Yesterday you were Mr. Hotshot. Let's see if you can do it today," he said. He sneered at me, threw me an AK and showed me where to stand. It was far from the trees and the plates and my heart beat hard.

"The gun's loaded. Be careful," said Mobuto with hard eyes.

I swallowed hard. The AK felt slippery in my wet hands. I wiped my hand on my shorts and then pushed the AK hard back into my shoulder. I fixed my eyes onto the plate and clenched my teeth. I must do this. I cannot miss the plates. If I missed I would be a dead boy. I must do this for Thandi. I cannot die.

I put my legs a bit apart and stood firm on the spot where Mobuto had showed me with the AK hard into my shoulder. I held my breath inside and then watched as the silver plate danced in the wind. I felt the breeze on my face and I moved with the wind and the plate. The plate was not good in the sight. I waited and tried again. My legs began to shiver. I did not know if I could do this thing. If I missed Mobuto would blow out my brains like Enoch.

"Shoot, you stupid boy," shouted Mobuto.

My heart beat harder as I took one more big breath and then stared hard at the plate through the sight and pulled the trigger. The gun jumped and threw me back. My ears rang and my head spun. I squeezed tight my eyes. I was too scared to look. I opened a crack in my eyes and stared at the trees. A big sigh came from my belly. Ropes dangled in the breeze. The plate was gone. My body shook. I must have hit the plate. I turned to look at Mobuto who grunted and pushed David to the place by me.

"You are lucky," he said. "Get back there."

I saluted and obeyed. David moved to my old spot and stiffened as he stared at the next plate. He had his legs a bit apart and I saw the gun jump as the bullet thundered out. I heard a clang and the plate moved and then hung from one of the ropes. I looked at Mobuto. Would he be happy with this?

He glared at David with narrow eyes. "You are lucky you clipped it," he said. "Next time be sure to hit it full on."

David gave a salute with wide eyes and moved back to join me.

Richard was next. Bilole pushed him forward. He stood with his mad hair blowing in the wind. His body was like a wood pole. I saw him take in a big breath and push his lips together. He lined up the plate and the gun shouted. The plate fell down. I was happy he had hit it but a bit cross he was a good as me.

Sipho was next. His thin legs shook as he went to the spot. He pushed the AK into his shoulder but his arm was shaking. I held my breath. He pushed the trigger and the gun thundered. I stared at the trees. The plate was still there.

I heard Sipho gasp and saw his eyes turn white. Mobuto's tooth glinted at us.

"So we have a no shot here," he said. "What do we do with no shots, Bilole?"

"We cut their fingers off, sah." Bilole laughed and he hoisted up his pants over his fat stomach.

My heart jumped. David gave a gasp and Sipho swayed on his feet. His eyes filled with tears.

"Pull him over there," said Mobuto with an evil grin.

Bilole grabbed Sipho who started to scream. He pushed him over to a tree stump and leaned his fat body onto him. Sipho was forced onto his knees. Bilole grabbed his hand and pushed it onto the stump.

"Splay you fingers," he shouted.

Sipho was screaming and squirming like the snake under Bilole's grip. His body was shaking and the tears ran down his face. I stared frozen. My stomach was sick. There was nothing I could do.

Sipho made strange noises as Mobuto marched over like an

evil crocodile. He took a machete from his belt and I saw Sipho's finger jump into the air before it fell onto the hot ground. Sipho screamed and clutched at his bloody hand.

I stared with big eyes at him. He was bent over and I felt the air around me grow close. I turned away. I wished I could help my friend and my stomach was fallen to my feet because I couldn't. I shook my head and looked down at my hands. Poor Sipho, he didn't have fingers like me anymore. My heart cried for him but I was glad it was not my finger jumping on the ground.

"So," said Mobuto coming back to us. "You see what we do to the boys who don't shoot straight. Take him away, Bilole. He will just be good for carrying our packs like a donkey."

Bilole kicked Sipho until he stood up. His face had turned white and he was swaying on his feet. Bilole grabbed him by the arm and dragged him away. My head was spinning and my mouth was full of water. I stared at the bloody machete in Mobuto's hand. I did not like the Rambo knife anymore. I hated these men and I hated this place. Why had they taken the finger from my friend?

"You shoot now," said Mobuto to Jabu.

Jabu went over with shaking legs. I kept my eyes to the ground. I did not want to see another finger jump off.

When I looked again the plate was gone. Jabu was lucky. His fingers were safe.

"Back to barracks," commanded Mobuto. "You'll train more later."

My mind felt dead as we marched back to the hut. Maybe they would kill Sipho just like they had Enoch. I wished I was back on the dump. I wished I was small again with Umama and Thandi. Why did this have to happen to me?

Chapter 14

"Richard," I whisper and shake him roughly.

"What?" he says, and he looks at me with blurry eyes.

"Get up and stay quiet."

"Why?"

I shove him hard so that he falls with a bump onto the green cement floor.

"Fuck you, Hotshot," he whispers fiercely. "What you doing?"

"We're going to break into the surgery. I need drugs."

Richard shakes his head at me. "You are too much!"

I clench my jaw. "Just follow me. Don't wake Trigger. I don't trust him anymore." I pick up a towel from under my bed and shove it up my shirt.

Richard looks over at the snoring Trigger and frowns at me, but he obeys and we creep from the dorm into the heavy, warm night air. I look up at the dark sky. There are many stars but the moon is half hidden behind the clouds.

"It is a good night. The moon's on our side," I say. "Let's go." I move my eyebrows towards the surgery. My body tingles as we edge our way against the buildings. I feel like a soldier again and I'm glad I've got Richard to come. I must make him remember who he is. Trigger is acting strange. He's trying to be the good boy now and won't want the drugs. I will think what to do with him later.

We creep forward and I point to the back of the whitewashed hospital building.

"We are going round back," I say.

Richard nods and follows behind me until we're below the wide wooden window of the surgery.

"Stand back" I say and take out my towel and wrap it around my arm. "Now make a sound like an owl."

81

"Why?" says Richard with a frown.

"Just do what I fucking say," I hiss.

He glares at me but purses his lips and lets out a low whoop of the owl and I push up on my toes and pull back my arm before moving it hard at the center of the pane. I feel the glass shudder.

"Do it again," I say to Richard.

He gives another whoop and I draw my arm back again and hit the pane harder so that this time the glass tinkles and cracks and then falls in a shower of sharp pieces around us. Richard smiles and I give him the thumbs up.

"Wait," I whisper as he moves towards it. "We must see if they've heard."

He nods and we hold our breath and listen. The night stays still and heavy with only the chirrup of the night crickets breaking through.

"This is too easy," I say with a sneer. "Now push me up."

Richard puts his hands like a stirrup and I stand on them and shove myself up to the shattered window. I push away the broken bits at the bottom and ease myself sideways onto the sill. A sharp pain shoots through my back as I twist and I bite my lip to stop the moan. Richard gives me a final shove and I fall forwards landing with a thump on the counter of the cupboard below. I clamber off onto the cold cement floor.

The room is quiet except for my breathing. I creep towards the door leading into the ward. All is dark and silent. I skim my eyes around the corners. Nurse Sophie's not there. There are two white humps in the bed. I'm not sure who they are.

"Hotshot?"

"Shut up," I whisper fiercely at the broken window. Fucking Richard, he's so stupid. "Just wait, don't talk."

I walk like the cat to the medicine cabinet. Its glass doors are locked. I stare at the rows of bottles behind. I take the towel and place it around my hand again and hit hard at one of the panes of glass. It breaks easily and I push my hand through and snatch at the bottles. It doesn't matter what I take – it will all be good. Then I feel a burning pain on my hand and my hand grows sticky with blood from the broken glass but I smile at the pain and stuff the bottles into the pockets of my shorts. I suck the blood from my hand and wrap the towel back around it. Richard crawls in the window and smashes onto the counter. I turn and frown at him.

"How did you jump up?" I asked.

"I found a rock to stand on," he says and smiles like he's Mr. Clever Boy.

I glare at him.

"You got some?" he asks.

I nod and point towards my bulging pockets.

Richard thumps me on the shoulder and grins but then notices my cut hand and frowns. "You hurt?"

I sneer at him and shake my head. How can this be hurt? Has he gone soft?

I empty the contents of the bottles onto the counter. Pink tablets I haven't seen before roll around with heaps of the small white ones which I know are for the pain. I grab up a handful. "Here, have five," I say, shoving a handful at Richard.

He stuffs the tablets into his mouth and chews. I do the same and we grin at each other with white chalky mouths. They'll do their work soon.

Suddenly I hear footsteps. We freeze and I edge towards the surgery window and peer through the pane. Nurse Sophie's back and moving about at the end of the ward doing something on the trolley. I turn to Richard and show him to go down. I creep to the corner and we crouch on the floor.

"We'll wait till she goes," I whisper.

Richard nods. The drugs are kicking in and his eyes are glazed. My mind is feeling warm and fuzzy all over and my body feels slow and weak. It reminds me of the glue. Richard and I relax on the cement floor and lean against the wall with stupid grins on our faces. I don't care about anything anymore. If Nurse Sophie comes in I will kill her with the broken glass. I sit dreaming about cutting into her throat and seeing the red blood pump out. It's been too long since I've tasted a kill. I drift away with the thought of blood so strong that I can even taste it.

When my mind returns the night has faded and faint pink rays are peeping in through the jagged window. I poke Richard in his side. He squeaks like the mouse. I point up and show for him to go. He nods and clambers up onto the counter before heaving his body through the broken window. I hear his soft thud and I pull my heavy body backwards through the window landing on my feet. We wait for a minute to make sure no one will see us. The light is misty and pink and the air is fresh. It clears my head a bit.

I peer around the side of the building, "Go, now!" I say.

Richard looks at me with his glazed eyes but obeys. We creep grinning back to our dorm and into our beds.

When I wake again the copper sun is halfway across the sky. A shadow flits across the doorway and I tense. Bengu is here.

"Modetse, Richard – Dr. Zuma wants to see you in his office now."

"Tell him to fuck off," I say and my voice croaks.

Richard laughs. I smile at him glad to see his old self is back.

"No, you must go," says Bengu.

"I told you. Tell him to go fuck himself," I shout.

Bengu clenches his jaw and refuses to move. My body tenses and I feel around for something hard to hit him with. The best I can find is my shoe and I throw it with disgust to the side. My fists will do. I lunge towards him but just then Tula comes up behind him. I freeze, turn and clutch at my bed to stop myself falling over.

Bengu shakes his head at me. "Hurry, the doctor's waiting for both of you."

He turns and walks away and Tula hesitates before giving me a small wave.

I'm hot all over and full with anger inside. I'll kill that bastard. Just you wait – soon I'll kill you and cut off your head to feed to the dogs, I scream at him inside my head.

"Come on Richard," I bark.

"They must know," he says.

"So what! What's he going to do? Kill us? They're too soft to do anything. I've no fear of them," I say, looking at Richard in disgust.

He looks down and shuffles into his clothes. I put on my sandals and walk out of the door towards the doctor's office like the proud lion.

I throw open the door and march inside.

"Yes," I demand.

Dr. Zuma gazes up from his desk and stares at me. I hold his gaze with hard eyes and a straight back even though it's painful to stand like that.

"Where's Richard?"

I shrug.

"How are you feeling?"

"Good," I say with an ugly smile.

He looks down at my hand and the crooked cut across the side by my thumb.

"I see you've hurt yourself," says Dr. Zuma.

I laugh out loud. "It is nothing."

"What you did last night is not nothing," says Dr. Zuma. "Tablets like that in big doses can destroy your liver. It's not good for you, never mind the theft."

"So what," I shout. "I've taken much worse than your stupid tablets. I told you we need the brown-brown or glue. I told you," I scream at him. "We need it. Our bodies need it. That's why I take it."

My head is thrown back and my body is like stiff like the AK.

85

I make a move towards Dr. Zuma to hit him. He stands up and in one big step he grabs both my arms and holds them behind my back.

"We won't have that here. You and Richard are going to clean up the glass and you are going to help Bengu re-glaze that window and then fit iron bars so you won't ever be able to do that again. I'm not pleased with you at all."

He stares at me with fierce eyes and holds my arms so tight behind me that I can't move. I look at him with hate eyes. I'm so angry that I feel my eyes prick with tears. No, I won't let him see that. I squeeze back the tears and continue to glare at him. I won't let him break me. I won't.

Richard comes to the doorway and stands staring with big eyes.

"I'm not happy, Richard," says Dr. Zuma. "You're both going to make right your wrong."

"Yes, sah," says Richard in a small voice.

I turn round and pull up my lip at him. Coward – he has no spirit anymore. All he's good for is the witchdoctor's fire.

He looks away from my stare of hate.

That afternoon the doctor comes with and guards me as I pull a face and help Bengu to fix the window. I put the putty on bit by bit and make sure I drop some. Then I try and break the new glass as I give it to him, but Bengu grabs it away.

"Leave the glass. You can do the iron bars," he says.

I pick up one and move my arm back to strike him with it but Dr. Zuma grabs my arm and pushes me over to the window. I try to resist but he's too strong.

"Richard come and hold this," says Dr. Zuma.

Richard shuffles over as if the doctor is Mobuto and obeys. Fucking coward.

"Good," says Dr. Zuma as we finish and clean away. "I'll show you some pictures of a diseased liver later and then hopefully you'll realize why we don't want to give you too many tablets."

"What do I care about my liver," I scream at him. "Fuck my liver. I'm a soldier. I take the brown-brown. I take the juju. I sniff the glue. You think some stupid tablets can break me. Hey? Hey?"

The veins are standing out in my neck and my fists are clenched. All the anger I've been keeping inside is exploding out.

"You must learn again to love yourself and your body," whispers Dr. Zuma. "It's my prayer that you'll do that soon."

"Fuck you and your prayers," I shout. "I don't need you and I don't need your God."

"Yes, you do." Dr. Zuma smiles. "I'm afraid we all do. Without him we are nothing."

I'm so angry at his words that my mouth just opens and closes like a fish. I put my hands to my face, throw my head back and scream. I hate him so much that I don't know what to do. I just want to be back with my L.R.A.

Chapter 15

It was two days and Sipho had not come. My heart was too heavy and I was sure he was dead. I was losing all my friends. I'd lost my family. Maybe Thandi too was dead? My body was going mad for the glue and I was sure just now I too would die.

I lay on my bed and stared with empty eyes at the doorway. David, Richard and Jabu were still in the shower. The sun was beginning to fall and the light outside had turned orange. Then suddenly I heard marching outside.

"Get in. You can join the boys for supper," shouted Bilole. A boy was pushed through the door and Sipho's big forehead came in front of my eyes. I jumped from my bed and ran over to him. I put my arms around him.

"Hey, Sipho, I was too scared for you," I said in a small voice.

Sipho pulled back and looked at me with wet eyes. He shook his head. "*Mimi nina* okay," he whispered.

I looked down at his hand. There was a brown bandage on it and it looked too fat. "*Samahani,* my brother. At least, they did not take your hand."

He nodded and shuffled over to his bed and lay down. I followed him with my eyes and then sat back on my own bed with a sore heart. The silence was heavy between us.

I cleared my throat and said, "Don't worry; we will soon get away, my brother. I will try and find a way."

"You think we can?" asked Sipho, lifting his eyebrows at me.

"*Ndiyo,*" I said with my eyes down. "We must just wait for the right time. I will stay with you Sipho."

Sipho nodded and stared up at the ceiling.

"We are brothers," I said, but he still just stared up at the ceiling. Inside my stomach was going round and round. I did not know how to help him and how we would ever get out of this place, but I must try. I must watch everything with clever eyes so

I could think what to do. Sipho needed me to lead. It had always been like that on the dump. Thandi needed me too. I gave a small sob. I clenched my fists. Why did this have to happen to us, why? Why had they taken my friend's finger? I hated these fucking men. I hated them so much.

I heard David's voice and turned as he came back into the hut.

"Hey, Sipho," said David, looking with sad eyes at him. "It's good you are back."

Sipho just nodded and said nothing. I pulled a face at David to tell him to leave him.

Then Richard and Jabu came in. They stopped and stared at Sipho and said, "Hey."

Sipho looked and turned over and lay on his side. I could see he did not want to talk to anyone and must be paining bad inside.

"Come, we must go eat," I said after a short while. "You will be better when your stomach is full."

We went to the dining hut and afterwards we walked back with heavy steps to our hut before the other boys. Sipho shuffled next to me with his head down. He had only eaten a small bit of the beef stew and left his bread.

"I'm tired," said Sipho as soon as we got into the hut. "My hand is paining. I'm going to sleep."

"Do you want a story to help you sleep?" I asked.

He shrugged his shoulders and lay down on his bed. I stared at him. His eyes were big and sad. My stomach hurt for my friend so bad. I knew he liked to have things always looking good and would hate his hand with no finger.

"I will tell you one about how the clever lion cub defeated the ugly hippo," I said, and then whispered, "It would be like us killing Bilole and Mobuto." I watched his face to see if this helped him.

Sipho gave a small smile and said, "Okay, maybe that will

help me to sleep."

I made up the story of the two ugly hippos called Bilole and Mobuto and the clever lion cub called Sipho. Sipho lion cub he got Mr. Modetse Crocodile to help play the bad trick on the hippos and make them fall in the trap so that Mr. Crocodile can bite their big backsides and make them run away. Sipho laughed as I made the big crocodile mouth and pretended to bite Bilole and Mobuto. I smiled at his laughter and was glad the story helped. I wished Thandi was with us to hear it. She always told me I was number one storyteller.

I closed my eyes so I could just pretend that we were all back in our sewer pipe house with me telling stories and Sipho, Enoch and Thandi all laughing and laughing. But then I felt my stomach jump and a big sob came out my mouth from deep inside. I could not pretend that for long. Everything here was so bad that I could never forget it. Enoch was dead and Sipho had no finger. What would happen next to us? I shook my head. I must not think these things. I had to stay strong or this place would kill me.

Soon Sipho was snoring. I hoped he would feel better when the sun came again.

The next morning Bilole screamed at us before the sun had awoken properly made us run and run around the field until our bodies were wet with the sweat. Sipho was lucky because he did not have to come.

We'd had to do this every morning for two weeks and I liked the routine. It made my mind strong and my muscles had grown hard. At the end of the two weeks I was able to run ten times around the field before I started to pant. It felt good.

"Phew, I am smelling," said Jabu as he lifted his arm to smell his sweaty armpits as we marched back to the hut after the last session. There were two black stains on his shirt.

I lifted mine and saw the same. "Stinko!" I said, and they all laughed.

Sipho was awake and lay on his bed staring at us as we came in.

"Hey, Sipho," I said. "You good?"

He nodded at me.

"At least you did not have to do the hard training," I said. "It was bad."

He shrugged and looked down at his hand. I knew he would have to carry the things for Bilole and Mobuto now and I knew that he must be very cross inside. I bit my lip and looked at the floor as I sat on the edge of my bed. I felt bad but there was nothing I could do.

"I will go and drink water and then we must rest. We must train again in one hour," says David.

Jabu and I looked at each other and nodded. He was like our father sometimes.

"I'm hungry. It's not fair that we can't have food until lunchtime," I said.

"At least water will fill our stomachs," said David.

I pulled a face. The hunger in my stomach had made me angry. I was glad I had friends but inside I was still hurting. If I told them the truth they would see that I just want to cry and run away from this place, but it was impossible. The soldiers were everywhere and they felt nothing to kill us. I would never really be able to help Sipho and me escape. My mind jumped again to Thandi and a deep cry came in my chest. Always it was jumping to her and nearly every night she visited in my dreams and left me with a big hole in my stomach when I woke. I shook my head to chase the thoughts away and hide my pain. I would have to try and be stronger. I must not let my mind break me otherwise I would die.

"You've gone quiet, Modetse," said David. "You okay?"

"Yes," I said, turning my head away. "Do you want to come get water, Sipho?"

"Okay," said Sipho.

We ran out to find the water and glugged and splashed its coolness all over us.

"I hate it here," said Sipho. He clenched his jaw as we walked back to the hut behind David.

"It's bad," I agreed, "but you must not let them break you." I looked down at his hurt hand. "You must try not to think."

"They make me a donkey. I don't like this life. I hate it. I hate it," he shouted as big tears flowed from his eyes.

"Shh, Sipho, don't shout," I said. "I know you hate it. I know you like things to be nice but there's nothing we can do."

Sipho put his head down and sobbed. "I want to die," he said. "I don't want to live anymore. I hated the dump and the fighting but it was not so bad as this. I hate it, Modetse, I hate it."

I put my arm around him. "Stop it, Sipho. I promise I will try and help us escape soon."

Sipho looked up at me with wet eyes. "Really?"

"Really," I said, and looked away with a heavy heart.

We walked on some more in silence and then I said suddenly, "Hey, let's play a trick on Richard."

Sipho lifted his eyebrows at me. "How?"

"Let's try to find the spider. I heard Richard tell Jabu he's scared of spiders. Let's find the big spider and put it in his bed."

A slow smile came on Sipho's face. "Where ?"

"They hide under the huts. Let's look this side." I crept around the back of our hut and Sipho followed. I got down on my haunches and looked under the dusty floorboards with hawk eyes. I was sure one must be there. Ay, I was too clever. There was a rusty brown hairy body of the big spider hiding with the stones and the dirt.

"Ay, something's smiling on us," I said, and giggled. "It's a baboon spider."

"A big one?"

"Ay, so big Richard will shit his pants."

"Where? Where? Let me see."

"Wait," I commanded. "Get me a stick."

Sipho looked around for a long twig and gave it me. I crawled under the hut towards the hairy bent legs which stuck out from the side of a stone. I stretched out my arm with the stick and held my breath as I gave the spider monster a poke. The stick made a dent in the soft body and I jumped back with a small cry.

"Did it bite?" said Sipho.

"No," I said, "it's okay; I think he's dead."

"You sure?"

I nodded my head but my heart thumped. I prodded the spider again and for a second it looked like it had come alive, I caught my breath, but then I realized it was just the stick that had moved it.

"It's okay," I whispered and grinned as I poked the numb hairy body again. I hooked the stick behind it and pulled it forward bit by bit until I could catch its leg. I held the hairy leg with my fingers and crawled out backwards.

"Take off your shirt. We can wrap it in that.

Sipho took off his T-shirt and gave it to me.

"Hey, this is a good spider for Richard." I laughed staring at the hairy body. "It's the big orange baboon one. His scarecrow hair will never go flat again."

"Good, I want to see his eyes pop from his head," said Sipho, and laughed.

"He'll be a monster scarecrow now."

We held our sides, bent over with laughter, and then walked like the main men back to the hut with our poison.

"Put your shirt under your bed," I whispered as we got to the door.

Richard, Jabu and David were in the hut but Sipho did well and just walked with big steps up to his bed and pretended to put his shirt in the basket under it. Soon it was time for supper and we all left the hut.

As soon as the food was finished Sipho and me raced back to get there before Richard and Jabu. David gave us a funny look as we ran from the dining hut.

"Quick, give me your shirt," I said to Sipho as we puffed into our hut.

Sipho pulled out the bundle and I unwrapped the hairy orange monster with its beady eyes and baboon fangs.

"Hey, this's too good. Richard will go mad." I laughed loud.

Sipho snorted as I pushed the baboon spider down to the bottom of Richard's bed. His feet would not be smiling tonight.

Soon Richard, Jabu and David returned. David gave me a long look and raised his eyebrows but I just smiled at him. I gave Sipho a sideways look. He looked back and smiled. I could feel his excitement and felt warm inside.

Richard and Jabu came in and I looked at them and said, "Hey!"

"Hey," said Richard, while Jabu grunted.

Richard settled on his bed and I held my breath.

"I'm going to sleep for a bit in case they call us for night training," I said, faking the big yawn.

"Good idea," said Sipho, also yawning and lying down on his pillow. I faced him and gave a wink. Our yawning made Richard yawn. He lay down and turned on his side. My body tensed and I bit my lip to hide my smile.

"It's cooler now. I need my blanket," I said, crawling under the coarse, grey wool.

"Me too," said Sipho.

"Tell us if we must get up David," I called.

"Okay," replied David with deep eyes and a frown.

Sipho's eyes bulged as we watched Richard lift up his blanket. I held my breath and waited.

"Aeeiou, aeeiou!" Richard's screams of terror cracked through the air. He jumped out of his bed and threw the blanket off. The spider flew up with it and landed on his foot. He kicked it, threw his arms up to the air and then ran screaming around the hut like a mad devil.

"Aeeio, fucking spider...fucking spider... The giant orange spider has bitten me. Aeeiou, I'm a dead boy...I'm a dead boy. Help me, help me...help me!"

He fell on the floor holding his foot and wailing with his eyes so big I thought they would pop out.

Sipho and I held our stomachs and laughed so loud that the tears fell down our faces. Jabu sat up and stared down at Richard and then his loud laughter joined with ours and shook around the hut.

"Richard...Richard," shouted David going over to look at the spider. "It's okay. It's dead. It's dead!"

But Richard was deaf to him and had hopped from the hut clutching his foot in his fear. David ran after him while Jabu looked us with smiling eyes through his laughter. I high-fived Sipho. His head was thrown back, his mouth was wide open in the big laugh and his eyes glowed. For a bit he had forgotten he was Donkey Boy and I was glad.

Chapter 16

The next morning Richard, ay he would not speak to us. We walked like a spider behind him and touched his arm to give him a fright until he was too cross.

"Fuck you, Hotshot. I'll get you back," he said, and pulled his face in a snarl like the mad dog.

"It was just a joke," said Jabu. "Leave Hotshot."

Sipho raised his eyebrows at me. All of a sudden Jabu was on our side. David shook his head at us and smiled.

"Leave it now, Richard. It's okay," he said. "Come we must go train. We can't be late."

Richard clenched his jaw but obeyed. Jabu ran behind him and made to kick him from behind and smiled at us.

Sipho gave a snort and I gave Jabu the thumbs up. I was glad he liked the jokes. Maybe he would also be our friend.

Bilole was waiting for us on the training ground, hitting his stick against his legs.

"You're lucky. One more second and I would've beaten you all. Run now. Ten laps and fifty push-ups. Go! You, Sipho – go over there and pack those things in that box."

Sipho nodded and moved to the trees on the side while we obeyed and ran with eyes hard in front around the big yellow field.

"Ropes!" shouted Bilole as we finished the last push-up.

We panted over to the long wooden frames with their dangling ropes. I felt my hands burn and sting as I pulled myself up the side and over. The muscles in my arms rippled and I felt my hard stomach give me strength. I was becoming strong and that was good. I must not lose hope. I must keep going so that one day I can get back to Thandi.

"Right, get to the teaching hut now all of you. Mobuto's waiting. Run!" shouted Bilole as we went over the last frame.

We saluted him and Sipho joined us as we rushed over to the big hut. Commander Mobuto was standing in front and we marched in silence past him, hands in salute and sat down cross-legged on the wooden floor. He stared with narrow eyes and marched with big steps up and down in front of us. We kept our eyes down so as not to offend. All of a sudden he shouted in a voice so loud that I jumped.

"We're going to watch a film today. You like films, you boys. You like Rambo. Today you will see who we're really fighting against. Start," he commanded.

We turned to see Nkunda starting the big projector. The light flickered on the white wall and then the faces of men appeared.

"These are the government pigs who want to kill us. Look at their ugly faces like diseased swine. They are like the tsetse fly who wants to come silently in the night and kill us. We're training you to stop them. You must not let us down. Do you hear?"

A big picture of the fly with evil eyes came on the screen. Then there were thousands of them and we saw the flies biting the children and then the children dying.

"This is you," he shouted. "The enemy will kill you if you don't kill him first. Are you ready to do the training hard to kill? Are you?"

"Yes, sah!" we shouted back.

I stared at these evil flies on the screen. My heart filled with hate as Mobuto screamed,

"You see. This is why we train you hard. You need to kill these flies. If you don't you are dead. You have not met the enemy yet. You have not seen their evil. Now you see them. Look! Look! They are killing you and your family. Are you ready to attack them?"

My body grew hard while Mobuto spoke. I stared at the flies with hate eyes and shouted, "Yes, sah, we are ready" with the others.

"Every day they are killing the people and destroying our country," shouted Mobuto. "They take all the money and make big houses for themselves. They eat like fat cats. If we don't stop them we'll be dead. Do you want to be dead soldier boys? Hey, do you want to be dead?"

"No, sah," we shouted.

"Good – you must learn to kill first. You're good killers. You have no fear. You're young and have long lives still. Will you kill well for the L.R.A.?"

"Yes, sah, we will kill well for the L.R.A.," we chanted.

"Good," said Mobuto. "You are lucky boys – now we'll do the L.R.A. ceremony on you and then everyone will know you are big soldier boys who belong to us. March to the field. Move!"

My mind buzzed with the pictures of the enemy and I could feel the hate growing in my heart as we marched behind each other to the field and lined up for Mobuto. Mobuto was clever. He knew these people. These people were bad. They were the enemy. If these people found Thandi they would kill her. They would rape her. The veins on my neck grew tense. I clenched my fist. My mind was black and full of blood. Mobuto was right. If they touched Thandi I would kill them. He was clever. I must listen to him.

"Take off your shirts, all of you!" shouted Mobuto as we reached the field.

We obeyed and ripped off our shirts and held them folded in front of us.

"Put them on the ground and stand to attention. Now!"

We placed the folded shirts on the ground and shuffled into a line, heads back and arms stiff by our sides. Bilole walked over like a bull elephant carrying something wrapped in a linen cloth. He slowly took off the cloth to show a big piece of jagged glass like a dagger. My breath froze in my throat.

"Ready, sah," he said to Mobuto.

Mobuto grabbed Richard and pulled him to the front.

Richard's eyes were white and staring and his thin body shook all over. He looked even more scared than when he saw the spider.

"Cut," said Mobuto as he clutched Richard's arm and held it out straight for Bilole. He came behind and made deep cuts into the arm like he was writing something. Richard threw back his head and screamed, but could not run; Mobuto held him too tight and laughed at his pain. I watched with narrow eyes as the dark red blood bubbled up behind the glass and my stomach dropped to my feet.

"Done," said Bilole, holding down the glass dagger, which dripped with the bright red blood.

"Good work," said Mobuto, looking at Richard's arm. He pushed him away to the side and called, "Next."

Bilole pulled David forward. Mobuto did the same, holding out David's arm for Bilole who smiled while he cut. David clenched his jaw and screwed his eyes shut as the glass went deep into his arm. He made a small cry and Bilole laughed and then pushed him away.

Mobuto grabbed me. I held my muscles strong and my jaw stiff. I must not look weak. Why were they cutting us? I wanted to be back on the dump. "No…" I screamed as the sharp glass cut deep into my arm. The pain was so fierce that my body went numb. My head buzzed and the yellow grass blurred in front of my eyes. I wobbled and felt Bilole push me over to Richard and David. I clutched my arm to stop the thick red blood shooting up. It ran out between my fingers. I looked at David and Richard. There was pain still in their eyes and I knew their arms were hurting like mine. I forgot the others until Jabu joined us, and then Sipho, both of them crying and shaking.

"Stop your sniveling," shouted Mobuto. "This is a badge of honor. You're lucky soldier boys. This will heal in a nice big scar and everyone will know that you belong to the L.R.A. Now, go wash yourselves and get back to barracks."

We tried to stop our tears and saluted him and then picked up our folded shirts and went to the shower hut. I shivered as the cold water washed over me and I let my tears come, glad that the water could hide them. I heard a snuffle next to me and saw tears running from Richard's eyes. He saw me looking and knew that I too was crying. I gave him a small smile and he smiled back.

When I lay in bed that night many thoughts fought in my mind. The writing would show everyone I was L.R.A., and if I escaped some people would try to kill me. But then I remembered the tsetse fly enemy. No, maybe it was better to be L.R.A. The tsetse fly enemy would kill Thandi if we didn't stop them. Mobuto had said so. I must listen to him. He is old and wise. He knows this enemy. He has fought him for many years. His eyes have seen what they can do. My mind jumped back and forward between these thoughts until I thought my head would explode like the grenade. I had seen the enemy on the movie. The movie did not lie. Mobuto did not lie. He was right. I must be proud to be L.R.A. that way I will stay tough and be able to protect Thandi. My spirit felt strong as I moved my fingers round the letters in my flesh.

After breakfast Mobuto told us to go to the parade ground and we had to run quickly from the hut.

"Today the General will come and see you," he said as we arrived panting. "You're lucky if you're looking smart. Any soldier boy who is not will be beaten before the General sees him."

I looked over my uniform and let out a big sigh of relief. It was very smart. I looked over at Richard. He was trying to smooth down his shirt to hide the creases. Fool, he didn't know how to be neat like me. I was glad Umama had taught me well. I smiled inside as Mobuto went over to Richard and hit him hard on the head.

"Go see Bilole and sort that out now," he shouted, kicking

Richard on his thin legs and hitting him in his ribs with a big wooden stick.

Richard doubled over and cried out but ran out fast to Bilole. Jabu looked after him and then looked down at his own uniform. It did not have creases but was still not so good as mine. I saw him look sideways at mine and stood straighter with my head high.

"Right, the rest of you, forward march!" shouted Mobuto.

We obeyed and marched in a straight line behind him to the parade ground.

"Nkunda's squadron's here," whispered David.

I saw Badboy with his braids of red and green beads in his hair standing stiff and smart in his uniform and hoped I would not have to be near him. I stared at him as we got close. His face and eyes were hard like the AK, which he held tight, and I could see he would feel nothing to kill us. He was taller than us and must be fourteen years. He felt my stare and turned with those eyes to glare at me. My stomach dropped. I looked down quick. I saw him sneer at me and narrow his eyes.

Two other old child soldiers from Nkunda were also with us. There was a very tall one I heard Nkunda call Bloodneverdry. He must be a quick killer. I drew back a little. They were tough these boys of Nkunda. I was glad I wasn't in their squadron. Jabu and Richard could be mean but they were not hard like these ones. I looked at a shorter one with dark skin, a square head and a fat nose. He had a scar down his cheek; maybe it had come from the battle. I heard Nkunda call him Trigger. I hoped that did not mean he could fire the AK quicker than me. There was also one called Shithead, who was short but strong, with big muscles in his arms and legs. He had the very big head and looked like he was fifteen years maybe. His skin was dark like Jabu's but he had many small holes on his face like pellets had been shot into him. I saw he had a sharp dagger on his belt and two Lieutenant bars on the beret on his head. He stood stiff and proud like a young lion.

"Line up here!" commanded Bilole showing us the area behind.

I smiled inside at this luck and took big steps into the second row, glad that I was away from Badboy and his cold eyes.

"Now, stand to attention all of you," shouted Mobuto. "The great General will be here soon."

We stood straight and silent as the hot morning sun burned into our heads and caused our armpits to grow wet. It felt like hours before I saw the General coming with his giraffe walk and mirror eyes. His uniform was still like new but now he wore the big hat on his head, which shaded his face with its sides, instead of his beret. He took big steps towards a wooden platform with a big standing umbrella over which Bilole had laid out for him. The soldiers around the platform saluted smartly and shuffled backwards. The General climbed the platform and looked at us behind his glasses. I shivered inside and wished again that I could see his eyes.

"Soldiers, this is your General. Salute!" commanded Mobuto, standing to attention himself and saluting.

We stood upright and saluted him while the drummers started up and the drums began to shout to the sky about his greatness. The "Boom, Boom, Boom" vibrated through the ground and caused my insides to shake.

"The General is our leader," shouted Mobuto. "He's our father, the protector and the one who makes the L.R.A. great. Without the General we are nothing. Today you will swear your life to him. If you ever turn traitor the spirits will come from the darkness and eat out your brains. You will never escape. Never! Are you clear?"

"Yes, sah," we said and saluted.

"Now, say after me:

Oh Great General of the L.R.A.
We swear to be good soldiers,

We swear to obey all orders and never betray the L.R.A.

May the spirits take us and eat out our brains if we ever break our oath.

You are our father, our protector.

We swear our lives to you."

We chanted each line loud after Mobuto and the drums joined with us, shouting their promise to the great man. The General stood tall as our voices bounced onto the mirrors of his eyes. My heart beat hard as the words came out of my mouth. The General whispered something to Mobuto, got off the platform and went away without looking back.

"Bilole, Nkunda – get the bottles," commanded Mobuto.

Bilole and Nkunda saluted and went over to the trees. They came back carrying two cool boxes and unpacked lots of small bottles.

"You will now seal your allegiance by drinking the blood of our enemy," shouted Mobuto. "This blood will help the spirits to build the dark power in your hearts and make you better killers for the L.R.A. Now drink!"

Bilole handed out the small bottles with the dark red blood inside. My body shook inside. I did not want to look at it as I lifted it to my mouth. I held my stomach, which wanted to jump out from the iron smell. The blood was rich and bitter on my tongue and slid thickly in strings down my throat. I had to force myself to swallow it and I pretended that it was lovely meat stew instead. At last it was done and I breathed a big sigh as my stomach calmed. I heard David retch next to me and showed him with cross-eyes to control it. They would kill us if we vomited the enemy blood. All over the boy soldiers were sighing and trying not to throw up.

"Take them back," said Mobuto.

"We can never leave now," whispered David as we marched slowly back.

I nodded He'd said my worried thoughts. I was scared of the

dark spirits. I had drunk them down. My body tingled and I felt sick. How would I get Thandi now? I could never leave the L.R.A. and escape the spirits. They would find me wherever I was and eat out my brains. I could only find her if they let me, and what if they would not let me do that? I had wanted to be L.R.A. because of the tsetse fly enemy on the film and because I thought it was the only way to save Thandi, but now I did not know anymore what to think. There was bad fear inside me. The enemy blood was in my stomach. The dark spirits had come into my mind. My heavy soul dropped to my toes and my eyes glazed over. The hot tears pricked behind them but I was too dead for them to spill over. I could not even run from myself now. The evil was inside me.

Chapter 17

I stared at the RPG and my body rippled. This was even better than the AK. It was long, polished and full of power. I wanted to learn more about these weapons. Already we had learned how to throw the grenades. Every day we were shooting our AKs at the targets and every day I was the best. When I got into bed at night I dreamed about the AK bullets and being the number one L.R.A fighter. I had the spirits in me now. I was strong like Rambo. Everybody was jealous because I was number one shot.

"The projectile goes here," said Commander Mobuto. "Don't stand behind or it will blow off your head like the angry buffalo. You must hold it like this."

He showed us to hold it on our shoulder. "You, Jabu, come."

Jabu walked over with big steps and a high head to Mobuto and took the RPG and placed it on his shoulder like Mobuto had shown. He looked strong and stood like Mr. Lion.

"Fire!" shouted Mobuto as he moved back.

Jabu pulled the trigger and a grenade hissed forward so fast it blurred and then exploded with thunder and fire as it hit the trees. Jabu was knocked back but he righted himself and did not fall. I frowned at him when he looked back at me with glinting eyes. Mobuto grunted and took the RPG away.

"David, you – aim for that old tank there."

I hoped David would shoot better than Jabu. Jabu mustn't think he's number one shot like me. David went over with a serious look and slow steps. He picked up the RPG. He held it well and pulled the trigger. The grenade hissed forward and knocked him back but he was okay and the tank exploded in a shower of twisted metal. I smiled. He was just as good as Jabu. I lifted my eyebrows at David as he walked back and he lifted his back.

Mobuto grunted and called, "Hotshot, come."

I marched over with a big smile at my new name and tried to grab the RPG but instead Mobuto commanded, "Throw this grenade over at the trees and make it far or I'll beat you."

I stopped and stared but saluted and took the grenade. I pulled a face and swore inside at Mobuto. Why could I not shoot the RPG? Why did I have to throw the fucking grenade only? I saw Jabu and Richard with a sneer on their faces because it was the Pineapple girls who throw the grenades mostly, because they're small and can run close to the targets.

"Pull the pin and throw it. Now!" screamed Mobuto.

I pulled the ring and made a wide arc with my arm, flicking my wrist to throw the grenade with all my power towards the far breadfruit trees. My aim was good and the bright flash parted the wide leaves and exploded the yellow fruit into the air.

"Okay, now try the RPG," said Mobuto.

I picked up the long tube and held it carefully. I wanted to make sure I could do it better than Jabu. I pushed it hard into my shoulder and put my legs apart before pushing the trigger in. The weapon jumped back into me and hissed out the grenade which landed by the trees with a flash and roar of fire. I stepped backwards but stayed strong.

"Not bad," said Mobuto. "Right, Richard."

Richard did okay but not as good as me. I glared at Jabu but he pretended not to see me.

"Now I want you all to take apart your AKs, Go!" shouted Mobuto as soon as Richard had put the RPG back down.

I grabbed my gun, which was well oiled and clean, and took it apart and lay it down for Mobuto to see. I glanced to the side. Jabu had beaten me. I scowled.

"Jabu name all the parts," said Mobuto.

Jabu rattled off all the parts of the AK and Mobuto smiled.

"Good. You remember the details well."

Jabu puffed up his chest and I glared at him.

"Put it back together. Now! Bilole, hit anyone who's late."

My hands blurred and soon my AK was back together smiling at me. Mobuto nodded at me and my heart felt proud. I saluted him and looked sideways at Jabu.

"The RPG's was good," I said as we packed our weapons away after training.

"We're lucky we shot well," said David.

I said nothing but knew he meant Sipho and his finger and my heart felt bad that I had forgot my friend's pain so soon.

"The RPG's better than the AK," said Jabu, giving me a sideways look.

"That's just 'cause you're not so good with the AK," I said, and glared at him with narrow eyes.

He clenched his hands. "Fuck you, Modetse; I'm just as good as you. I put it apart before you and I know all the parts better!"

"So, I hit much more targets than you."

"You talk such shit – I've hit just as many," shouted Jabu, coming at me with his fists. "I'm older than you. Don't think you can be better than me."

"You're only one year older," I shouted back. "That means nothing. You don't have to be old to be the best soldier. I am better than you."

"Fuck you," shouted Jabu, launching at me.

David caught his arms and pulled him back. "Stop it, you two. You'll make trouble for yourselves.

"Hey, you boys – Mobuto wants you out now. Move! If I find you fighting I'll fuck you both up."

We turned to see Badboy standing at the door. He glared at us with his cold eyes. He had his hands on his hips and I saw his machete glint at his side. He saw me and kept his eyes hard as he put one hand around its handle. I froze and Jabu jerked back. The air between us crackled as Badboy looked from me to Jabu and then back again.

"I told you to move; now go or I will cut you and drink both your blood."

I gave Jabu the evil eye but marched over quickly and picked up my AK. I did not want to test Badboy. I slung it over my shoulder and showed for David to follow.

"Be careful of Jabu," whispered David. "He had big brothers and is used to fighting. He will want to beat you."

I nodded and gritted my teeth. I knew David was right but I was not weak. I would not let Jabu beat me. I didn't care if he knew how to fight and was hard; so was I.

Mobuto was waiting outside with a movie in his hand.

"To the movie hut," he shouted. "We'll watch the enemy pigs," he said with a grin. "You'll see the dirty pigs from the bush who try and kill us. The evil ones who kill your mother and father and stick their dirty big cocks into your sister."

"Yes, sah," we said. We hurried to the hut and sat on the floor with our legs crossed and our AKs across our laps. My mind was excited at the thought of seeing the tsetse fly enemy again and I forgot about my fight with Jabu.

This time the movie started with a village with lots of children running around. The men were sitting drinking beer and the women were making food in big pots, hitting them with long wooden sticks. All of a sudden soldiers, dressed in uniforms of the government crept from the bushes. They were wearing the government badge and had green paint on their cheeks.

"Watch as the enemy pig kills your family," screamed Mobuto. "See how they cut out their hearts and eat them and pull out their eyes with their dirty fingers."

We rose up in anger as we saw the soldiers rush into the village and begin shooting, stabbing and raping the people. Every hair on my body was full with fury. My muscles screamed with hate and my face twisted with my anger.

"You must kill the dirty enemy pigs. You must kill them. They're killing your family. Look they're sticking their big dirty diseased cocks into your mother. You must kill them!" screamed

Mobuto. His eyes were bulging and his fat stomach heaved up and down.

My anger grew inside. Mobuto was right. I could see the dirty enemy pig on the screen. He was attacking the young girl like Thandi who was only five years. He was beating her with his gun until she was lying bleeding on the ground. I wanted to tear him to pieces like the wild dog.

I jumped up and shook my fist at the screen. The enemy cut the throat of the girl and I opened my mouth and roared, "Die! I will kill you!" at the screen.

We screamed together as the enemy stabbed the women and tore their clothes. Every boy wanted to kill. "Kill the pigs. Kill the pigs!" we shouted and the hut vibrated with our anger. I watched the enemy rape the young girl and the film went blurry in front of my eyes. My fists clenched and my whole body tensed like the wire spring. It was Thandi up there! The rage in my belly burst forward like the mad black rhino. I screamed as loud as I could, "Kill the enemy pigs. Make their blood spill out. Drink their blood. Take out their eyes!"

The whole room was alive with our hate. Even David wanted to kill.

"Kill the pigs, take out their eyes!" we shouted together after Mobuto. All I felt was the power of the L.R.A. My body was alive for the killing. I was a killing machine. I felt David next to me and Sipho. Jabu and Richard were there too. We were all true brothers of the L.R.A. We were the army who would fight and destroy the evil enemy pigs who took our beautiful land. Too long the land had cried tears of blood because of what they have done. That's what Mobuto told us. We would take their blood and make the land free again from the evil regime of the enemy. The General and Commander Mobuto would lead us to victory.

"*Maisha Uhuru*," shouted Mobuto.

He raised his AK high into the air. We copied him.

"Freedom lives," we shouted.

"Maisha Uhuru!
Mungu yu pamoja nasi,
Sisi Ni Jeshi La Mungu,
God is with us, we are the God Army."

Chapter 18

"Modetse, come quick."

It was David. He looked at me with big shining eyes and panted with excitement. I looked up at his happy face. "What's up?"

"Jabu's has found some meat for us. He says we must come fast before the soldiers come back. Where's Richard and Sipho?"

"They're at the dining hut with Trigger. They have to do the cleaning duty for Bilole."

"Okay – let's go."

I followed David through the tall yellow grass and past a clump of acacia trees to a thatched mud hut at the back. David ran like a gazelle on his long thin legs and I took big strides behind him. It was late in the afternoon and the sun was moving down the sky.

"Here, quick," said Jabu as his head peered out from the back of the wooden hut. He put his fingers to his lips and showed for us to come to the back of the round mud hut. We crept around its circle wall to a strong fire, which still smoldered with the smell of the burnt meat. My mouth filled with water; the smell was too good. There was a big leg of buck lying across the red coals. The soldiers had cut chunks from it but there was still good juicy meat on the bone. Jabu grinned and his brown eyes shone.

"You're too clever, Jabu. How did you find this feast?"

He puffed up like a rooster when I asked this.

"Ha, you are not the only clever one. I saw Nkunda coming from here with the other officers. Their mouths were shiny with the oil from the meat. I knew there must be a big feast."

Jabu talked through a mouthful of the meat, his cheeks round like two mud huts. The meat it smelt too good and I pulled out my sharp dagger and ran to the buck. I stabbed the teeth into it, cut big jagged slices of the bloody meat and stuffed it into my mouth. It was soft, fat and oily and tasted like the heaven.

"My stomach dances from this meat. I've never eaten like this," I said as I tore a big piece of red meat from the bone with my sharp knife and gave it to David. He pushed the whole chunk into his mouth. His cheeks bulged and he had to chew it with his mouth half open because there was so much. We were laughing with our fat mouths as we ate.

"Give me more, Modetse," said David. "My stomach wants more."

I'd never seen him so excited. He was jumping up and down.

"I'm sharing it properly, David. You must wait."

I kept my head high. I felt like the officer and my heart inside was as strong as a bull elephant. I felt different inside now from my oath and drinking the enemy blood. If I thought about blood now it did not worry me anymore. I liked the smell. I was like Rambo and a true soldier. I think the evil spirits had eaten my weakness.

"Cut it properly," said Jabu.

I glared at him and cut the meat slowly. He must be careful. I could stab him with this knife. Just because we were friends now did not mean I would let him think he was in charge. I gave the meat to David. He smiled at me with his kind eyes and took it from my knife.

We sat on our haunches like a pack of baboons and ate more of the juicy meat. My mouth was full with it and the blood and oil ran down my chin and over my hands. The smell was so sweet and rich. It was like the blazing fire and my heart felt strong. I cut more juicy meat from the leg until the white bone showed through and handed some to David and Jabu. After that I let out a big burp and Jabu did the same. We laughed at each other.

"Shall we keep some for Richard and Sipho?" said David.

Jabu wiped his hands on his shorts and jumped up. "No, we must go," he said. "Nkunda'll be back soon."

The mention of Nkunda's name made my body feel cold.

"What will he say when he sees the meat's been eaten?"

"Maybe he'll think the hyenas have taken it?"

"That's stupid, Jabu," said David. "The hyenas will tear the meat with their teeth not cut it cleanly with a knife."

"It's Modetse's fault," said Jabu. "He cut it too quickly and did not think!"

"Liar," I shouted. "You'd already eaten some. Don't try and blame me!" I shoved Jabu in the chest with my hands.

He angrily shoved me back. "You always think you're right, Modetse. You always want to take over."

"That's because I'm better than you," I said pushing him again.

We glared at each other with clenched fists. I wanted to smack him in the mouth and make him bleed. I wanted to see his blood and knock his teeth from his jaw. I made a move towards him but David grabbed my arms and shouted, "Stop it! We're idiots. They'll know we have eaten it. We must think what to do."

We went quiet. My stomach had been so happy to see the meat that my head did not think to make it look like the animals had eaten it. Now I felt afraid. Nkunda would be angry because we had taken his meat.

"Maybe we must take the bone off the fire and drag it into the bush. Then they'll think it is the hyenas."

"Good idea, Modetse. Come, let's fetch it," said David.

I snatched the leg from the fire and turned to run to the bush but stopped suddenly as strong footsteps thudded from the bush towards us,

"Quick, they're coming. We must run round to the front.

We turned, but it was too late. Nkunda and his men had seen us. My heart fell deep into my boots. My oil mouth was frozen. I stared at him. I was holding the leg in my hands. I dropped it to my side. Nkunda looked at me with cold eyes. He was not wearing a shirt but had a string of AK bullets across his shiny brown chest. There were three other soldiers with him. They were all quiet and looking at us with cruel eyes and evil smiles, waiting to laugh at our pain. I prayed to God that he would not kill us. I thought my heart would jump from my chest. I breathed heavy and my legs shook. I looked at David and Jabu. They were frozen like me.

"You mustn't show your fear," I whispered to David. "You must be strong. You must not cry otherwise they'll kill you."

David looked at me with his big eyes and I could see he'd understood. I hoped he would be able to act well. I did not want to lose my friend.

* * *

The rope cut hard into my wrists. The hot sun beat down on my head. Nkunda had taken my shirt from my body and was standing with a rawhide whip in front of my face.

"So you think you can rob your Captain?" he shouted in my ear so loud that my head rang. I could feel my legs shaking and the sweat jumping all over my body. My heart was full of fear but I knew I must not show it otherwise I would be food for the hyenas.

"We...we're sorry, Nkunda. The smell of the meat was so good we did not use our brains."

"You have no brains. You are fucking stupid boys. What're you saying? Do we not give you enough food? Hah!"

"No, Nkunda. You give us good food. You are too good to us. We just saw the meat and then we did not think. We thought it was left for the animals."

The sharp crack of the whip hurt my ears and then I felt the pain sink deep and hard into my body. Red blood splashed up onto my face and dripped down onto the ground. "Thwack!" again the pain tore into my body and again. The sharp tail of the whip smacked me in the face and I closed my eyes tight against the hurt and the blood. I bit down hard on my lip until the salty taste of blood filled my mouth. I must not cry out or he would hit me more.

"Why would we leave meat for the animals? Huh? Huh? Do not play the clever boy with me. Do you hear me?"

"Yes, Nkunda. I am sorry. I've been wrong, Nkunda. I'm sorry."

I cried out loud to Nkunda but this made him hit me even harder. The whip tore into my skin like a crocodile for the fifth time. I thought I would die soon from the pain. My spirit wanted to climb out from my body to escape the hurt but I knew I must not let it. I must live for Thandi! The memory of our chubby mouths and chicken came back into my mind and I let it fill my thoughts to try and escape from this pain...

"Enough!"

It was Mobuto's voice.

"I'll take it from here."

I never thought that I would be glad to hear Mobuto. We were his boys. He would not like it that Nkunda had taken us over. Mobuto took the whip to me again and I felt it crack across my back causing me to scream out. Then he turned to David. I felt a cold splash of water on my face and my body. Someone was untying my hands. I fell onto the soft ground and felt the red dust on my tongue.

"Carry him back to the hut. I'll deal with him later."

"Yes, sah."

I felt two strong hands lift me up and put me over a shoulder like I was a sack of corn. I opened my eyes and saw Mobuto finishing with David and starting to whip Jabu. I was glad it was not Nkunda. I smiled to myself and then the darkness came and took me away from the hurting.

Chapter 19

When I woke I found that I was on my bed and the room had darkened in the weak light of the setting sun. I sat up.

"David? Jabu?" I whispered.

There was no answer. They were not here. A cold fear came over my body. I hoped Mobuto had not killed them.

"Richard? Sipho?"

There was no answer. Then I heard the door creak and I saw someone limp in.

"David. Is that you?" I whispered.

"Yes, Modetse. It's me. Stay in your bed. Mobuto may come in."

"Are you okay?"

"I'm paining, but I'm okay. Stay well, my brother."

"Where's Jabu?"

"Mobuto just finished with him. He'll be okay; he's not screaming and Mobuto doesn't want him dead. I heard him tell that to Bilole."

"We are his soldiers. Only he can kill us if we do wrong, not Nkunda," I said.

My heart was so glad to see David. I looked over his face. It was swollen and I could see the big cut on his cheek. He stumbled over to his bed and fell down on it.

"You are right. We must never do wrong to him otherwise we'll have no hope," he said. He lay back with his arm across his head.

"We're too stupid. But the meat she was good, hey? Better than the fat woman," I said to try and cheer him up.

David laughed. "You're too much, Modetse. You're too strong. That strength will get you into trouble."

"It makes me the strong soldier."

David looked at me and gave a strange smile. I think he was a frightened of me sometimes. I was not so scared anymore of the big men now. When I saw the new children come and get beaten my stomach did not jump into my mouth. Richard and Jabu were so jealous; I could see it in their eyes. They also wanted to be like me but I was the only hotshot and I would tear their bodies with my AK bullets if they tried to steal my prize. I was glad Mobuto liked me because he sees that I've become a hard one who's clever. That was why he did not let Nkunda kill me. He needed his number one shot. My stomach grew warm with these thoughts and I smiled.

"What're you thinking, Modetse?" asked David.

"Nothing," I said, and closed my eyes until the door creaked open again. It was Jabu. He was limping. He looked at us in the dim light and then put his finger on his lips. He went quickly to his bed and sat on the bottom. I heard the thud of boots and saw the elephant body of Mobuto filling the doorway. He put the light on and I put my hand in front of my eyes against the strong glare from the bare bulb.

He stared at us in silence and then sneered. "So, you devils, you want to play the big soldier men. You want to eat the fat juicy meat like you are Captains. Well okay, devil boys. Soon you'll act like the big soldier men you think you are. In a few weeks we are going to the Thokozo village to find more boys and girls. We hear that the villagers are hiding the food and the weapons for the rebels. We'll burn their fucking houses and kill their women. The graves of our enemy are not yet full. We need more bodies. You'll come and blow out the brains of the fucking dirty village pigs. You'll find the weapons and burn their fucking mud huts. You fucking solider boys want to be men. Okay you'll be men. Only then will you earn the meat. I want you up at five a.m. Is that clear?"

He shouted so loud that it made my ears ring. We jumped from our beds and saluted him. My body throbbed inside and I was scared and a part of me did not want to hurt the villagers, but the other part of me was excited. I would really be a proper soldier now. I would go with the big men. I could show Mobuto properly what a hotshot I was. I wondered what it would feel like to put my AK bullet into the body of a real person and see their blood fly out, maybe their brains too if I got a good head shot? Ay, it would be too good. My heart beat very fast. I had drunk the enemy blood. I had made the oath to the General. The dark spirits were in my soul. I had the power in me now. I could kill even better than Rambo. I felt Jabu's eyes on me and looked over at him. He stared back with angry eyes like it was my fault we'd got caught. I looked back with hate. He must be careful. I would feel nothing to kill him too.

"You'll have to make it good, David, or they'll kill you," I whispered when Mobuto left the room. He was just standing there staring down at the floor. He looked up at me and nodded.

"Yes, Modetse. I'll have to make it good on the outside but on the inside I'm not good."

"You're a fool, David. You've sworn the oath to the General – you must make your spirit strong," I whispered.

"I'll try."

"I'm strong," I said, and laughed. "I'm Mr. Hotshot."

"Yes you're such a stupid Hotshot that it's your fault we're caught," shouted Jabu behind me. "I'm sick of you, Modetse. You think you're so big and that you're the favorite."

"You're just jealous because I'm better. You found the meat Jabu. It's your fault."

"Stop it!" said David. "You'll bring Mobuto back."

Jabu and I glared at each other but shut up. We did not want Mobuto back. I stomped back to my bed and turned my back on David. I did not want to talk to them anymore. Tomorrow would be a big day and I must be ready for it. I must prove myself to Mobuto. I would have to be the best.

Chapter 20

"Hotshot!"

"What?"

I jerk around to Trigger coming in the doorway. He's smiling and looking relaxed and I scowl at him. What's he looking so happy for? Something's been changing in him. He's not having the bad dreams and he's always in the Art hut thinking he's number one artist. I stare hard at him looking so fresh from his sleep. He's definitely brainwashed or this art thing is helping. He doesn't want to even talk about the L.R.A. anymore. I clench my jaw. It's that fucking doctor. I know he's been talking to him many times. I'll have to take control and train Trigger to love only the L.R.A. again.

"There's a baptism down by the river. Nurse Sophie she says you must come," says Trigger, looking at me with big eyes.

I pull a face. I've no idea what baptism is but don't want to ask. "Tell Nurse Sophie to go fuck herself."

Trigger looks down and goes silent. I'm right about his brainwashing. If he was good L.R.A. he'd laugh. I must talk to Richard about him. If he doesn't want to come back to the L.R.A. we must kill him.

"We're all there; even the girls," says Trigger.

"So? I'm not interested in Pineapple girls. I've had enough of them," I sneer.

"That Tula's there."

My body jerks at her name. I feel my cheeks grow hot.

"There are good spirits coming, Hotshot," says Trigger suddenly in a small voice.

I stare at him. The mention of spirits makes my heart beat fast. What does he know of good spirits? This baptism must have something to do with them. They will know if I'm not there.

I stand silent in the dim light of the hut while Trigger shuffles

119

his feet and waits for my answer. I can feel the spirits inside me waking. Maybe they will want to war with these others. Maybe they want me to go to this baptism so they can show their power. I have nothing to fear. I will show Tula I'm the strong one.

"Okay, I'll come," I say.

Trigger gives me a thumb ups but I ignore it. He turns quick to run back down to the river like he can't wait to get away from me.

I walk through the forest to the river with heavy steps. My head is sore and the talk of girls has made me think of Thandi. My belly aches as I try and count the years. She must be seven years now. I hope the glue hasn't harmed her. Who has looked after her? Is she even still alive?

My heart jumps at this thought and I squeeze my eyes shut to try to push it away. No, I will not believe she is dead. I must find her. She will be there.

The picture of Thandi and me walking through the rubbish is clear in my head. I'm carrying her and she is laughing because we're going to eat KFC. I look at the picture of me like I don't know me. I'm not that boy anymore. I have changed so much. I don't know if she will even know me now. Not even Umama's spirit would recognize me. I'm so hard and I've killed so many. I can never go back to that boy. Never!

I shake these flies from my mind. Where did those thoughts come from? No the L.R.A. are right. The dark spirits are right. It was right to kill. I don't have to be that boy again. He was weak. He let himself get caught and left Thandi. It is better to be a soldier and soon I'll be strong and then I'll go back and find my squadron. We'll go to the dump and find Thandi and if anyone's hurt her we'll cut them to pieces with our AK bullets. Thandi will be proud I've become so strong.

I take big steps and soon I'm at the river. Everyone is standing near the bank. I can see Miss Owl Nurse Sophie surrounded by the Pineapple girls like she's guarding them. I look past her and squint my eyes in the hot sun to see where Tula is. My heart beats fast as I find her. She's standing a little way behind wearing a short white dress. She looks so good. Two of the small girls, Zinzi and Lily look over at me with big eyes but I look away so they can't see I'm staring at Tula. Her face is fixed on the river and I'm glad she hasn't seen me yet.

I push past Nurse Sophie and stand next to Trigger.

"I'm glad you're here," says Nurse Sophie, but I ignore her.

Then the stupid bitch whispers, "The baptism ceremony and the Holy Spirit will help take away the dark sinful life and make you a new creature. Remember you're just a child. It's not your fault."

I hit out at her but Trigger catches my arm.

"Leave me alone," I hiss. What the fuck's she talking about? Who is this Holy Spirit? I hate her so much and I bet Tula saw me want to hit her. Now she'll think I'm a bad one. I wish I'd just stayed in the hut.

"It's okay, you don't need to go in." Nurse Sophie smiles. "You just watch from the bank."

"Come, Trigger," I say, and march off with my back as straight as I can to join Richard who's standing a bit further down the riverbank.

"Hotshot, have you seen the girls?" asks Richard with a big grin as we get to him. He lifts his eyebrows at me and looks over at the group of girls.

"They're just fresh meat. When'll we take them?"

Richard laughs. "You're right, Hotshot, and you want that Tula. Maybe we'll have them in the forest?"

I push my shoulders back and join the laughter. "That'll be good. We can all have a turn," I say. "Even you, Trigger, or are you a good boy now who does not want to rape?"

Trigger goes red and shuffles his feet. "These are not Pineapple girls anymore, Hotshot. They've changed."

"They're Pineapple girls you idiot. They'll always be that. They're girls and we're men. We can have them if we want."

"Nurse won't let us. She's watching all the time so that we can't be alone with the girls."

"I've seen some boys alone with girls," says Richard.

"They're good boys who've been here a long time."

"They've betrayed the L.R.A. They go to the stupid church on a Sunday and believe in that Jesus. Is that what you're doing, Trigger? Hey? You a traitor too?"

He kicks at the ground when I'm talking with fear in his eyes. He is not like the Trigger I knew in Nkunda's squadron. What has happened to him?

Suddenly singing rises up from the forest edge. I turn to look. Dr. Zuma is leading a line with Mama Zuma and some girls and holding high in the air a big wooden cross. They're dressed in long white robes and heading for the river. "Hallelujah, hallelujah" they sing with clear voices as they wind their way down the bank.

"Sit down all of you," Dr. Zuma says to us as they file past.

We squat on the soft muddy bank and watch as they go towards the water. The air around me grows still and heavy. A knot rises in my stomach and my skin prickles. I wish I hadn't come. There are strange spirits here. I can feel them in the air.

Dr. Zuma pushes the wooden cross deep into the soft river bank and wades slowly into the brown water until it's waist high. The girls form a line on the edge. Mama Zuma waddles her big white robed body into the water so that it rises up around her like a sail and stands next to the doctor.

Tula moves down and enters the water. Her white dress floats up around her and I wish I could be under the water to see her pants. I stare hard at her thinking of this until she looks up and sees me. Her cheeks go pink and she looks away. She goes over to stand with Doctor and Mama Zuma.

"Come, Patience," says Dr. Zuma to one of the Pineapple girls.

"You're a poisoned child but you've repented of your sin and this is a sign of leaving that old life behind and becoming a new creature in Christ Jesus. The water will show how you die to the old life and be born again to the new."

He takes her hand and helps her into the water and then places both hands on her forehead and prays in a loud voice. "Patience, I baptize you in the name of the Father and the Son and the Holy Spirit."

Then he pushes her backwards under the water and Mama Zuma and Tula grab her shoulders and help her back up. She comes up spluttering. Her head is back and her eyes are shining. Then she opens her mouth and starts to sing with strange words. Dr. Zuma puts his hands on her head and speaks in the same sounding words. Patience sings loud to the sky with fiery eyes.

My skin grows cold. What is she seeing? Is she talking to the spirits? My heart beats hard and my breath sticks in my throat. I watch as Tula puts her arms around her and guides her back to Nurse Sophie on the bank. I stare at her face. She is shining as if she is clean inside.

My stomach knots. My spirit is not happy. There is something happening here that I can't understand. These other spirits have power. I hold my body tight for it wants to run away, but I can't do this in front of Tula because she'll think I'm scared. I push myself into the muddy bank and fix my eyes with a blank stare. I won't let anyone see the strange fear I feel inside watching this.

The doctor is shouting loud to the sky in this strange language and now Mama Zuma is saying words like that. Everywhere around the people are talking and shouting "Hallelujah." There is power in the air and my body grows hot and wet. These spirits will hate me for what I have done. They can see the blackness of my soul and will war with my dark spirits. But how can I kill them? How? My mind shivers; this spirit war will kill me.

Then I feel a space next to me. I turn and see Trigger walking to the river. He joins the line at the edge of the water. Dr. Zuma goes over and gives him a white robe to put over him. Traitor! He's left the L.R.A. I knew something was wrong. I will kill him for this.

All of a sudden my head spins and my eyes blur. The river's turned red with blood. Dr. Zuma is pouring blood over Trigger's head.

"I baptize you with the blood of Jesus," he is saying. Now he is pouring the blood all over everyone. He is coming for me with his hands full of blood.

"Come, Modetse, come," he is saying. "Come to the blood...come...let the blood on the hands of Jesus cleanse you."

My ears hum and a thundering "takka, takka" vibrates through my head. I cannot have this blood. It is magic enemy blood. Dr. Zuma is helping them. They are coming with their gunships to take back the blood which I have drunk. They're trying to kill me! My chest closes. My eyes blur and my head explodes.

"No!" I scream. "No! Leave me alone. Leave me alone."

I jump up from the riverbank and run. I must get away from these spirits, this blood...the bullets and hands are chasing me. "Where's my AK? Where's my AK?"

Then I feel someone shaking me and I hear the voice of Nurse Sophie.

"It's okay. It's okay," she is saying, but her voice is far away. She keeps shaking me and then I feel like I'm coming back from somewhere outside myself.

I shake my head and look at the ground. My head is still spinning. I take a deep breath and look up. I'm sitting under the guava tree. I look down at my legs; they're shivering and so are my insides. I don't know what has happened.

Nurse Sophie shakes me again on the shoulder and squats down next to me.

"It is okay," she says, looking deep at me with her owl eyes and giving me a sad smile. "You've had a flashback, Modetse. The pictures aren't real. Your mind's tricked you. It's jumped back to the past."

I stare at her. Is this true? Has my mind tricked me? I look around. There's no enemy and the doctor is not chasing me. My cheeks grow hot. I've made a fool of myself.

"Just leave me alone," I mumble.

"The doctor can help take these away. You must talk to him. He's helped lots of soldiers."

I clench my jaw and say nothing but inside my stomach knots and my head spins some more. I don't even know if I'm awake or asleep anymore. Everything feels so strange and I'm growing weak inside. I can't let that happen. All this talk of Jesus and sins is troubling me. What is happening with these spirits in the water? Why are all the boys and girls changing so much? These people will make me mad. They will take away my power. I must make my mind strong again. I must call on the darkness to help me fight them.

Chapter 21

The night was dark because the moon was hiding behind thick clouds. Commander Mobuto said it was good because we were going to taste the magic and meet with the great witchdoctor of the L.R.A. This made my heart beat hard like the drums I heard in the bush.

"I want total silence," shouted Mobuto, as we assembled ready to leave. "The magic doctor does not like noise. You are to move like the leopard through the forest. I don't want to know you're even here. Is that clear?"

"Yes, sah," we said and saluted. "There'll be many animals in the bush. You will see their eyes glowing at you if the moon she comes out. Just keep behind me. We're going to a dark and secret place and you'll only find it if you follow me. Bilole let's move."

We followed behind Mobuto through the forest like a pack of leopard cubs following our father. Mobuto was dressed like the chief with a leopard skin around his waist. His fat belly smiled at us over his belt. He still carried his AK and the rope of bullets lay strong against his bare, brown chest.

David was behind me in the dark bush and Sipho came behind him carrying the pack for Bilole.

"I hope you've scrubbed like me, Modetse. We mustn't let the great doctor smell anything bad," whispered David as we pushed through the dark vines.

"I have. Bilole told me to clean well. I won't let the witchdoctor smell me out."

"We mustn't get left behind," said Sipho, stumbling over a tree root.

I saw Mobuto's fat shadow fading from us in the dark and went faster. Bilole, Richard and Jabu pushed through the bush behind us and we went on quiet, picking our way through the fig trees and the wide fans of breadfruit tree leaves. I heard the chatter of the monkeys and many times we saw the bush move as the buck darted through it.

"Lion," whispered David as we heard a distant roar.

"I'm glad Mobuto's got an AK." I said. I was more scared of the lion than the enemy. After we'd gone a long time, stumbling often over the roots and stones because there were few stars and no moon to guide us, I smelt the smoke of the fire and through the dark jagged leaves of the trees saw the fire behind. I heard the fire talking and then all of a sudden with a "Dum-de-Dum," the big drums began to talk.

The tall drum engalabi called to us. It shouted, "Boom, Boom, Boom" and then all the drums joined in. They got louder and louder, calling us to them. Mobuto moved fast and we had to take big steps to keep up. The line we made through the forest thinned out. I grabbed David's arm before he disappeared ahead of me.

"I'm scared," whispered Sipho.

"We mustn't show fear. Mobuto says he'll give us magic to protect us from the bullets of the enemy," I said.

"But sometimes the noses of these magic men, they smell the fear," whispered Sipho.

"Well, then don't be afraid, stupid."

"Silence," shouted Mobuto.

We reached the end of the forest and the dark fig trees spat us out into a big round clearing. In the middle stood a blazing fire, which jumped and crackled high up in the air. It was red, yellow and orange and the heat of its flames reached out and tried to singe our bodies.

I looked at Mobuto. His face glowed red in the light and his fat body was high and straight; his eyes were narrow and his face firm as he waited to see the great doctor. Even he looked a little afraid.

"Don't show your fear," I said to David and Sipho, but inside my stomach shivered and the air around me grew hot.

David nodded and Sipho looked at me with big eyes. I looked at Jabu. He looked back at me and nodded. He was clever that one and wouldn't show his fear. I tried to stand straighter. Richard stood close next to Bilole as if he'd somehow protect him.

I looked beyond the thundering fire and saw three big thatched mud huts. They were round, like fat women and had yellow, blue and red triangles on their walls. Their thatch was thick and new and sat on them like pointy Basutho hats.

Tall young men, with brown muscular bodies, sat next to the drummers. They got up and threw big sticks on the fire. "Yieee," they shouted as the flames of the fire, strong and red, shot high into the air. They hit each other in fun on the shoulders and then went back to gather more sticks.

The flames teased the leaves of the bush and it drew back from their fury. The dark night sky became red and I could see clearly. Many soldiers were seated on the far side of the fire. I could see Nkunda and I was glad that Mobuto was with us. The General was sitting on a big wooden chair near the main hut; his presence filled the air.

The drummers wore the skins of the antelope around their waist. They had dried brown seedpods on their wrists and ankles, which jingled, jingled as they drummed, and they wore wide bands of nyala skin around their heads. One drummer was like the vervet monkey and beat three drums almost at once. "Dum-de-dum, Dum-de-dum, Dum-de-dum."

I had never seen men move so fast and beat the drums so strong. Their bodies shone with sweat in the firelight. Their eyes were wide and white. I could see that their spirits were one with the drums. I couldn't stop staring at them.

"You must not talk when the Great Leopard comes from his hut," Mobuto said. "You must keep your eyes to the floor. He will not be happy if you look in his eyes. The great doctor will give you strong medicine and make you like the powerful bull elephant where the bullets cannot pass. You are lucky soldier boys tonight, hey?"

"Yes, sah. We are very lucky," we all said. We watched Mobuto with big eyes. We did not want to do anything wrong.

He smiled at us and said, "We're the God Army. We have the special magic that will make you invisible to the bullets of the enemy. You're lucky that you're in the God Army and not that of the enemy. Now follow me and don't make a sound."

We crept behind Mobuto with our eyes on the ground. I did not want to look at the hut for I was afraid I would make the great doctor angry if I looked at his house. The fire spat blue and red flames high into the air as we came near. The flaming tongues licked out at us and the fire cackled like a great fire witch. I felt the hot hand on my face and my heart jumped. We sat cross-legged on the side next to the boys of Nkunda. The General lifted his eyes at us and we saluted. He stared and said nothing.

The drums beat harder and harder, louder and louder, "Be-dum, Be-dum, Be-be-dum." Two wizards came from the huts on the sides of the big hut. They wore the skirt of lion tails and beat shields of the springbok. I couldn't see their faces because they had the big wooden masks with the slant eyes and big scowling mouths on. I could see the quills of the porcupine on their heads and there were many dried gall bladders around their waist. I knew these had powerful juju inside. Maybe it was this that would give us the magic.

They danced round and round the fire and the colored beads and brown dried seeds on their ankles and their wrists shook to the rhythm.

Faster and faster they went while the big drums called, "Dum-de-dum, Dum-de-dum." The fire grew bigger and bigger. The wizards went round the fire, faster and faster. They were so fast that my eyes were swimming. They screamed "Aieee, aieee," at the fire. My heart beat like the drums. My head whirred round and round like the dancing wizards. I was scared that just now I would fall backwards from the spinning.

The soldiers clapped with the drums. I looked at Mobuto and he showed for us to clap. We clapped, clapped, clapped with the rhythm of the drums. My spirit sang with the drums. I felt like I was flying around the fire with the wizards.

Then the women came out.

"Ulololo, ulololo, ulololo," they screamed.

Their voices were high and clear above the beat of the drums. They had skirts of red and black and their big bare breasts, covered with many beads, jangled in time to their dance. They wore bracelets of red dried seeds around their feet and wrists which made music as they moved.

They danced with the wizards. Faster and faster. All of them danced and screamed while the drums shouted louder and louder. We joined in by clapping. The noise was so big that I thought it would break the sky and then the big drum shouted, "KABOOM!"

Suddenly there was silence. I held my breath and waited. We all waited. A big shadow came in the entrance of the middle hut. It moved away and then the great doctor himself came out.

He stood in front of the hut. All I could do was stare at him with my mouth open. His spirit was so strong that it took over the whole place. He was very tall. I'd never seen such a potent man before. He was much greater than the General. Everyone was afraid, even Mobuto.

"Aiee, he's very powerful, Modetse," whispered David.

"Yes, David. His spirit will eat us."

"We must be careful, Modetse. We must make sure he likes us."

I nodded. "Whisper to the others."

I could see Sipho from the corner of my eye. He sat still next to David with wide eyes and an open mouth. Jabu and Richard too were frozen. David whispered in Sipho's ear and he nodded.

The great witchdoctor had moved to the fire. He held a tall baubled stick with many beads on it. He had fat legs and a big belly like the hippo. He had a crown of tall black and white quills of the porcupine on his head and the band of the leopard across his forehead. His skirt was made of the tails of many leopards. It shone gold in the firelight. Around his ankles was the skin of the lion and I saw that his wrists had shining colored beads that jangled as he walked.

The drums waited. We stayed still. The night too was silent. The moon hid this night for fear and only the fire dared to speak as the great doctor paced around it. He looked at all of us soldier boys. His steps were heavy and the red ground vibrated as his fat feet hit into it. The air was thick around me. My heart had jumped inside my mouth. I think it was stopped beating from the fear.

"Aeeiou," screamed the witchdoctor suddenly. His voice was shrill and hard and tore the silence of the night in two.

"Aeeiou," he screamed again and held his beaded stick high into the air. He had many gall bladders around his waist. He took one and threw it in the fire. The flames caught it and laughed. The magic made them jump up high in the air and scream and scream. The light was bright now so that the great doctor could see us like in the daylight.

My breath was trapped inside my body. My mind was numb with fear.

"David, I am very afraid of this man," I whispered.

"Don't look at him, Modetse," whispered David.

His eyes were big and wide and his body was stiff. We were all filled with terror. I was excited to come but now I wished that we'd not come. It was too dangerous to talk. I clenched my jaw and kept my eyes on the fire.

The drums started up again. "Dum-de-dum, Dum-de-dum. Dum-de-dum. De-de-da. De-de-da, Deda, Dada, Dada." They were louder and faster now. I let my mind dance with the drums.

Round and round; faster and faster. The drums shouted to the forest and the sky about the power of the witchdoctor.

Then the doctor stopped and looked at us boys and I could see his yellow eyes and his big toad nose with its wide nostrils, sniffing, sniffing.

He moved around the circle, "sniff, sniff." I knew that he was smelling out the rotten boys. My body shook. What if he thought I was rotten and threw me on the fire? What if he did not like David because his heart was too soft? Or Sipho or Jabu or Richard? What he if threw all of us on the fire like we were the evil witches? I'd heard that the great witchdoctor called the rotten boys witches and burned them on the fire.

My eyes were big and my heart was in my mouth. The witch-doctor came closer and closer. I could see the fat on his belly. It jeered at me. He bent down and I could smell his horrible breath that stank like the dead chicken. His yellow eyes came towards me and I looked down. I kept my breath stiff, inside so he could not see my fear. I had to stay strong. "I'm a big soldier now. I'm Mr. Hotshot. I can shoot the magic bullet. He will not smell me for a witch," I told myself over and over in my head.

I felt his fat face come closer and saw the leopard tails swing in front of my face. He was breathing hard into my face but I held it firm with my eyes looking to the ground even though my stomach had come into my mouth. My nose twitched. I held my hands tight and kept my face firm. I could not let him see that I could smell his stink. I looked at his fat feet with their seedpods.

He pushed under my chin and made me look up. I kept my eyelids down so that my eyes were not wide open. I could see his fat body, which was wet with sweat and shone in the fire.

I felt his eyes on me like they were looking right into my spirit and inside I screamed in fear. The other wizards stood behind the witchdoctor.

Suddenly he shouted, "Juju!"

The wizards jumped and took out a pouch and gave it to the

great doctor. He squatted down and opened the pouch. I could see a brown powder in the pouch.

"Howwaath," he shouted. "You are a lucky soldier boy. Make sure that you are a good killer for the L.R.A. The magic juju will make you invisible but if you do not kill well for us the juju will eat your flesh."

My body shook and I bowed my head to the great doctor to thank him. I had been careful not to look straight in his eyes. I'd done everything Mobuto told us to do.

The witchdoctor took out a small sharp knife with strong silver teeth from under his skirt of leopard's tails. He pushed the knife onto my forehead and cut it in deep. I felt a sharp pain shoot through my head and felt the hot blood come down into my eyes. I locked my jaw to stop my scream.

"Good blood," he shouted. "Good clean cut for the magic juju."

He pulled both my arms apart and made two deep gashes into their soft upper flesh just below my L.R.A. scar. The wizard gave some more magic juju to the great doctor and he rubbed it deep into the wounds. It pained me but it also felt good. My mind started to smile. It reminded me of the glue. My head got light but my legs were heavy. I felt strong now. I could do anything. The magic medicine had made me too strong for the bullets of the enemy pigs. My ears were buzzing.

"Ha, ha. Now you're strong with the magic medicine, hey, Mr. Hotshot," said Mobuto. "You're lucky that the doctor did not smell you for the witch."

I was very feeling lucky but I hoped that my friends would also be lucky. The witchdoctor moved to David and my skin prickled. I did not want him to kill my friend.

"Please don't be scared, David," I prayed in my head. I saw the wizard give the powder and my heart sung again. David was safe. The great doctor cut deep into David so that the blood of my brother flowed out thick and red. I saw him put in the magic powder and rub it deep into the wound. David smiled and my heart was glad. The doctor moved to the next and the next. Jabu also got the juju and so did Richard.

Then the doctor suddenly stopped and screamed. He pulled a boy out by the hair. I saw a big forehead sticking out in front and my heart sank.

"Aeeiah. A witch. A witch. He will bring bad luck. He will talk to the enemy. Burn him. Burn him," he screamed in a high-pitched whine.

Sipho had shown too much fear and the doctor had smelled him. Sipho screamed and his white eyes met mine. I stared back in horror but there was nothing I could do. My heart hurt my ears and my breath stuck in my throat. I looked away.

I heard David catch his breath. All the soldiers started shouting, "Burn him. Burn him."

They were on their feet and stamping them as the drums started up again. "Dum-de-dum," they shouted as if they too wanted Sipho to burn. "Burn Him, Burn Him. Burn Him," everyone was shouting now.

I joined in, hitting my crossed legs with my fists as I shouted but inside my heart was crying for my friend. My eyes were fixed on the fire. Why was it Sipho and not Jabu? Why Sipho? Bitter water flowed into my mouth and I quietly retched and swallowed it down.

The soldiers and the drums beat loudly calling for his death. Commander Mobuto and Nkunda pulled Sipho screaming to the cackling red fire. He was shaking all over and squirmed and screamed and dragged his feet against the red soil as if somehow it would swallow him up and save him.

His voice was so high and shrieking that my ears hurt. I closed my eyes tight so I could not see him but my ears couldn't close. His screams stabbed through my head like the steel of the AK bayonet.

Then my nose drew back from his burning flesh and my

stomach somersaulted. I turned to the side and vomited into the red sand. I tried to take my mind away but the smell and the screams were too strong. I don't know how much time had passed when the screams stopped.

Sipho was dead and the great doctor was moving again. I watched as his big shadow moved to the end of the circle and I held my breath as he smelt the last boy. My body was numb and my chest heaved up and down with short breaths while my mind whirled with horror. My spirit felt like it had come out of my body. Everything was dizzy.

The great doctor finished and the drums started to beat again but this time they were not so loud. I saw the women come from the huts on the side with big boards of food. There were two springbuck on a spit at the side of the left hut and other women cut the big pieces of sweet smelling meat from the bones. The great doctor was hungry. He moved to a big wooden seat near his hut. The women ran and put down grass mats for his feet. I could see one of them preparing a big plate of meat for the doctor and I could smell the oily flesh.

"You'll not stay for the feast," said Mobuto. "It is only for the General and the officers. But don't worry, little soldier boys, you have the magic juju which will keep you safe from the bullets. Bilole take them back. You can give them beer to celebrate."

"Yes, sah. Up and get in a line. You'll follow me."

We saluted the General and Mobuto and followed Bilole back into the dark forest. I felt like it had been a horrible dream. I could not believe Sipho was not with us. I walked in silence beside David. My nose could still smell the burning and my ears rang from his screams. I think we were all confused what to think of this night.

I turned to David and whispered, "I feel sick." I couldn't bring myself to say Sipho's name but my heart cried hard for him.

David gave me a sad look and shook his head. "It's bad,

Modetse. My heart's heavy."

"Mine too," I said. "I don't know why the doctor smelled him."

David shrugged his shoulders. "It was his fear."

Jabu and Richard ran up behind us and Jabu poked his head over my shoulder. "The juju is good, hey." He didn't seem worried by what had happened to Sipho and I glared at him.

"It helps me forget," said David, but he also glared at Jabu.

Bilole had also had the juju and began lift up his knees and arms and chant,

"*Mungu ni Mani,*
Mungu yu pamoja nasi
Mungu yu pamoja nasi.
God is with us.
God is with us."

The others joined in, holding their fists high into the air and lifting their knees as they danced behind Bilole through the bush. I walked faster but could not bring myself to sing. My head spun from the juju and my steps felt light, but the stink of Sipho still burned in my nose.

"We've the magic of the God Army in our blood.

We're the chosen ones of the L.R.A." chanted everyone.

I tried to chase Sipho from my mind as they chanted. I was a soldier. I must only think of that otherwise I too would be a dead boy. I stomped onto the soft ground. Then the juju buzzed in my mind. The chanting carried me away. I was a magic soldier now. I had the magic juju in my blood. The bullets could never kill me.

Chapter 22

Early the next morning, still strong with the magic juju, we followed Mobuto through the dark green jungle with its many breadfruit, fig and wattle trees full of the damp smell of the morning. The waking sun had painted its dark pink rays across the sky the sharp karook-a-rook of the turtledove rose among the trees. My body felt strong from the juju but the smell of Sipho's roasting flesh had come back to my mind and caught at the back of my throat. I retched.

"You okay?" asked David.

"It's just Sipho," I said, spitting the bitter water onto the red ground.

David nodded. "Try not to think."

I looked at the ground, said nothing and then retched again. "My nose can still smell the burning," I said, and my voice croaked. My eyes went red and I gave a sob. David squeezed my arm.

"The smoke would have made his mind sleep," he whispered. "He won't have felt the fire."

I swallowed the sob and looked up at David with a frown.

"My mother, she told me of the burning tires the people use to kill others – those who are burning don't feel the fire."

"You sure?"

David nodded and my stomach relaxed. I hoped he was right and Sipho's spirit was gone already before the fierce flames ate his flesh. I shook the smell from my brain. I must try and be strong. My mind jumped from one side to the other. I hated what they had done to Sipho but if the great doctor had smelled him out then maybe he was bad and could jinx the L.R.A. I could not question the great doctor and his magic. I must only think about killing the enemy pig. Sipho was gone and I must try and forget. I could not help him now. But my heart stayed heavy and my mind went round and round as we marched through the thick jungle.

"Look, I'm a flying boy," said Jabu, pushing past us. He held his arms out wide to the sides and started to zigzag through the forest like an airplane and Richard coming up behind him laughed.

"Shut up you fools," hissed Badboy from behind. "Mobuto said no talking."

I pulled a face at Jabu and Richard who shrugged and pulled faces back but they obeyed and fell in behind Badboy who had joined us from Nkunda's squadron for our first raid. I stared at Badboy. His hair still had the braids with red and green beads on each side, but now he wore his Lieutenant's beret with his two bars and had put stripes of green paint on his cheeks. He marched very straight and when he turned to look back at us I flinched. His eyes had the same cold look like the General. He would feel nothing to kill us. I looked down quick and fell behind Jabu with David behind me. I saw him sneer at me and narrow his shark eyes.

Bloodneverdry and Trigger were also with us. Bloodneverdry was marching by Badboy and they shared a joke and laughed. Then Bloodneverdry looked back at me. I met his eyes. I would not let them think I was weak. I could be just as bad as them. Bloodneverdry gave a sideways laugh and turned back to talk to Badboy. Trigger was just behind me. He came alongside and lifted his eyebrows at me as we crept forward through the bush. I gave him a small smile back. At least he was not a bad one. I felt sorry for him to be with those two in a squadron. Many of us had nicknames now and it was better. I did not feel like Modetse anymore. I did not want that name again until I could be back on the dump with Thandi. My mind jumped back to the dump with its stink and its rubbish. The time was so long ago it did not seem real anymore. I felt my stomach jump and I pushed the thoughts away. I could not remember too much. It made me weak, and if I let myself be weak, I would die. I was Hotshot now. I was the soldier and I liked to be Hotshot. My muscles tightened. I was such a number one shot that Mobuto gave me that name. I must be proud of myself and I knew that Richard and Jabu had green eyes because I was so good. David was called Cleverboy and Jabu was Grenadelauncher because he was good with the RPG. His back and shoulders went straight when they called him that. He thought he was such a big deal with that name. But Richard was called Scarecrow because of his hair and he hated it. It was a good name and made me laugh because me and Sipho we always said he looked like the scarecrow. I was glad he didn't have a name to puff him up. The thought made me remember Sipho again and I shook my head to chase it away. I must not think of him; all I must think of is this mission.

I looked hard in front as we stalked like the leopards through the thick bush. All my muscles were stiff and ready for the kill. My ears were sharp and I darted my eyes from side to side in case any danger was hiding from me.

Suddenly Mobuto put up his hand and stopped. He crouched down and showed us with his arm to get down. We obeyed and fell to our haunches. He turned to us and whispered, "Keep down, we're nearing the camp. I want no sound. Be careful your boots don't break the twigs or roots. Now get down flat. We'll leopard crawl from here."

We sprawled silently on our stomachs in the long grass, boots curled into the damp soil ready to push forward on our elbows. I pulled my AK up onto my back and kept my face low. I had two spare cartridges taped like the buck horns on my AK. Ay, I would have plenty of bullets to kill with.

I watched Mobuto crawl through the grass and copied him. Bit by bit we crawled forward. My dark spirit was alive and happy with me. I could hear the rustle of the wind through the bush and the insects running for fear.

I made my eyes thin and looked hard in the yellow dawn light through the swaying grass. Far in front I saw the orange glow of small firelight. I lifted my head and sniffed the crisp air. I could smell the wood smoke and cooking and I smiled to myself. This was the village of the enemy. Soon they would taste our power and revenge.

I looked back at David. His body was tense and his face serious with deep eyes. Badboy and Trigger were grinning and Bloodneverdry was licking his lips. They had been on these kills before. I was happy that now I too was with them.

Mobuto shuffled his fat body forward in the soft sand until he had a good view of the village. He turned to us with his finger to his lips and whispered, "No sound now, we must take them by surprise. Wait until I give you the command and then follow me. Bloodneverdry, you take Hotshot and Cleverboy and hit from the left. Badboy, you take Grenadelauncher, Trigger and Scarecrow and hit from the right. The rest of you follow behind me."

I frowned at David and pulled my mouth in a snarl. Why couldn't I lead? Mobuto liked Bloodneverdry because he was so fierce but I could be a better killer than him. I saw a picture in my mind of me shooting all the villagers and running fast in front of Bloodneverdry who couldn't keep up with me. Then I felt him next to me.

He glared at me and then whispered, "Right, sah," with a proud smile on his lips.

He showed for us to follow him and I looked with hate as he crawled low and quick through the bush like the rattlesnake, but I had to obey. He had his AK high on his back and his dagger was caught between his teeth. I took out the dagger from my belt and put it in my mouth too, and smiled inside. I was sure I looked better than him.

As we moved forward I saw the enemy village clear through the grass with its thatched huts and cattle lowing behind in the kraal. My heart beat so fast I feared it would jump out of me as I saw the shapes of the people near the huts and around the small camp fires.

I bit down on the dagger and suddenly wished I could just shoot my bullets instead. The thought of touching the body of the enemy scared me now that I could see them but I chased the fear away. I mustn't let Bloodneverdry know because he would tell Nkunda and Mobuto I'm weak. He knew Mobuto liked me too and he would want to see me die. I must be careful.

Suddenly Mobuto commanded, "Forward. Move!"

Bloodneverdry jumped up and took the dagger from his mouth. His body pounced forward and he screamed, "Now!"

I took out my dagger as we leaped up, charging forward out of the bush and screaming with our heads thrown back and mouths wide open, "Aiee, Aiee, Kill the enemy pig. Kill, kill, kill!"

The fierceness of our screams cracked the morning like many broken eggs and our crashing thundered through the bush. The villagers went stiff with the fear, screamed high-pitched and began to run everywhere. The chickens squawked and scattered sending feathers into the air. Everywhere was madness.

I ran like a devil with every part of my body awake. I put the dagger back between my teeth and shot my AK so fast into the air that it danced in my hand. I panted as I shot and spit sprayed out from my mouth. Everywhere the people screamed and ran like a herd of wildebeest from the lion. I zigzagged behind the running figures, firing my devil bullets. Some of them flew up in the air and I saw their blood splatter around them. My body was alive with power and energy. No one could stop me.

People ran to the huts for cover but Mobuto threw grenades at them and they exploded with mad flashes of fire. The flames rose up all over and ate the thatch. We shot a fierce storm of AK bullets into the village. Some of the smaller boys with Mobuto could not fit the AKs on their shoulders and tucked them under their arms as they ran forward, shooting everywhere.

The loud bangs of light from our grenades flashed in front of my eyes as I ran and their booming made my ears dead, but inside my body was strong and fierce and ready to kill. In front the villagers screamed with their fear and pain and ran in mad circles round their huts of fire. Their eyes were big and wide and many held their ears and heads from the big noise. My heart beat with excitement. They were filled with fear of me. I had the power over them.

I pushed my AK back into my shoulder and held it steady. I took aim at the running villagers and fired too many bullets at them. I watched and smiled as one by one, they fell under my aim. It was like magic. I killed people and no enemy bullets could stick to me.

Bloodneverdry ran up behind me and shouted, "Follow me, Hotshot."

He went like the mad rhino through the fires and I put my AK onto my shoulder and followed him over to the far side of the village. We saw an enemy running to the thick bush behind the village.

Bloodneverdry shot forward and grabbed the man by the neck, pulling him back onto the ground. The man kicked and screamed. He made funny noises in his throat and I saw a big wet patch appear on his pants.

"Dirty enemy pig," I screamed in my mind as I clenched my dagger between my teeth. The man's face was a blur to me. All I could see was the enemy face from the movie and I pulled back my lips and screamed. Bloodneverdry held the enemy with one hand and took my dagger out of my mouth.

"Now, Hotshot, cut!" he screamed. "Let's see if you are as good as you think."

He pulled the man's neck back like a chicken. I had to hold my hand tight to stop it shaking. I could not let Bloodneverdry see my fear. This was the enemy who would rape my Thandi. He was the evil one who would kill my brothers and my people. I had to kill him and drink more of the enemy blood.

I drew the sharp teeth of my knife deep into his chicken throat. I heard him babble and saw the dark red blood jump from his throat like a waterspout. His eyes went white and his throat gurgled goodbye to his soul. I could feel his hot enemy blood on my hands and it gave me power. I was a killer. I had killed an enemy pig.

"Aiee," I screamed, and held the dagger high into the air. I rubbed the blood onto my face and laughed with Bloodneverdry. I had proved myself and he rewarded me with a high five.

"Good work, Hotshot. Let's find another one."

I ran with Bloodneverdry and we caught another enemy who was hiding in the hut. I stabbed and stabbed into his shivering body. He would never touch my Thandi. He would never hurt my family. Now I was a true killing machine. I drank deep from the evil inside me and grinned. Now I was a real L.R.A. The General and Mobuto would be proud.

Chapter 23

"Wake up, Modetse." It was David calling to me but his voice was far away.

"Wake up you are screaming. You'll make Mobuto come in."

I turned my head and stared at David. His face looked like it was underwater. My head still buzzed with pictures of blood and killing. I was killing everyone and the blood was flowing from my hands until a warthog rammed me hard in the stomach and my insides tumbled out. I shook my head to take away the horror.

"Are you okay, my brother?"

"I mustn't sleep again," I mumbled.

"The dreams; they're worrying you?" David looked sad at me.

I nodded and turned my eyes away. "I think it's the brown-brown," I whispered in a small voice. Why did I have this fear inside me? Why had the dark spirits not chased it away? I tensed my face and stomach. I must not let myself be weak. I had the magic inside me. The bullets could not kill me anymore.

David came over to sit on the edge of my bed. "I think the brown-brown makes the mind see bad pictures," he whispered. He stared at me and then asked, "Who's Thandi?"

I froze. "What you mean?"

"You were saying the name in your sleep."

"Oh?" I said and looked away. I had never talked of Thandi before because it was too hard to think about her and it made me feel weak, but she still she came to visit in my dreams.

David looked at me, wanting me to speak.

"She is my sister," I said after a while.

David nodded like he understood. He smiled sadly and said, "When I sleep I also see the blood. I've had enough!"

"Shh," I said quickly. I looked around the room but the humps of boys were quiet. "You must be careful. You can't trust anyone. If they hear you they'll kill you. We're L.R.A. You must be tough."

David nodded and then stared far in front. "Yes, Modetse, I know," he said with sad eyes. He shuffled his feet and looked at the floor then whispered, "I'll try and be a good L.R.A. boy."

I looked at David with worried eyes. He was my friend and my blood brother and I had to protect him, but he mustn't be a traitor. Traitors they burned on the fire and I did not want that to happen to him. If it was any other boy I would kill him or tell on him to Mobuto but not David. He was lucky we were blood brothers.

"I can't sleep anymore. Let's go outside?" I whispered.

"Okay," said David.

We crept out of the hut into the dark night. There were stars scattered high in the sky and the quarter moon hid behind thin clouds. The night air felt cool and fresh. I took a deep breath, which calmed me, and I heard David do the same.

"We've been here many moons. You should be stronger, David," I said. "You must listen to Mobuto and hate the enemy pig."

"I'm trying. But sometimes when there's so much blood it makes me want to break." David's face was pained. He frowned and his eyes began to water.

I glared at him. "The enemy must bleed. They made us bleed, David; why don't you hate them?"

David stared and said nothing.

"If you break, they'll kill you. You know that!" I whispered fiercely. "I also pain inside David. I pain for my sister. I want to become the officer so I can find her on the dump. I must stay strong so I can do this."

David looked at me in surprise. "You seem so tough, Modetse. I didn't know you were paining for your sister."

"Why do you think I have the bad dreams? But we must fight for the L.R.A. If we don't fight then the enemy will come and kill us and then no one will help Thandi. The General's our father. We've have sworn to him and you cannot break it. The spirits will eat your brain, David. You must listen to Mobuto, David. He's shown us what the enemy do. We've seen their rebel camps."

"I'll try, Modetse," said David. He patted me on the shoulder. "Come, we must go back. There are guards over there."

I looked across the dark fields. Tall figures were patrolling the boundary. I nodded at David and we crept quietly back inside. I lay on my bed with my eyes open. My jaw was clenched after talking with David. I tensed my fists. David must be careful. He must not betray the L.R.A.

I lay for a long time staring up at the dark ceiling. Thandi was alive again in my mind. She was hungry and crying on the dump. I tried to push the pictures away until the morning sun began to eat away the night, then I closed my eyes for a bit until it was time to rise.

* * *

"Hotshot, you and Cleverboy go see Mobuto now!"

I scraped the last of my porridge from the bowl and saluted. David did the same and we ran across to his hut and saluted him from the doorway. He was lying on his big double bed with his head on a pile of white pillows. He looked at us for a long time. I kept my eyes firm to the front. My stomach fluttered. Had we done something wrong? Had he heard about David's heart?

"So, soldier boys. You're doing well with the kills, yes?"

"Yes, sah," we said as we clicked our heels together and saluted again.

He puffed out his chest and looked us up and down.

"Good. Yes good. Now, there'll be a few changes. Cleverboy, we've decided to send you to Intelligence. You can help Lieutenant Bandi there. Hotshot, you'll stay with the squadron. He got up and hoisted up his trousers over his fat stomach and looked at us with narrow eyes.

146

"Now move!" he shouted suddenly, and I jerked backwards with wide eyes but inside my stomach was warm.

We ran off and I turned to David and smiled. I could see the gladness in his eyes and deep inside I felt the same. He would be safer over there where he did not have to kill. We reached our hut panting and David took my hand and gave me the strong double handshake.

"Go well, Hotshot," he said with a big smile. "Take care in the battle."

"Stay well, Cleverboy," I said. "I'll be okay."

He shook his head and laughed. "It's my prayer that you will be my brother."

Then he turned and walked away towards Intelligence HQ. I watched his straight back grow smaller. I would miss him but I was proud that Mobuto had chosen me to be the fighter.

Bilole came from the side of the hut and I turned quickly and saluted him. He nodded at me and smiled.

"So, Hotshot, we've another assignment. This'll be a special one. Commander Mobuto says we leave in one hour. Be ready."

"Yes, sah." I saluted with a fast hand. I wondered why it was a special mission and my body buzzed with excitement.

Chapter 24

I followed Commander Mobuto onto the yellow grass field. Richard and Jabu were lined up with Bloodneverdry, Trigger, Shithead and Badboy. There was also a fat one with a bad skin called Uglyboy.

"Stand here in front," called Bilole.

I moved to where he had shown me in the front with my head held high. I felt their jealous eyes on my back but I clutched my AK by my side and was glad I'd made sure that my uniform looked smart.

Mobuto strutted past our lines like Mr. Chief Lion. He looked us up and down and we all stood stiff and tall knowing we mustn't make him anger. He lifted his fat stomach up from under his belt and put his hands on his hips. Then he suddenly shouted at us, "We're going to find a village that are helping the enemy pigs. We're going to make them pay."

"Yes and you soldier boys are going to help us. Today you will be true men of the L.R.A."

I turned to see who had spoken. It was Capt. Nkunda. He glared at me and I kept my eyes fixed to the front. I did not want to upset him. Mobuto looked fierce at him.

"These village hyenas will pay for their treason with their hands and their feet," continued Mobuto with a sneer.

"Yes." Nkunda laughed. "The hands they do the work and the feet they do the walking. We're going to take away the hands of the enemy pigs so that they cannot work."

"What will we do, soldier boys?" barked Mobuto.

"We will cut off the hands and feet, sah," we all shouted.

"Why will we do that?" he shouted.

"The hands they do the work and the feet they do the walking. They help the enemy pigs!" we shouted back. Mobuto grinned at us and I went warm inside with prouding.

148

Mobuto showed for us to fall into line behind him. We were going on foot and not in the trucks so that we could take the villagers by surprise. We followed him, clutching our AKs and packs, across the field and through the gate into the thick green forest behind that smells of wee from the monkey vines.

The cool damp of the forest felt good on my skin because the uniform was hot. The forest was full with the sound of the rainbirds, honeyguides, hornbills and ground crickets who were all singing hello to us. I looked up high in the trees. The baboons, they were sitting watching with careful eyes and long yellow teeth but I was not afraid of them. I had my AK and my silver machete in my hands. I could cut out their blue balls and eat them if I wanted. They were scared of me that's why they hid and watched, just like the enemy pig.

"Hotshot, cut off the bush that way. Uglyboy, you follow him. You must cut quick and quiet."

"Yes, sah." We saluted.

I sliced like number one solider through the bush with my machete. I wore a red bandana on my head, which looked good with my uniform, and strong brown polished boots instead of the old rubber sandals. My muscles were hard now like the lion's and my heart was strong from the brown-brown. I was a true killer machine for the L.R.A. and my AK did not feel heavy now. I had the magic juju in me and the dark spirits. I could do anything. I told myself this again and again in my head so that the fear deep inside would go. The more brown-brown I took the better it got. It took all the feelings away so that I could be empty inside and just want to kill. Mobuto's words buzzed in my ears. We were going to get these tsetse fly villagers. They would not help our enemy again.

The thoughts helped my darkness inside to grow and I cut and cut at the sticky green bush, my whole body like the lion ready to kill. I looked sideways at Uglyboy. I wanted to cut faster than him and I was in charge. I wanted to be first one for

Mobuto.

"Shh, down," said Mobuto, suddenly stopping.

I'd been so busy with my thoughts that I hadn't realized we were nearly at the village. Mobuto turned and showed us with his hand to get down. We knew what to do now and obeyed him instantly, falling on our bellies in the long yellow grass. Then, very slowly, we crept forward, pushing ourselves bit by bit with our legs. We were so clever and so quiet the enemy would not hear us.

I pushed myself on my stomach through the long grass. I felt it tickle my nose and cheeks but I kept my eyes fixed in front. I saw the tops of the thatched village huts through the grass.

I moved forward another foot and then through the gaps of the reeds I saw the whole village. The women were making maize porridge on glowing fires. They sat on tree stumps with their big black iron pots in front of them. "Thump, thump, thump," they went as they hit the wooden sticks into the pots to grind the porridge.

I saw little sparks fly from the fire as they thumped it. The smell of porridge was thick in the air.

There were children running around and making a noise nearby. They were hungry for their breakfast and my heart softened. I did not know if I wanted to kill children, but then I remembered that they were from the enemy who would kill us first and my heart grew hard.

I could not fear to slay them. I could not see their men so they must be fighting with the army against us and these children would grow up and kill us Mobuto had said. He told us we had to kill their women and children and make them suffer or they would make us suffer.

"Hotshot, Uglyboy," whispered Mobuto. "Take the huts on the left. Bloodneverdry, you take five of the others and get those on the right. Shithead, you and Trigger guard from the back in case the men come back and I'll take from the middle. When I say

'GO' we attack. Are you ready?"

"We nodded at Mobuto. My body was tense. I would tear the village with my AK.

"GO!"

I ran screaming from the bush, my head thrown back and my teeth showing. Every muscle in my body was alive. I pushed my AK back into my shoulder and headed straight for the huts Mobuto had pointed out, shooting my fire bullets at them.

The women jumped up in terror. They were so frightened that they nearly fell in the fire. One woman grabbed her child and started to run and run, but I was too fast. I pulled her red skirt and she fell in the dust.

"P-p-please don't hurt us. Don't hurt my child," she screamed, covering her terrified face with her trembling hands and pulling up her knees to her chin like a baby.

Her pleas just made me want to hurt her more. My mind was filled with madness. "Enemy pig bitch," I screamed, and kicked her in the head. "You help the enemy pig. You're the people who rape and kill my family."

"No, we're not," she pleaded. "We're just living in the village."

"Liar," I shouted, and hit her hard with the butt of my AK.

She rolled over onto her side, clutching her head and wailed.

"Put her on her stomach and pull her arms in front," commanded Mobuto coming up behind me.

"Yes, sah," I said as Uglyboy and I pushed the woman onto her stomach with her arms stretched out in front. She was crying so much that she was eating the dirt and bubbles of mud were coming from her mouth. We kicked her and laughed.

"Now watch," said Mobuto. He lifted up his machete high in the air and brought it down hard on the woman's hand. The hand jumped away and the red blood fountain spurted high into the air. The woman screamed so loud that it hurt my head, but I was not scared of the blood, even if it was so thick and red.

"Now it's your turn, Hotshot."

I lifted up my machete with both my hands high above my head. I held my breath in so that I could steady my arms. I focused my eyes on her shivering brown hand. Uglyboy was holding her arm flat on the dusty ground. He looked up at me with a warning. He did not have to worry. My aim was good.

I pulled my arms back over my head and then like lightning I brought down my machete. The hand jumped far away. The red blood leaped and pumped from her arm. I felt a surge of power and pride. I'd hit it spot on.

The woman was groaning with the blood running away making her weak. I kicked her. She was an evil thing and I'd done well; she would not work for the enemy again. Mobuto grunted and turned away from her squirming body. He patted me on the shoulder.

"Good work, Hotshot. Your aim was excellent."

"Thank you, sah," I said. "I'll cut off many more hands for you."

Chapter 25

That night as I lie on my bed dark spirits fill the dorm. My heart beats hard and sweat breaks out all over me. There is a shadow bending over me and another at the end of my bed.

I try and scream but nothing comes out. I am frozen. What is happening to me? Help me please.

I try and scream again but all that escapes is a croak. My body grows wet with sweat and my heart pounds so hard that my ears hurt. Help me somebody. Richard...Trigger...help. The thoughts scream away in my head but still I cannot move or speak. The face of the shadow is over me now. I can smell the stink of rotting flesh. Its red eyes filled with hate drill into my mind like knives. The other shadow is crawling over my bed towards me. The devil has sent his spirits to take me. They will suck out my soul.

I cannot stop them. I cannot watch them do this. I squeeze my eyes tight. My breath is loud and hard. Then the hands come. Bloody hands rise up in front of my closed eyes. They hit my face. Their iron smell is strong in my nostrils. The blood is flowing into them and down my throat. It is trying to drown me. No...no... Then my body moves. I kick my feet and thrash my hands. My mouth opens wide and I scream and scream, "No...No...help me, help me."

Hands shake my shoulders. A face comes in front of me. I stare up at Richard's big eyes. Trigger comes beside him.

"Stop screaming," Trigger shouts. "It's okay. You're having a nightmare."

"Wake up, Hotshot. Wake up," says Richard.

I stop screaming and turn my head to the side away from them. I stare at the far wall with a heaving chest as tears prick behind my eyes.

"I thought I saw something," I say, and my voice croaks. I feel my face grow hot. "It's okay. Go back to sleep."

"Try and not worry," says Trigger. "It's just the nightmare. You must talk to the doctor."

I tense my body and say nothing. Every night I'm dreaming bad things like these bloody hands. The dark spirits are laughing inside me. They don't want me in this place. They want to take me back to the darkness. That's why they tried to take me just now. How will I get away from them? No, they are in me. I must stay with them and do what they want.

I give a big sigh. If I do that then they won't harm me. They won't suck out my soul. The doctor he knows nothing. He does not have the evil inside. How can he help? How? I hate him. I wish David were here to help me. He would understand. The thought of David causes a pain in my stomach. I close my eyes and try and push his face from my mind.

"Try and sleep," says Richard as he and Trigger go back to their beds.

But I can't sleep and toss and turn until the sun rises. Then I get up before the others and go to the washroom. I splash cold water on my face but inside my heart remains heavy and full of fear. I can't get this Holy Spirit from my mind. Maybe that's why the dark spirits are angry. There is fear deep in my belly, which I can't chase away. It follows me and attacks by making my heart beat from my chest and sweat break out all over my body. I want to run screaming but I don't know to where.

It's school today again and I give at sigh. At least that is one thing that helps me. I want to learn more and more so that I can become a Commander one day in the L.R.A. I see Mobuto's big body in my head and my belly pains. He was clever. He could read and do many sums. I will one day be like him.

I sit at my desk as Mama Zuma hands out the sums from last lesson. We did multiplication and division and I look with eager eyes. There are many red ticks through my book.

"Good work, Modetse, you have them nearly all right. Do

your corrections and then we're going to do some English."

I nod and do my corrections with a firm face. Next time I want full marks. We learn how to do Swahili phrases into English. Mama Zuma says that English is an international language and it is important that we learn it. I'm happy to do this.

Mama Zuma comes and stands over me as I work through the phrases. She smiles and says, "Very good work, Modetse," which makes me feel warm inside but then she looks so deep into my eyes that I feel she can read my soul. I shift on my seat and frown.

"You okay," she whispers, bending over me.

"Of course," I say quickly, and pull a face. My heart beats in my ears. She knows this Holy Spirit well. She can see the dark spirits have been worrying me. I don't know what to do. These things are too big for me to deal with. I can't kill them with an AK or my hands. They are an invisible enemy. How will I fight them?

"Dr. Zuma will help you," she whispers as if she can read my thoughts. "I think it is time you speak to him."

I glare at her and say nothing. She has spoiled my day. All I want to do is my schoolwork. I don't want to think about the doctor and I don't want to think about any spirits. How will he be able to fight this invisible enemy? He is no different to me.

She sees my anger and pats me on the shoulder. "Keep up the good work. Do the next page now. You will get through it."

I shrug her touch away and turn the page fiercely. I know she means more than the work but I don't believe her. I finish doing the phrases but inside my stomach is tight and my head finds it hard to concentrate. I just want to run away from everything but how do I run from myself?

Chapter 26

Mobuto marched up to me while I sat and cleaned my AK.

"Hotshot," he shouted. "I've good news for you."

I jumped up and saluted him quickly. My heart jumped. Mobuto stood and smiled a sly smile making me wait for a few minutes. "We've decided to promote you to Lieutenant. You've been here eighteen months now. It is time for promotion." He gave a big laugh. "You are happy, no?"

"Yes, Commander, I'm very happy," I said as I pushed my shoulders back and stood up straight. "Thank you, sah," I saluted again. Inside my heart was dancing. I was an officer now. Soon I would have the power to ask Mobuto if I could fetch Thandi.

"I'm coming, Thandi girl," I said in my head. "I'm coming." Ay, maybe this could really be true? Soon I would find her. My stomach was happy and a big smile broke out across my face. Thandi would be waiting for me. She knows that I would never forget to look for her.

Mobuto grunted and walked over to pin my lieutenant bars. He patted me hard on the back so that I fell forward a bit.

"Make sure you lead well, Lieutenant Hotshot. You have a squadron of new boys under you now. Fetch them from Bilole and take them to the field for training." Mobuto turned and took out a big hat for the sun. He gave it to me.

I saluted and put the hat on my head lifted it proud like the General. "Yes, sah." I saluted again and marched off smiling inside to find my squadron.

I found Bilole and saw six new boys from the village standing behind him looking scared.

"These my boys?" I asked puffing out my chest.

"Yes, Lieutenant," said Bilole. He smiled with big teeth. "Take them away but be careful. Commander Mobuto said the General will be here tomorrow. You must make them look good for him;

156

if they don't you will pay."

I shrugged but then saluted and swaggered over to the group of boys. They all looked about eight or nine years and were standing shivering on thin legs and looking at me with big eyes.

"My name is Lieutenant Hotshot," I barked. "You are in my squadron now and I'll train you hard. What are your names? You first," I said, poking the smallest with my finger. He was very thin with a round stomach and round head like a gem squash. His eyes were so big that they looked like they covered nearly his whole face.

He nearly fell backwards and stammered, "Joshua, sah."

"You and you?" I said to the other two. They were both about nine and also thin.

"Bongi, sah," said the first one. He had a scar down his arm and another on his cheek. There was a bit of his ear missing at the top. I stared at it with narrow eyes.

"You from the streets?"

He nodded. "I am from Kampala," he said in a small voice.

My spirit flinched. Thandi was still in Kampala. "From the dump?" I said.

He shook his head. "No, sah, from the West side."

I stared at him and then looked at the next one.

"I am Vincent, sah," he said.

He had a thin face like an antelope and looked at me like I was a hungry lion. I saw his knees shaking. His shorts and shirt were dirty and torn. He stood close to Bongi like he knew him and must also come from the same streets.

"Right, now move, you fucking goats. Take up those stones over there. Put one on each shoulder and you must run fast round the field. If you drop one of the stones I will kill you. Do hear me? I will kill you. Now move!"

"Yes, sah," they said with their big frightened eyes.

I watched them with a straight back and narrow eyes. My stomach was warm inside and my mind smiled. I would make these boys strong like me and make sure my squadron was the best. When they were strong from the stones I would teach them with the wooden AK and then I would let them fire their first magic bullet. I would show Mobuto and Bilole that my squadron was the best.

I made them run for an hour. The sun was hot and high in the sky but my hat helped. I had to show the General my squadron one day and I couldn't have any weak boys to let me down.

"Run, you fucking pieces of shit. Run. One two, one two. Faster, faster."

I watched them sweat I laughed inside because they found it so hard. They looked like they were tough even though they're small. Vincent was the fastest and he held his stone so tight his knuckles were white. His jaw was pushed forward as he panted around the field. Joshua's big eyes stared hard in front and his chest moved hard up and down as he ran but he kept going. Bongi looked tough. He had a firm face and narrow eyes and held his stone close to him with tight arms as he ran around. As they bobbed up and down with their big eyes and panting hearts I remembered when I carried the heavy stones. I glanced down and flexed my arms with their strong muscles. I'd grown tall and every fiber in my body was taunt and ready to kill. I looked out at the running boys. After a few months they would be different. It was hard for them now but they'd thank me later. They were city boys. The little hyenas would be okay.

"Sit down," I shouted after they'd been running for thirty minutes.

The boys dropped the stones and looked at me with big eyes and panting mouths.

"Move to the river. You can drink the water and then you'll come and watch the magic bullets fly from my AK. You must come in one hour," I shouted.

"Yes, sah. Thank you, sah," they said, and saluted.

I saw Vincent give a big smile and then he and Bongi high-fived with weak arms. Joshua followed behind them with quick steps and a panting chest.

I walked to the Officer's Hut. It felt good to have my own boys and I was very excited that for the first time I could go there and eat and drink the beer. There was also Jamba to smoke. They let us have lots of Jamba but we were not allowed to drink beer with the officers. Now that was gone. Now I would feel the beer in my belly and the Jamba in my brain.

"Ho, ho, Hotshot, you can come to the Officer Hut now. That must make you happy?" said Mobuto as I mounted the stairs. He was sitting on the cool veranda with Nkunda and Bilole.

"Yes, sah," I said with a big smile.

"Have you finished training your squad?"

"Yes, it's too hot. My stomach's crying for the beer."

"Good. Bilole, get a tusker for Hotshot."

Bilole grunted and hoisted up his fat body to bring me a cold Tusker. I felt very proud to take it. I was like a man now. The Tusker was strong and gold and I licked the foam off the top so that my lip has a white moustache. Mobuto laughed at me.

"So, are you ready for another raid, Lieutenant?"

"Always, sah. I want to cut off more hands and feet for you, sah."

"Yes, Hotshot, we will find some new ones for you. I heard there's a village on the other side of the Gokwa river where the enemy pigs are getting food. It'll be a two day trek for us but it'll be worth the pickings."

"Lots of new hands that will do no more work," I said, and gave a devil laugh.

"Yes, my friend. Soon there will be no more hands to work for the enemy," said Mobuto. His gold tooth glinted at me.

"Hotshot – you can have the meat now," said Bilole.

He dished himself a big plate and stuffed it in his mouth.

"Yes, go get some and give me more," said Mobuto. He threw me his empty plate.

I went over to the big black pot filled with warthog stew and dish up two plates full. The rich smell made my stomach dance. I was a lucky soldier to be an officer now.

"So, Hotshot, tonight Nkunda and I have a better plan for you."

"Oh, what is that, sah?"

"Yes, Lieutenant, this will be better than the beer and the meat," said Nkunda with a sideways mouth.

"Or even the hands," laughed Mobuto.

My mind was frowning now. What could be better?

"Tonight your man will taste your first ladylove, Hotshot. You're fourteen and we'll see if you can shoot the magic bullets with your snake and not just your AK."

"Ha, ha, ha. That's good, Mobuto, maybe he has an AK for a man," laughed Nkunda.

"You mustn't shoot the bullets too fast, Hotshot, otherwise there'll be no fun."

I felt my cheeks get hot. I laughed with them but they made me feel small. I didn't want a ladylove.

"My AK's my ladylove," I said.

"Ha, ha, your AK's your ladylove. No, Hotshot, you must feel the soft brown flesh of the Pineapple girl," said Mobuto.

"Yes, you can choose any girl you want. There're some good new ones with pretty mouths and big brown eyes who have come to the camp," said Nkunda.

"After your first time you will want more and more, Hotshot. You'll shoot your magic bullets into all the girls. Here, smoke the Jamba. It'll help to make you ready," said Mobuto. He shoved the joint at me.

I pulled the blue smoke deep down. It chased the fear away but my heart still thumped because I knew that Mobuto and Nkunda would watch me have my first ladylove and I would need to do it good like a man.

"Can I get another Tusker?"

"Ha, ha, yes go get another Tusker but don't have too many or your AK barrel will droop," said Mobuto. He threw back his head in a belly laugh and his fat stomach wobbled. Nkunda joined in the laughter and I laughed too with hot cheeks and a sound that was too high. I leaned back in my chair with my beer and took another big sip hoping its coolness would take the redness from my face.

"My cock's talking to me," said Mobuto. "You'll take her first and then I'll have her and then Nkunda."

"She'll be lucky this pineapple girl to have us three, heh?"

We pushed back our chairs and went to the grenade hut where the Pineapple girls worked. Mobuto threw open the door and the girls stopped and quickly saluted with big eyes.

"Line up. You are lucky girls for our Lieutenant Hotshot has come to choose a ladylove."

The girls they stood and looked at me with big brown eyes. Some were too young and looked like only nine years. I didn't want to look at the young ones. They made me think of Thandi. My heart beat hard. What if Thandi was caught? Would they want to make her a Pineapple girl if I brought her here? I shook my head to chase away the thought and looked through the line of girls with my breath stuck in my chest.

I saw one girl near the end who had light brown skin and big round eyes. She looked about twelve years. Her lips were full and her ears were small. She held her hands together and shook and couldn't look me in the eyes. She looked like she was a city girl and she would be okay. The city boys had probably already taken her.

"I want her." I pointed, trying to make my voice sound loud and strong.

"Good choice," grunted Mobuto. "Take her. We'll go to my hut."

I grabbed the girl by the arm and made her walk behind Mobuto and Nkunda. I threw her on the bed in Mobuto's hut and began to take off my pants. Mobuto ripped her panties from her and he and Nkunda held her legs wide for me with her dress up. The girl lay and stared up at the ceiling like she was somewhere else. That made me angry. This was my first ladylove and she was lucky to have me. I felt myself growing hard like the barrel of my AK and then I climbed on top and I thrust and thrust until I made her scream and I screamed too.

"My turn," said Mobuto gruffly.

I looked at his manhood. It was big and brown. The girl she cried when he went in her. Then it was the turn of Nkunda. The girl cried and cried. I bet she wished it was only me. Now I was a true man. I could have anything I want.

Chapter 27

The bush has come alive.

"Ambush!" screams Mobuto. Move back!"

Bullets fly out from the trees. There's a flash of green headbands. Rebels jump out of the bush. I scream and shoot my AK. Noise is everywhere. Fire is everywhere; eating us, burning us.

BAM! A grenade blasts in my ears. Aiee, Bloodneverdry is in the air. His back is broken. There's blood everywhere. There are the bodies everywhere; some with no heads. Whose body is that? My mind screams with fear. The fear eats me up.

"Retreat," shouts Mobuto. "Retreat."

I'm stuck to the ground. Death has swallowed me like the hippo. I can't escape. "No..." I scream. "No..."

Then something's shaking me. A voice is calling to me. "Come back," it calls. "Modetse, come back."

My body is wet with the sweat and my mind is full of the clouds.

"It's not real," says the voice.

I blink my eyes. I'm lying on the grass outside my hut. What's happened?

I turn to look. The voice is Mama Zuma's. She's sitting cross-legged on the ground next to me and shaking my shoulder.

"It's okay, my child," she says. "Here, sit up. Have some water."

I push myself up and my arms shake but the cool water helps my dry mouth.

"They happen to all of you," says Mama Zuma with a smile. "They'll go in time."

I just stare and say nothing. I do not want to talk.

All of a sudden she puts her fat arms around me. She pulls me to her and pats my head. "It'll be okay," she whispers.

I widen my eyes. I feel like I am a child again back with Umama. I just want her to make everything better, to take away the pain. The tears start to visit my eyes. I fight them back. No, I'm a soldier. I won't cry.

"I'm fine," I mutter, trying to push her away, but she refuses to move.

"Is there a lot of blood in your dreams?"

"Too much," I say as the memories come back into my head like the strong river. My hands sweat and I catch my breath.

"Do you want to tell me about it?"

I don't want to but I can't stop myself. It just comes out of me. "It's bad blood. It comes from the dark spirits," I croak. "It's trying to drown me. Sometimes I can smell its iron smell so strong I'm sick."

"Does it scare you?"

"Yes. I think it'll kill me."

"It's over. It can't kill you now, Modetse. Perfect love casts out fear. The dark spirits have no power against it."

I grow angry with her. What is this perfect love? What does she know? Before, when I was in the L.R.A., I felt nothing, but now the guilt attacks me. What does she know of guilt? She didn't cut off the hands. She doesn't have dark spirits inside who come out and attack her. The air around me grows heavy. I hate this mission. They've made me feel this guilt. I hate them! I try to get up but she touches my arm.

"Stay, please a bit longer. Blood can also be good maybe. Do you think so? Like with a blood brother maybe?"

I flinch as David jumps back into my head and a deep pain rises in my belly.

"Did you lose a blood brother?" she whispers.

"The enemy killed him. That's why I hate them," I shout.

David's dead body is back. My muscles grow hard and I clench my fists.

"It's sad, Modetse, when young lives are lost. That's why war's so evil on both sides. Maybe the L.R.A. killed someone else's blood brother. Have you thought of that?"

My eyes widen and my stomach goes funny. I say nothing and we sit in silence. Then Mama Zuma puts her arm around me.

"Blood can be cleansing. It has great power," she says. "That's why it is used for sacrifices and to ask for forgiveness. It's a great mystery. Does it help to think about the good side to take away the bad?"

I shrug my shoulders. She has made my head spin.

"You're forgiven by the blood, Modetse. Right now you might have mud on you from the past but the power of the blood of Christ will wash that clean away. There is no greater power than that, nothing. Darkness flees from that power. You must always remember it was not your fault. God will not hold it against you. You must go and speak to the doctor. Please tell me you will."

I nod, but my mind spins. I want to believe what she is saying but she doesn't understand. There is nothing that can chase the darkness away. Blood comes from the kill. There is no power to clean in the blood. What is she talking about? My body grows like iron and I hold my arm tight so I don't hit out at her. She just makes me feel bad inside. I jump up and brush the grass and sand from my body.

"I need to walk," I say.

Mama Zuma nods and smiles at me with sad eyes.

"That's a good idea. Come to my kitchen afterwards. I'll go and bake a big chocolate cake for you. Remember go see the doctor."

I nod and walk away my mind going round and round. Good blood, bad blood... This blood talk is making me sick. How can blood make you clean? But inside I'm scared she could be right and maybe these other spirits have more power. This blood they use has a power I don't understand. Will it kill me or clean me? Maybe I should see Dr. Zuma.

Chapter 28

"Dr. Zuma's ready for you, Modetse."

I glare at Nurse Sophie and walk into the cool thatched hut. My body is filled with anger. I wish I hadn't listened to Mama Zuma and her stupid story of the blood.

Dr. Zuma sits in a big black leather chair at the far end of the hut. There's a small wooden table with books and a flask of water with two glasses in front of him. He smiles at me and gets up and puts out his hand.

"*Kuwakaribisha*, Modetse. Good to see you."

I nod, but play stupid to the hand he gives me.

He looks at me in silence for a few seconds and then says, "Please sit down here."

He points to a big blue armchair opposite him. I sit hard down into its soft cushions and stare at the ceiling. Dr. Zuma sits back down in his chair and we stare at each other. I move in my chair and look at the ceiling. Then he makes a noise in his throat and asks, "I believe you're doing well in school?"

I stay quiet. What game's he playing?

"Mama Zuma tells me you're a talented mathematician. You could go on to university one day, you know."

I try to stop it but his words make me happy inside. Then I realize that he is being the sly jackal. He's trying to stop me from going back to the L.R.A. by lying to me and making me think I can do things only rich people do. I glare at him.

"I'm a soldier. I don't need university."

He smiles and says, "I hope we can change that, Modetse. It's time for a turning point. What happened in the past was not your fault."

"You're not L.R.A.!" I shout with spit shooting from my mouth. "What do you know?"

"The L.R.A. is over, Modetse," he says, looking me straight in

166

the eyes.

"No, it's not over," I shout. "I'll be the new leader."

This man knows nothing. He's just trying to brainwash our soldiers and stop them going back the L.R.A.

I jump out of my chair and kick over the square wooden table in front of us. The flask and glasses break hard on the clay floor and water spills out across it. I kick the overturned table so that it flies up against the shelf at the back of the hut. Books fall to the floor. I pick them up and throw them against the wall. I turn on him like the fierce lion and scream, "I'll destroy you and everything you have. I don't want to talk to you. I want to go back to my family. Where's the L.R.A.? You've made me a prisoner of war and you're trying to brainwash me with your Jesus. The L.R.A. will find you and kill you. I'm Lieutenant Hotshot! They need me!"

This pig doctor he just sits there and says in the quiet voice, "The L.R.A. has left the area, Modetse. The Government's defeated them. They've poisoned your mind and we must undo that. True cleansing will come from God in your own time. It's not your fault what happened. You were only a child."

He doesn't seem worried by my shouting and just gets up and picks up the books and the table. I clench my muscles and scream, "I'm sick of people telling me it's not my fault! It is my fault! I want to kill. I like to kill. I want more blood!"

I feel like I'll explode. This doctor knows nothing. He's not a soldier. He doesn't know what it's like to belong to the L.R.A. He's just a stupid city man. What can he know of killing? I breathe hard. I clench my fists until my knuckles are white. My head spins round and my heart beats like a drum in my chest.

"Let the anger pass. I understand how you feel, Modetse," says the doctor.

He's so calm that it makes me want to cut him to pieces. I tense my arm to stop it lashing out and grind my teeth together.

"How can you understand? You're not L.R.A," I say, and spit

on the floor to insult him.

He ignores my spitting and answers in a quiet voice,

"You're right, I'm not L.R.A. but when I was a young man I was also a soldier. I've been in conflict before in the Congo. I've also seen horrible things, Modetse. So you see I can understand a bit."

I look at him with wide eyes and an open mouth. That explains why he could hold me so tight.

"You were an enemy?"

"No I wasn't an enemy. This was before the L.R.A., but no war is nice. I wouldn't like to be in one again. I've also had to ask Jesus for forgiveness."

He looks deeply at me for a while and I stand frozen.

"Will you sit down now, Modetse? I'd like to hear about your role in the L.R.A."

He pushes the chair for me and I clear my throat, shuffle down to it, and sit with my head down and elbows on my knees.

"When you're ready, Modetse," he says in a soft voice. "Start maybe with telling me how you get the name Hotshot."

I give an evil grin and spit out, "I was a hotshot and the best man for cutting the hands of the enemy."

I stare at him, waiting for him to look shocked, but he just continues to look at me calmly and asks, "You cut lots of hands off?

"Yes," I shout. What's the matter with this stupid doctor? Why isn't he shocked at what I've done?

"Was there a reason for cutting off the people's hands who were not soldiers?"

"Yes, because the hands they do the work. If they've no hands then they can't work for the enemy."

"What if they're not helping the enemy?"

"All those villagers were helping the enemy," I say. Ay, this man is stupid.

The doctor goes silent for a moment and then asks, "Do you

dream about cutting off hands now?"

I flinch. Aiee, how does he know my dreams this man? I'm worried that maybe he has some special powers because he's also a priest. He was talking to the spirits in the river; that means he can find out things and have power over me. Maybe he's sending the hands and dark shadows to my dreams? My heart beats fast and I clamp my lips. He smiles at me, looks down at his paper, and writes something.

"You know, Modetse, sometimes even now I dream about the things I saw thirty years ago. I shot people who didn't deserve it. They still come back to haunt me. It would not be unusual if you dreamt about hands."

Now I understand. He has no powers. He's just clever because he's also been a soldier. I give him an angry stare.

He just smiles back and asks, "Do you dream of them?"

"Yes, sometimes."

"Are you cutting them in your dreams?"

"No."

"What're they doing?"

"They hit me."

"Oh? They want revenge?"

"Yes."

"Is it many of them?"

"Too many."

"Yes, I understand. Of course they'll want revenge, but that can only be if it really was your fault. And, Modetse, this is a very important point. You must listen to me." He leans forward and looks me deep in my eyes. "It was not your fault. You were just a child and as a soldier had to follow your orders. You were brainwashed into doing what you did. You must not blame yourself."

I stand up and scream, "I wasn't brainwashed and I'm not a child. I'm the best soldier to cut off the hands of the enemy and I wanted to follow my orders. I'm good L.R.A. I do what I'm told and I'll go back and I'll cut off all the hands and feet of the enemy pigs. I'll cut off your hands and the hands of Nurse Sophie and everyone…"

I shout so loud that my chest heaves up and down. My breath hurts in my chest. My head spins.

I stand up and kick the blue armchair so hard that it squeals right across the wooden floor. It nearly knocks a pot with green palm leaves over. The doctor jumps up and steadies the pot. Then he moves the chair back to its place and sits back down in his chair. He shows me with his hand to sit down again.

I shake my head and shout, "I won't talk to you anymore. I'm strong enough to sort out my own dreams. I don't need your help."

I run from the hut back to the dark green forest where I can hide from everyone. I don't want to think about anything but inside my head spins. I don't know what is right. If what he says is true and it's not my fault then the L.R.A. is wrong and it's their fault. But that can't be. No…it is the enemy's fault. It's their fault…not mine. I don't want to lose my power. I can't lose my power. I don't believe in their forgiveness it will make me weak.

Chapter 29

"I like the crafts," says Richard as we make our way to the Craft hut that afternoon. "Mama Zuma says I'm the talented artist."

I frown at him and grunt. Trigger and he keep telling me to do the stupid crafts. My mood is still black from visiting the doctor; I don't want to talk or hear his stupid boasting. I'm only going because Tula will be there.

We go in the long Art hut with its mud walls and straw roof. It is cool inside and smells like the cows. On the floor are many long yellow mats of straw. Next to them stand big wooden boxes filled with red clay, colored beads and buckles. The new leather smell relaxes my mind. The air is full with the noise of the children chattering like small chickens.

My eyes walk around the hut. The girls are sitting far from the boys. My heart beats like a bongo drum. Tula is with the small girls. They are playing with many bright beans.

"Modetse, Richard. Over here," calls Mama Zuma. She shows us to sit on a long yellow straw mat with strips of brown leather in front.

I lift my eyes at Richard and pull a face. I want to sit by Tula. He smiles back and we make our way past the girls to the mat. I can feel Tula watching me as I walk past, but I stare hard out in front and pretend not to see her while my drum heart hurts my ears.

"You boys will make belts today," says Mama Zuma with a happy smile. "Here, choose some nice buckles."

"Are they for us?"

Mama Zuma smiles some more. "I'll tell you in a minute. Now sit down."

I take a shiny buckle from the pot and sit down in front of the strip of leather. The buckle is round and silver like the moon. It has many markings on it all around the edges and must cost much money. I look down with big eyes. Ay, it is too good.

"Bengu's here," whispers Richard, poking me in the side.

I frown and look up to see Bengu walk like Mr. Main Man into the hut. He's wearing a Coca-Cola T-shirt and smart khaki shorts with zips and buckles on them. I look at his shoes. They are white Adidas with a bright blue stripe and look new. He's put black and white beads around his neck and braided his hair like he's Bob Marley. I hate him. He thinks he's so cool. I see him look sideways at Tula and smile. She smiles back and waves at him. I hold my teeth so that they hurt. I glare down at my buckle. It doesn't make me feel good anymore.

I hear Tula laugh. I look up. She's making clay pots with the two small girls Zinzi and Lily. The red clay is going everywhere so they are full with it on their faces.

"What a mess," says Mama Zuma with a laugh. "But I can see a good pot coming. Your father will be proud, Tula. Now he'll want you to be a teacher."

I see Tula pull a face but she says nothing.

Bengu turns to look. "Yes, Dr. Zuma will like that one," he says, and laughs showing his straight white teeth.

My body stiffens like the angry lion. My fist wants to hit him. He talks like he's one of them.

"He thinks he's too good," whispers Richard.

I nod and glare down at the floor. "Fuck him," I whisper back.

My mood is dark again. I pick up the leather strip and begin to hit it hard with the stone like it is Bengu. I cut a deep pattern into it with the stick. Richard takes my buckle and tries to put it on. I grab it back.

"Fuck off!"

"I am helping. You are making a mess."

"I am not," I shout. "Leave it alone!"

I can hear my voice talk back around the hut. All the eyes are looking at me. I see Tula look up and I feel my cheeks go hot. Then I see that Bengu with an ugly proud smile. I get up and stomp out of the hut. I want so bad to stab Bengu until all his blood runs out.

"Modetse. You okay?"

"Fu…" I stop. Tula is here. My cheeks grow hot. I don't know what to say. I just nod. She's wearing blue jeans shorts and has a black T-shirt with "No Problem" in white writing. There are colored beads around her neck and dangly ones in her ears. She looks too good.

"My mother says to come back in once you feel better. We're going to make Christmas presents," she says, and smiles.

I nod as if I knew that and say, "I'm coming now."

She smiles again and I give a small smile back before she goes inside. She has made me sad inside. So many moons have gone that I don't know how long it is since I lost Thandi. Christmas makes me think even more of her. I would always save some of the money to buy the good food from the KFC shop and lots to drink. Umama always made Christmas special for us. A heavy stone sits in my stomach. My heart pains for my sister. How will I ever find her again? No, I will find her. I will get strong and use the LRA to help me. I won't let these weak thoughts live in my mind.

I march back into the cool of the Craft hut keeping my eyes on the ground so I don't have to look at anyone. Richard moves to the side so I can sit back down in my place. He's put my belt in front with the buckle resting on it. I sit back down pull a face pushing it out of the way.

"We're going to make each other presents," says Mama Zuma. "It's nice to have presents that have been specially made by us. There'll be other presents too which we have bought for you. It's going to be a great time."

"Christmas! That'll be good hey, Modetse," says Richard. "I hadn't thought it was Christmas."

I just look at him and say nothing. I wish he would just shut up.

"Okay, boys and girls," says Mama Zuma, clapping her hands. "What we're going to do now is pick the name of someone from this pot. Whoever you pick is the person who is going to get a present that you are going to make now. The ones you have just made are for you to keep yourselves. You can now choose to make any craft you want to match the person whose name you draw," she says. "Tula, will you please take the pot around?"

I watch as Tula unwinds her long legs and walks over to her mother. She takes the big red-brown clay pot around and everyone puts in their hand to draw a folded name.

"Dig down deep, Modetse, and choose a name," she says, and smiles at me.

I put my hand down into the cool clay and take a folded piece of paper from the pile.

"Unwrap it to look, but keep it secret," says Tula, putting her finger to her lips.

She gives me a wink before going over to Richard. My stomach trembles and I give a small smile. I look down and unwrap the folded paper.

The name Bengu stares back at me and I breathe in sharply. Bengu! I don't want to give him a present. The only thing I want to give him is an AK bullet. Why him? I glare down at the name and crumple it in my fist.

"What?" says Richard.

"Nothing," I mumble. I shove the paper aside and dig down in the buckle pot until I find the most ugly one I can. It's square and dull. Good it won't look nice on him.

"Who you got?"

"Bengu."

"Oh, now I see," says Richard, and laughs. "You must make him an ugly belt."

I give a sly smile. "I will make it very ugly. I think I'll write 'Fuck you' on it."

Richard laughs. "You would, too. I know you."

I begin to stab the leather with my stone like I'm smashing in his head. All of a sudden my mind jumps. The stone's become a bayonet. I can see myself like my spirit has left my body. My face is the devil face. My eyes are like the mad hyena. My mouth is open in the ugly scream. I am stabbing a body with my bayonet. Stab, stab, stab! There is big blood on my hands. There is the small child screaming. I've killed her mother. I'm laughing at my kill. "No...I don't want to be this boy. What have I done? What have I done? But the body is not the small child. It is the enemy. I must kill him or he will kill me.

I begin to scream out my hate but Richard shakes me and throws water on my face.

"You are screaming," he says. "Shh."

My spirit is back. I shake my head. I am shaking. What is happening to me? I am numb and my cheeks feel hot. I look around the hut. Everyone is talking and busy with their craft. They are not looking at me but I know they are just pretending. Inside I feel sick. My body is wet and my mind is full of clouds. I don't know what to think anymore.

I see Richard staring at me. I want to smash his face in. What's he looking at? If the darkness is wrong then we are all killers and are black inside. I get up and run from the hut. This time I won't come back. I'll run to the forest so that I can be alone.

I run over the hard red soil as the hot tears prick behind me eyes. I reach the thick forest and keep running. The cool of the breadfruit trees and the hands of the palm trees make me better inside. I run and run until I'm deep inside like a cave. I sit hard on the soft leaves. My body is wet with sweat. My mind thinks back to the camp. Inside a voice is asking how did I change so much? I was a good boy. I was Thandi's big brother; Umama's only son. How did I become so bad?

But then another voice tells me No, it is right to kill. I must not be weak. I feel the darkness rise up in my soul. It will give me strength. The blood comes in my nostrils. Its iron smell makes me retch. I don't want it anymore. I'm sick of the blood. I shake my head. I wish the darkness would cover me so that I can sleep and never wake again.

Chapter 30

The jeep screeched into the camp and five soldiers jumped out with their AKs held high. They ran over to Mobuto and handed him a paper. He read it and turned and showed for me to come. I hurried over.

"Go get some of your squadron and the others. Give these instructions to Bilole."

"Yes, sah." I saluted. I took the instructions and found Bilole before running to call Richard and Jabu and three of the boys from my squadron.

Jabu and I jumped into the front jeep with Bilole driving and Richard got in the one with Nkunda. I put Joshua, Vincent and Bongi in the back.

"Hold your AKs high," I said. "And keep your eyes straight."

They nodded at me with big eyes as we spun off bumping onto the dark jungle path. The jeep climbed the trees roots like a mountain goat. Jabu and I held out our machetes to slice away any thick vines which dangled in our way.

"Where are these rebel bastards hiding?" I said as we bounced through the jungle.

"Near the river," said Bilole. "We're going to make the ambush to kill them."

Jabu and I lifted our eyebrows up and smiled. This was the first time we'd laid one; it was going to be too good. Suddenly Bilole switched off the engine and the jeep jerked to a stop. We fell forward. Vincent and Joshua let out a shriek.

"Shut up, you fools, before I beat you," I said. I held up my hand as if to hit them and they cowered before me with big eyes. I glared at them and then turned back to Bilole.

"We're stopping here. Nkunda is staying further back on the other track in case they go that way. We'll hit the lead truck; he'll get the end one. Get out," said Bilole.

I obeyed and shouted at my boys to do the same. They jumped out and stood to attention. I marched over like the main man with Jabu and we squatted next to Bilole who was busy unwinding a long cable for the claymore trip wire.

"Crawl there, Hotshot, and tie this across the dirt track. Jabu, you go behind Hotshot and help and then take his boys and go lay the mines over there."

Bilole pointed down the sand track.

"Put them all in and make sure you cover them well with the soil. Brush the soil in an untidy way with the palm fronds after."

"Yes, sah." Jabu saluted.

He took the rucksack of mines from Bilole and put them on his back. We fell to the ground and crawled like mambas through the bush. Sharp rocks and stones pricked my stomach but I ignored the pain. Through the gaps in the yellow grass I saw a track in front where the jeeps rode.

"We can tie the rope low around that lala palm," I whispered.

Jabu nodded. I leopard crawled to the edge, keeping my ears tuned and my eyes sharp for any sound or movement. Nothing! I slithered fast across the track and hid my body behind the thick rough trunk. Its sharp pineapple edges hugged the rope and I secured it easily. I gave Jabu the thumbs up. He nodded and showed for my boys to follow.

They crept onto the red soil and dug to hide the mines. Jabu smoothed the soil down and then brushed it with a palm frond, which I threw him to make it look like nothing was there. I showed with my eyes for us to go and we slid back through the bush to Bilole.

"Done," I said, and made a big grin.

"Good work," said Bilole. He gave me a nod. "Now send your boys to keep watch. They must give the signal when they see the jeeps coming. We'll lie in wait downwind."

"Yes, sah. Boys here," I commanded.

"Yes, sah," they said, and ran over to salute me.

I narrowed my eyes and looked at them. "You're going to be the meerkats. You'll hide in the thick clump of leaves of those marula trees and watch for the jeep of the enemy pig. When you see them coming in the distance I want you to give a call like the rainbird. Do you hear me clear?"

"Yes, sah. We are clear, sah."

"Do the call now. You, Joshua – let me hear."

"Boo-o-o-o, boo, boo, boo, boo," said Joshua, closing his big eyes and holding back his head with his fat lips pushed out in an O shape.

"Okay," said Bilole. "That sounds good. Now go."

I turned to my boys and looked at them with hard eyes and a firm face. "Remember if you fail I'll kill you! Come! I'll show you where to wait. Get down!"

I crept through the bush towards a clump of marula trees to the side of the track with my boys creeping behind me. The branches were full, with thick green leaves and bunches of small orange berries. They would give good cover.

"Joshua, up that one, Vincent – there, Bongi – you that one. Go!"

The boys saluted and scattered to climb up the trees like baby baboons. Seconds later they were well hidden among the leaves. I stared at them and suddenly felt a deep ache in my belly. Thandi had come back in my head and was asking for me. Where had she come from? Why did she come into my head now? My stomach went weak and I shivered. I frowned and jerked my head. This was not the time to think of Thandi. I was a soldier. I had an enemy to kill.

I stood still and smelled deep from the musky jungle. I closed my eyes and imagined a picture of dead rebels full of blood. The thought of their blood made my heart beat fast and I smiled and straightened my back. I was already a Lieutenant. If I did this kill good then in a few months I would go higher in the LRA and be a Captain. Then I would ask Mobuto if I could go back and get

Thandi. I could not allow any weak thoughts in my head to stand in my way.

I blinked and stared back at the jungle. The afternoon sun was bending down towards the earth but the bush around us was still hot and my uniform stuck against my body. The air hummed heavy with silence and the sweet scent of the jungle vines.

I shuffled on the ground and stared hard through the bush at the waiting road. "Come on, you bastards," I whispered. "Come on. I want to blow your fucking brains out." I looked over at the lala palm in the distance. Where were they? Why were they taking so long? Maybe we had got the wrong place?

Bilole shifted uncomfortably and glared at my questioning eyes. Then all of a sudden we heard Boo-o-o-o-o, boo, boo, boo, boo.

Bilole gave me the thumbs up. My boys had done well. Seconds later the distant drone of jeeps could be heard. Jabu and I smiled at each other like jackals.

The sound grew, and through the trees I saw a line of enemy jeeps full with government rebel soldiers. They were holding M16s high in their hands and talking loudly to each other.

I held my breath. "BOOM!" Nkunda's claymore mine exploded under the last jeep sending out many spikes of steel in a shower of fire and dirt high into the sky. The forest trees cracked and splintered and bits of bloody bodies flew up and fell back to the ground like broken pigeons. I put back my head and laughed. Nkunda had done a good job.

"AMBUSH," screamed one of the rebels as the jeeps in front screamed forward towards us, thinking the ambush was only at their back. The rebels fired like the mad people at the bush behind them.

Then Bilole shouted, "Now!"

Jabu and I kept down low and pulled hard on our hidden rope.

"KABOOM!" our bang was bigger. The first jeep jumped,

twisting its steel and throwing the rebels high in the air.

The brakes of the second jeep screamed and the rebels jumped from it and began tearing the palms and marulas apart with their bullets. The ground sprayed hot and high in the air and bark and leaves splintered around us.

"Go!" I shouted to Jabu and Bilole and we jumped out of the bush and fired back at the rebels. They took fright like we were forest devils come to life and madness broke out with them shouting and thudding through the bush as they tried to flee from our killer bullets.

They darted through the forest and turned back to fire on us but my aim was too good and one by one I shot down their fleeing backs, splattering thick red blood onto the green leaves of the forest.

"Boys, fire!" I commanded at my soldiers who had slid down from their marula trees.

They put their big AKs under their arms and fired madly with no fear after the enemy knowing that the magic juju would protect them. Vincent held his AK at his chest and ran forward with his arms tense around it and his small finger stuck on the trigger. The bullets flew out like fire in front of him. Joshua's gun was pointing up but that was okay because he was so small. His bullets flew across the bush and joined with ours. The rebels had no chance. We pushed on through the bush firing at anything that moved.

Rainbirds and honeyguides flew upwards, squawking their terror at the killing. The forest was scattered with bloody bodies. Good – this would give the rebels a clear message not to mess with the L.R.A. Next thing we'd visit their villages and cut the lips from their girls. My body bristled with excitement and I gave a sly smile as I saw their bloody faces in my mind. This was too good!

I exchanged high fives with Jabu and Bilole and gave the thumbs up to my boys.

"Let the rebels come find their dead," I made the ugly face and kicked one of the mangled bodies lying in my path. The iron smell of blood and broken flesh was strong and I breathed it in deep, feeding power to my dark spirit.

"They'll be waiting for their five jeeps by the river a long time," I said, and gave a devil laugh.

"We've hit them hard," said Bilole with a sneer. "How many bodies you count?"

"More than thirty," I said. "It is a good kill."

We grinned at each other and high-fived again.

"Mobuto will be pleased," said Jabu with a grin. "Let's go tell him."

I nodded and we jumped back in our jeep and headed back shouting our victory to the jungle.

Chapter 31

Mobuto was happy with our ambush and gave me the day off. I put the piece of grass in my mouth and whistled as I went over to the clump of high pine trees where Jabu was sitting playing cards with Bilole. They were sitting nice on sawn off tree trunks with a middle one for the table. My head smiled at the sweet pine smell of the trees. I went to the shade. My boots crunched over the dried needles.

"Hey, Hotshot, you want to play?"

"Deal," I said, taking five silver shillings from my pocket and throwing them into the shining pile in the center of the log.

Jabu gave me slit eyes but threw down an upside down card. I turned it over and smiled inside as the black king card showed himself to me. I kept my face tight and still.

"Deal," I said again, and Jabu slapped down another card. This time it was an ace. Ay, the spirits were smiling on me today. I put down my two cards and pretended to flick the insect from my trousers.

Bilole stared and was quiet for a second then said, "Deal."

Jabu put his lips together and said nothing. Then he dealt another one for himself. I kept my body tense and still. I was sure they could not tell anything from my face even though they were looking at me with intense faces and inside I laughed at my jackal soul. They were fucking idiots compared to me. I waited until they were looking with serious faces at their two cards and then slapped over my black king and ace.

"Ha, ha," I said as I took the pile of silver coins and stuffed them into my shorts. "Come deal again."

"Fuck it," said Bilole, getting up and kicking the log table with his brown boot. "I haven't got time for this shit."

He marched away with a sour face towards the dining hall. Jabu scowled at me and also got up.

"You're idiots," I shouted. "Just because I'm better than you."

"Fuck you, Hotshot – you're just lucky. One day your luck will stop," said Jabu, pulling back his top lip.

"You're just jealous because I'm better than you."

"Fuck you," said Jabu. He turned and came at me with his fists up.

I jumped up and darted from foot to foot, facing him with upturned fists. "Come, come," I shouted, "you're no fucking match for me. I'll make your head spin with your blood. I'll turn your eyes black and red so that you'll be only good to be fed to the dogs. Come, you fucking bastard. Come, try me, try."

Jabu, he exploded like the grenade. He hit out his fists at me. I ducked to the side and rammed the side of his head with my fist so that my whole body vibrated and the bones of my hand shouted out. I ignored the pain and pulled my arm back and hit him again before I pummeled him with both hands.

Jabu hit out like a wounded buffalo, roaring and pushing against me with his hands up, trying to hide his face. I jumped backwards and was ready to go in for the kill when all of a sudden I heard drums and David's voice calling. I stopped and dropped my hands. Jabu too stopped and jerked around. David came panting up to us.

"The great doctor has sent the diviner. Mobuto said we must all go to the river now."

Jabu and I exchanged glances and I nodded at him. He accepted the end of the fight and nodded back. His right eye was swollen and a big blue lump sat on his head. I grinned at David and lifted up my eyebrows. David frowned.

"We must hurry," he said.

I patted down my uniform and tucked my shirt neatly into my trousers. The talk of the diviner made my belly flutter. A slow prickle of fear moved over me.

"Do you know why she's coming?" I asked David as we ran over.

He shook his head.

"Hey, Hotshot, Grenadelauncher, where the fuck you been?"

Mobuto glowered at us with fierce eyes. He hit us both on the head as we saluted.

"Get down to the fucking river now. You're lucky you just made it. One second later than the diviner and you'd be dead!"

I winced and ran down as fast as I could to the river. My squadron were lined up on the riverbank and they saluted smartly as I came down. Joshua stared with his big eyes and both Vincent and Bongi looked pale showing their fear inside, but I could see they were trying to stand stiff and look brave and they looked happy in their eyes to see me.

"Good, you're lucky you're here," I shouted, "otherwise I'd kill you fucking goats."

They saluted again with big eyes and chanted, "Yes, sah."

I snorted at them and walked proud over with David to join Scarecrow and Trigger standing on the riverbank.

The high cries of "Ulaloo, ulaloo..." cracked the morning air. We tensed and turned to look at the thick green pine and willow trees on the far riverbank. A row of five women with white clay faces, jangling seedpods around their wrists and ankles and blowing skirts of green and red, came out from the deep greenness of the forest like a long viper. They wound their way down to the water. Behind came the "dum, dum, dum" of drums as strong men with glistening brown muscles appeared behind them holding tall drums of cowhide which they beat to the rhythm of the snaking women.

The women reached the brown foamy water and suddenly stopped their loud wailing. We stood silent and still, staring at their white faces and red eyes. The air around was thick with spirits. Ay, my body was too full with the fear. Even the kingfishers and honeyguides were afraid and stopped their chirping. The only sound in my ears was the beat of the drums and the whooshing of the brown river water.

I looked sideways at David and Scarecrow. Their faces were frozen. Then the diviners entered the water. The chief diviner threw up a fountain of brown, foamy water and shrieked to the spirits of the sky.

"Ulaloo," she screamed. "Ulaloo."

My ears went numb at the sound of her scream. It was that of a witch not a woman and my heart leaped in my chest. I heard David take in a sharp breath and saw Jabu wobble on his feet.

Memories of Sipho flooded my brain and I shook my head and tensed my stomach as the stink of burning came back to my nostrils. No, there was no fire here. They could not burn us.

My chest grew tight and stiff as I watched the diviners hit and splash the water. My mind saw me going under and being held there by the white witch faces as they laughed at my drowning lungs. I shook my head to try and make the pictures go away.

"Attention!" shouted Mobuto.

We jerked upright and saluted as he sauntered in front of us.

"The General is pleased with our battle," he shouted. "The great doctor has heard of our victory and sent the diviners to bring the spirits to lead us on to greater kills. Now line up. You will enter the water to meet with the spirits. You, Hotshot – go!"

My breath stuck in my chest and I saw Jabu smirk. Fuck him. Why did I have to be first? I looked with big eyes at Mobuto, saluted and marched quickly down to the river. I kept my head up straight and my eyes staring ahead.

The cool water seeped into my uniform and stuck it like mud onto my flesh. The five diviners had made a semi-circle in the water. They glared at me with their small, red eyes and white clay faces. My heart beat harder and my breath came out in short, sharp pants.

The one in the middle came at me with her arms in front. I could see long yellow nails on the ends of her hands and small rotten teeth, which peeped out from her fat lips. She grabbed my hair and pulled me into their circle. I bit down hard on my teeth to stop any sound and clenched my eyes tight.

I drew a sharp breath as I felt the cold water close over me. The fear ate me as they held me down. There were hands all over me, pushing, pushing me down, down until I felt the hard stones of the riverbed against my back. Inside my lungs were burning and screaming for the air. My head started to swim and I felt my muscles go weak.

Then all of a sudden I was pulled hard up and slapped across the face by the one diviner, then another, then another. My head spun. I opened blurry eyes to see five white faces screaming at me. The chief diviner held up long green strings of weeds, which stunk like sick, and rubbed them all over my head. My stomach jumped. I gulped the bitterness back down.

"Let the spirits lead you to kill. Make rivers of blood for the L.R.A. Fill the graves with the flesh of the enemy. Kill, Kill, Kill," she shrieked as she rubbed the stinking weeds across my face and body.

The other four diviners joined in, clawing me with their long nails and grinding the curses deep into my spirit. My mind grew black. I felt the power of the spirits move strong through me. I breathed deep before being pushed from the water by the diviners.

I turned to see David, waist deep in the water waiting his turn. I leered at him. "Good – this is what he needed. The spirits would help to grow the blackness of his soul."

Chapter 32

Christmas morning is already hot even though the yellow sun has only moved a small way across the empty blue sky. We have to go to church today Dr. Zuma says, even me. Caterpillars gnaw at my belly. These church spirits scare me and part of me wants to run away but the other part wants to go so I can see Tula.

I get up and pick out my best clothes.

"You are looking smart this morning, Modetse," says Trigger, lifting his eyebrows at me as I put on a clean white shirt with black buttons and new khaki shorts, which feel nice against my skin. I pretend I haven't heard him and take out some red and black beads I've made to go around my neck. I wish I could also braid my hair and have some Nike trainers but at least my leather sandals look okay.

"You look better than Bengu," says Richard, giving me a thumbs up.

"It's Christmas. We must look smart," I say, keeping my eyes turned away but his words warm my stomach.

Trigger comes close to me and whispers. "I think you're looking good for Tula not Jesus."

"Think what you like. I don't care," I say, and pull a face at him before making for the door. He draws back but gives a small smile.

"Come on, boys," said Nurse Sophie outside the door of our hut. "We can't be late."

I finish combing my hair as we walk along in the hot sun. I open the top button of my shirt so that a bit of my chest shows. I've brushed my teeth well and they are shining white against my brown face. My muscles have grown stronger. They show through my white shirt. Tula will be impressed.

"Right, in we go," says Nurse Sophie as we reach the wooden steps of the chapel.

188

We go inside. It's cool and dark with rows of wooden benches. There're already many children here and it's alive with noise and chicken chattering. I look at the big wooden cross behind a red covered table. It's very big and hangs high from the ceiling. It gives me a funny feeling in my stomach as I look at it and I turn away. On the side is a long wooden stand with an open big black book on it. In front and near it is a small wood table covered with a white cloth. On it sits a small manger filled with straw and a doll who is baby Jesus.

I stare at the little statues of sheep and cows. There're three little men wearing long cloaks. They must be the wise men that Mama Zuma told us about. There are also little shepherds. I glance at Trigger. He is staring at those.

"I used to look after the cattle," he says. "My father was the tribal leader and we had many cattle."

"I hope they were not small like those," I say, and he laughs.

"It was a good life," he says. "One day soon I will try and find them again. Dr. Zuma says he will help me."

I feel jealous inside that he has hope but then I push it away. He has become weak. He is not like a strong soldier anymore. My eyes search through the rows as I look for Tula. My eyes find her. She's sitting next to Mama and Doctor Zuma in the front row. They are dressed very smart and Mama Zuma has a red and black scarf on her head. I walk like the proud one to sit on the bench behind and she turns around and gives me a big smile. I smile back and wave. Trigger and Richard squash up next to me and Richard digs me in the ribs and shows me big eyes. Trigger leans forward and grins. I ignore them and look around the benches. I can't see Bengu anywhere. Good, he's not here yet and will have to sit somewhere else.

Tula's braided her hair with red and green beads and silver tinsel and is wearing a red dress with little white dots on. I look sideways at Richard and Trigger who're grinning at me.

"She looks good," whispers Richard, and pokes me again in

the ribs. I poke him back and make a face to tell him to shut up. I stare at the braids of her hair. The silver tinsel makes her look like an angel. She must feel my eyes on her head because she turns around to smile at me. My legs go weak.

"Maybe she'll give you a Christmas kiss?" whispers Trigger, seeing her smile.

"Shut up," I hiss.

We start to sing "Away in a manger." I've a good voice and I sing loud so that Tula will hear me. After that we sing "O Little Town of Bethlehem" and "Hark the Herald Angels Sing." Mama Zuma has made us learn all these words at school. Then Dr. Zuma stands up and we hear the story of baby Jesus and how he was born to save us from our sins, and how the power of his blood can do that. He tells us that no matter how bad we've been in the past God still loves us and will forgive us, and he points to the big wooden cross. He understands the evil which makes us do things because it comes from the devil. I feel a knot in my belly at his words and my heart starts to beat fast even though I try and stop it. Faces of the people I killed flash before my eyes and I try to push them away. I can't think about them. I don't want to remember their blood.

Richard takes a sharp breath next to me and I turn to look. He's staring straight in front and his eyes are wet with tears. Maybe he's also feeling the guilt inside like me? I look at Trigger. He's got his eyes closed and his hands together praying to this God. His face is calm and smiling. There is something different with him now, ever since he had that baptism. Why does he not have the guilt? I feel angry inside that he can be okay and not me. Maybe these other spirits are real.

Dr. Zuma thanks Jesus again in a loud voice for our forgiveness and the mystery and power of his blood. There is a fierce churning in my belly and my heart is beating fast. This talk of the devil has caused fear to grab my mind. What if these dark spirits come from him? What if they are stronger than these other spirits of Jesus? If that is true the Jesus Spirit will not be able to stop the dark spirits. They will kill me. They will eat me and throw me to this devil and I will burn in his fire.

Dr. Zuma talks more about this devil. How he has brought sin on everybody; how only the blood of Jesus can set us free. My skin is alive. My head is spinning. Inside the dark spirits are attacking me. "Lies," they are shouting. "Don't listen to the lies of Dr. Zuma. I stare at Dr. Zuma but his eyes are shining. His voice is strong and full of power.

"There is power in the blood," he shouts. "Redeeming power. Power no devil can stand against. Call on the name of Jesus. All authority in heaven and earth lies in his name. Call on it and the devil must flee. He must. The choice is yours. It is your free choice to make."

Dr. Zuma is shouting out these words. His head is thrown back and his eyes are full with tears. My heart is beating so hard I feel it will jump from my chest. Inside I want to pray to this Jesus and his blood and scream, "help me, help me" but the words won't come out.

There is a strong power all around me. It is a buzzing power, which feels good, but I don't know what to think. I shake my head. Is this true? Can I call on the power of Jesus? Is that what I feel or is my mind just playing tricks? Can this Jesus really hear me and save me from the devil? Is he true or is this all just a story like the ones I can tell? Is he stronger than the devil? Inside something is telling me deep inside that it's true but there is still darkness in my mind that says "No."

I shake my head. I cannot think anymore. I don't know how to make this choice. What will it do to me if I do? Will it make me weak? I stare at the back of Tula's head. I will just think of her. I hope she's listening to the words of Dr. Zuma. I hope she believes him that Jesus can forgive me so that I can be good enough for her.

Mama Zuma goes to the piano and everyone starts to sing "O

Come All You Faithful" and then Dr. Zuma gives us his blessing and tells us to go in peace. I let out a sigh and look down at the floor. My hands are shaking.

Then everyone starts to shout, "Presents. Presents." Richard and Trigger start shouting too and jump up.

Richard turns and grins at me. "I hope I have a good present," he says.

"Me too," says Trigger clapping his hands. "I want some new clothes."

"They've made things not bought them," I say. "You'll probably get an ugly belt."

"That's okay," says Trigger with a shrug. "I wonder who's made one for you."

"Maybe it's Tula. You'd kiss it all night if she's made it." Richard laughs.

"He'll make love to it," sniggers Trigger, jiggling his backside forward and back.

"Shut up, you idiots," I say hitting Trigger hard on the back. "It doesn't matter who's made it as long as it's good." But secretly I hope that they're right. It'd be good if her hands had made me something nice.

We go into the big hut which has many tanned straw mats around the edges. In the middle is a big branch of a pine tree. Its sweet pine smell fills the hut and it's shining with lots of red, blue, silver and green tinsel all over. There're also many sparkling colored balls and at the top sits a big silver angel with wide wings. The little children have put on the decorations. The shaking in my body stops. I'm glad all the talk of spirits is over.

"Ay, it looks good," says Richard. "I've never had a tree like this."

"It is good," I say. "I bet that Tula's helped them to make it because it is so beautiful."

We sit down on the mats around the back. The small ones sit in the front. I see the two little girls called Lily and Zinzi that Tula looks after. They've big eyes and are staring at all the colored presents wrapped around the bottom of the tree. The Pineapple girls Patience and Grace run up like the small children to join the group. Their eyes are wide with excitement and they all squeal together, even Tula. I shake my head at them but inside I'm excited too. I've never had a Christmas like this before.

Tula turns and looks around with her eyes like the almonds and I quickly look down. I wonder if she's looking for me or just looking around the hut. I wish I could've drawn her name instead of Bengu's. I've made his belt very ugly with that buckle and a horrible pattern. I don't feel bad about that. He doesn't deserve anything good. He's my competition and I know he loves Tula and he's better than me. I'll beat him up if he touches her. I frown and my body tenses with anger. I hate him. He's even spoiling Christmas for me.

"Right, Merry Christmas, everyone, and welcome," says Dr. Zuma, walking over to the big Christmas tree. Mama Zuma joins him. She beams at us with her round face like the pumpkin and claps her fat hands to make the little children quiet.

Dr. Zuma's wearing a red hat with white fur and a red shirt of Father Christmas for the small children. He has a white cottonwool beard around his face but he is still wearing his glasses and I'm sure they are not fooled, but it's nice he's trying. He stands in front of the tree packed high with presents and picks one up.

"It's present time," he shouts, and all of us cheer, even me; I cannot help it.

"Yay," the little ones shout. They jump up and down clapping their hands hard and shrieking. My stomach churns. I feel like I'm a child again but I don't want to show it. I look sideways at Richard and Trigger. Their eyes shine and I see their hands clench with excitement. We all feel like the little ones inside. I want to be like them and jump up and down and shout, but I can't. Tula will think I'm stupid. Inside I wish so much that

Thandi could be here. She would love this even better than KFC.

Lily screams, "Presents, presents, presents," with her little head thrown back and her mouth wide open. Patience and Grace join in shouting and clapping their hands hard. We all start chanting, "Presents, presents, presents." It is madness in the room.

"Now whose name do I have here?" says Dr. Zuma, shouting over the noise. He picks up one of the big parcels wrapped with red and green paper. It has a big silver bow on top. "Ah, this one is for you, Lily."

Lily screams with excitement and grabs the present. She starts to rip off the paper and Dr. Zuma snatches up more.

"This is for you, Zinzi, and for you, Patience, and Grace, Merry Christmas!"

The girls tear the bright red and green colored paper with the small snowmen on. The paper flies everywhere. Mama Zuma laughs and looks at them with her shining honey eyes as she bends and picks it up. Lily screams and jumps up and down as she holds up her present. She's a doll and so does Zinzi covered with colored beads. Lily's eyes shine as she holds her doll to her chest and sings to it. She's so happy. Zinzi rocks hers to and fro. They like playing mothers and it makes me smile but also feel pain. I wish Thandi could be here and have one of those. I give my head a shake. I must try not to think. Next Christmas I will find her. I must just think of that.

Patience and Grace have new dresses, white with red straw-berries on and red ribbons. Patience holds it up against her like it's the best thing in the world. Grace does a little dance and runs over to hug Mama Zuma. She laughs with her fat body wobbling and hugs Grace back, like a big mother monkey, and then goes over to give Patience a big hug too.

I don't think much of the Pineapple girls but it's good to watch them. My cheeks grow hot when I think what we did to them in the camp. Maybe they're not so bad.

Dr. Zuma finds other presents for the small boys. Some of them have wooden cars and some have carts you can sit in. They're just as excited as the girls. Mama Zuma puts one of them in his cart. His name's Patrick and he looks like he's about seven years. She pulls the cart around the hut and we all clap and laugh. The little ones are throwing tinsel on all of us. Richard's covered with blue and silver tinsel. Lily throws some silver tinsel at me. I tie it around my head like a band and smile at her.

She chuckles. "You look like an angel, Modetse."

I pull a scary face at her and she screams in delight and pretends to run away. I squeeze my eyes to chase away tears as her face turns into Thandi's. She is always with me. I can't chase the pain away. This Christmas is bringing her alive too much.

"Modetse, this is for you," calls Dr. Zuma.

My heart jumps. I get up. Everyone is watching me as I go to the front. My cheeks grow hot. I give the doctor a double handshake and take the present. It's wrapped in blue and silver paper and has a silver bow on top.

"Merry Christmas, Modetse. This is going to be a blessed year for you. You deserve it."

The doctor makes me feel funny inside. He speaks to me like a father.

Mama Zuma comes up to me and hugs me. "This is a new start, my son," she says.

I nod and fight back the tears as they prick behind my eyes. Ay, this kindness is too much.

"Now, go open that present quickly," says Mama Zuma, giving me another hug.

"Richard, your turn," calls Dr. Zuma as I make my way back to my place keeping my eyes fixed straight in front.

I sit down cross-legged and put my present on the floor in front. It's small and soft. I don't want to tear the blue and silver wrapping like the little ones. I take the stick bits holding the paper with slow fingers and open the paper. I can smell leather.

"What you got, Modetse?" asks Trigger. He's still waiting for his.

I peal back the wrapping. There's a leather wallet lying there with a pattern of the sun and stars on it. It's dark brown and has been polished so it shines. I lift it to my nose and smell the strong cow leather.

"Open it. What's inside?" asks Trigger.

I pull it open. It's soft light brown suede inside. At the bottom is a big silver coin, which smiles at me. I gasp and lift it out. It's round and shiny. I've never had such a beautiful present before. I wonder who has made it.

"Ay, it is a good one," I say.

"Ay, me too. I've a good belt," says Richard. He's come back and ripped off his red paper with the green Christmas trees on. He's not careful like me. "Look it has red and green gem stones in it."

"You are lucky," I say. Bengu will not be happy with his. It's nothing like the one that's been made for Richard.

"Trigger. Your turn," calls Dr. Zuma.

Trigger jumps up and runs to the front. He grabs a big parcel in the same paper as mine and runs back to us tearing it open as he runs.

"I have sandals," he shouts. "Look, amazing sandals."

He has some brown leather sandals with three straps and a gold buckle. Ay, they are smart ones. He puts them on his feet and does a dance.

"How did they know my size?" His face is like the sun.

I shrug and smile at his dancing. He's so happy. I look back down at my nice wallet and touch the soft leather.

Richard leans over. "That's a good wallet," he says. "You are a lucky one. That coin will make you rich."

"Yes, now you can start a business and become a rich business man," says Trigger, and laughs as he sits back down and stretches his legs in front so he can look like Mr. Proudman at his sandals.

"And then marry Tula," says Richard.

I pull a face at them. But inside I feel warm. They've given me an idea of hope. Maybe one day I will be rich.

"These are good presents," I say. I look around the room and see if Bengu's got his. He's come to the tree and has gone to sit next to Mama Zuma. There's wrapping paper all around him and I can see the belt lying in front on its paper. He hasn't put it on. That means he's not happy. My cheeks feel hot and I hope he thinks that one of the small children made it. I feel small bad because everyone's so happy with their presents. I look away. I don't want him to catch my eye.

Dr. Zuma has more presents for us now. I take another parcel wrapped in gold paper covered with silver stars. I unwrap it bit by bit and look at a big brown leather book. It has the name "Holy Bible" printed in gold on the cover.

"That's a wise book," says Tula.

My heart jumps. I didn't see her come over.

"You must try and read it."

"Yes, I know," I lie. I've never seen one before but I don't want her to know that.

"This is a good-looking book," shouts Richard unwrapping his. He strokes the brown leather cover with its gold writing. "This must have cost a lot of money," he says with a big grin.

"They're expensive ones," agrees Tula. "We're lucky."

We've all got the same brown leather ones except for the little ones who've Children's Bibles with bright pictures on the cover. They're all opening the Bibles, looking at the pictures, and pretending they can read. I'm glad that they've given us the grown-up ones and not treated us like the children. I open the first page. It's written in Swahili and I can read some of it. Mama Zuma has taught us well. Richard and Trigger are tracing their fingers bit by bit across the words. I turn the pages and see that there are drawings. I find the ones of Jesus as a baby with the sun over his head. I turn more pages. Every time he's shown with the sun over his head. In the one picture he's walking on the water like he's got special powers. I see Tula watching me and smiling and I turn the page to the writing and pretend to read fast. She grins at me and comes to sit near me and I feel my body grow hot.

"What did you get for your other present?"

"A wallet with a silver coin," I murmur, cross that my voice shivers while I speak. I clear my throat.

"That's lucky," says Tula, giving me a big smile and showing me her white teeth. "It's a good omen."

I nod and smile to myself. I hope she's right. "What did you get?" I say looking up into her eyes.

"A nice bracelet and earrings," she says, putting out her arm to show a brightly beaded bracelet with red, blue, yellow and shiny green beads and long dangling earrings with peacock feathers, "and a traditional dress from my mother," she says, and then pulls a face.

"You don't like it?" I say and laugh.

She shakes her head and her almond eyes twinkle at me. "I hate traditional things. I don't want to be a traditional wife."

I look deep into her eyes and bite my lip. She doesn't realize how lucky she is to have her mother still in her life. I see her frown and quickly say, "You don't like being told what to do?"

She laughs. "You've read me well. I hate being told what to do. I've got my own mind and own ideas."

I give a smile while my heart drops. She has big plans this one. She won't want someone like me.

Dr. Zuma comes over to us and smiles. "The Bibles are donated to us by a charity. They wish all of you a blessed Christmas. Mama Zuma will teach you much from it in school but right now I think it's time for mince pies and then lunch."

"Yay," shouts everyone. Our stomachs are ready for our food and the chapel erupts in a blur of bodies racing to get out of the door.

Chapter 33

My body was strong and my mind had no fear now. The dark spirits were living deep in me and were my strength. The enemy and their bullets were nothing for me. I lay on my bed after training with these thoughts running through my head.

"Hey, why you smiling?" asked Richard, coming into the hut.

I shrugged. "Nothing."

"You thinking of the Pineapple girls?" he asked with a jackal smile.

"Fuck the Pineapple girls," I said. "I'm thinking of killing the rebels. I want another ambush."

Richard lifted his eyebrows and gave a half-smile. "Maybe you'll be lucky. I heard Bilole saying they're going to attack a village in Koboga. Maybe your squadron will go."

"Of course my squadron will go," I said, and pulled my lip at him. "My squadron's the best."

Richard looked at me and said nothing. I could see fear in his eyes and my stomach grew warm. Good, he must fear me. They must all fear me. I was the number one killer.

"Modetse," said Jabu, marching into the hut, "Bilole wants you."

"See," I said to Richard.

"Hotshot thinks he's going on the raid," said Richard, looking at Jabu with his eyebrows up. Jabu looked at me with jealous eyes and I glared back as I pushed past to go to see Bilole.

I heard them whisper as I left the hut. "Fuck them. They were jealous because I was the chosen one. Just now I would kill them too.

"Ah, Hotshot," said Bilole as I stood by the door of the office and saluted. "I have instructions for you from Mobuto. Sit."

I sat down on the wood chair and waited while Bilole settled himself in his big chair and leaned back to look at me.

"The General has told us that a village in Koboga called Nigiri are hiding food for the rebels. It is on our way to the Nakaseke region where we're getting more ammo and guns from. You and your squadron will come with us. You are to attack the village and cut off the hands of these fucking bitches. See if there's anything good that you find to bring back. Badboy and Shithead will go with."

"Who's in charge," I asked with narrow eyes.

Bilole looked at me, said nothing and then gave a big laugh. "You are," he said. "But you must do good for Mobuto otherwise you won't be officer boy anymore. You hear."

"Yes, sah," I said with happy eyes. "I will do good. I am hungry for more blood."

My stomach glowed warm. Badboy was also a Lieutenant and Shithead had been here longer then me but still I was in charge.

Bilole looked at me and laughed again from his belly and shouted, "Go – get your boys. We leave in one hour."

I rushed and got my squadron and soon we were in the jeeps bumping on the dirt road towards the bush. Bilole was driving my jeep and Nkunda had Badboy and Shithead with him. Joshua, Vincent and Bongi sat watching with big eyes and holding tight to their AKs. I glared at them. They had better do good for me!

"We will drop you two kilometers from the village and then you must go through the bush," said Bilole. We'll pick you up on the way back. You have four hours. Make quick or I'll leave you."

"Yes, sah," I said. "You hear that, boys," I shouted. "We must be fast."

It was their first raid and the boys nodded at me with wide eyes and I saw their knuckles go white as they clutched their AKs even harder.

The jeeps shot off the road and we started bumping hard into the bush. Bilole squealed to a stop. "Get out," he shouted.

I heard Nkunda screech to a stop behind us. Badboy and Shithead jumped out.

"Behind me. Now," I shouted.

Badboy looked at me with narrow eyes. "We'll watch from the back, Hotshot," he shouted. "Move, you boys. Do what the Lieutenant says."

I nodded and stood tall as I took out my machete. I showed for my boys to follow. "Keep your AKs pointed up and don't touch the triggers," I commanded.

They saluted with big eyes and copied me as we cut forward through the bush. My heart was beating fast and every piece of my body was alive and my ears sharp. The rebels could be like the leopards and come suddenly from nowhere. This was my raid; I wouldn't let anything stop me. I would look after my boys and help them taste the rebel blood.

"Down – on your stomachs," I whispered as we came near the end of the bush. I could hear the rumble of voices through the long yellow grass. We got down under its cover. Good, they would not see us come. I smiled inside and turned to look at Badboy. He showed with his head and eyes to hit the village from that side. I nodded and put my machete in my mouth. I kept my eyes like slits and peered through the grass as I slid forward like a king cobra.

My boys were close behind and I could hear their breathing. Then I saw smoke and huts. I stopped and lifted my eyes so I could just see over the grass. I counted five children playing near four women who sat cleaning corn. There were big sacks next to them. Bitches, they were feeding the rebels. I looked across the huts and to the ends of the village. An old man and woman were outside by the end hut. I couldn't see any other men. They must be fighting us with the rebels. That was why these villagers are feeding them. I watched as an older fat woman came out the hut on the other side with a young girl half-hidden behind her. They turned away from us, moved to the trees on the far side, and bent over with their backs to us to collect sticks and twigs for the fire. My veins tensed and my breathing came fast as I turned to my squadron.

"You are to shoot anyone who comes near you," I whispered to my boys. "You must go in the huts and get any food that's there. Keep your eyes alert as you go. Shoot to kill."

The boys nodded with frightened faces. I saw Joshua's hand shake as he held his AK. He was small and very thin. I think the AK was heavy for him but if he fucked this up I would beat him hard.

"You do well," I said with fierce eyes, "otherwise you're dead boys. You hear!"

"Yes, sah," whispered Bongi, while Vincent and Joshua saluted with big eyes.

I could hear the fat woman singing to herself as she picked up the brown sticks. The young girl bent over with her back to us. I felt the power strong in my body. If I gave the command they would be dead. I looked back at Shithead and Badboy. They waited like fellow cobras ready to strike. My heart jumped in my chest. It was time for blood. I wanted to kill. I made my arm in a forward curve and screamed, "Now!"

The grass parted as we jumped from the bush, machetes in our hands, screaming like demons with our heads thrown back.

"Shoot," I screamed to my squadron and they started firing everywhere with wild eyes. The women by the huts wailed and tried to run around the side. My boys ran after them and their AK bullets cracked through the air.

"Shoot in the huts," I commanded as I ran forward with Badboy and Shithead.

"Get those," I shouted to Shithead as I saw the fat woman and girl by the sticks drop them and run deeper into the trees. "I'll get the others."

Shithead ran to the fleeing backs of the woman and girl as they reached the far tree line. He grabbed the girl by the legs. He threw her face down on the ground like a lion catching the deer and brought his machete down hard on her hand, which lay in front.

"No...leave her...please..." the woman screamed as he chopped off the girl's hand. She screamed and Shithead pulled the other hand and chopped it quick. Then he turned to the screaming woman and was on her like a bullet to chop off her hands.

I laughed loud as their red blood spurted out and then turned to run after the women who were cleaning the corn. I caught one by her legs and dragged her back. I screamed with my face pulled back like a devil as I chopped hard down on her foot with my machete. The red blood sprayed up around me and I felt it splatter onto my face. I breathed deep from its smell and stood on her back as I hacked off her hands.

"Find the food," I shouted to my boys.

They ran to the doors and fired lines of red thunder into the huts. The thatch flew off and the mud shot out from the sides around the village. Some of the woman and children had escaped screaming into the bush. Badboy and Shithead took off after them.

I stood and looked with shining eyes around the village. The bodies were spread out over a wide area, their blood still coming from their half arms and legs. They would be dead soon.

"No more Nigiri village," I screamed at them lying on the ground. "You see what happens if you feed the rebels. You are dead people because you have betrayed the L.R.A. It is your own fault."

I turned to Joshua, Vincent and Bongi who were coming out of the huts with big sacks of corn and beans. Joshua's sack was so heavy for him that he was nearly bent double but Vincent carried his on his back and came fast. Bongi had one on his back and pulled another one behind him. "Move. We're done here," I commanded.

They walked faster and stared forward with fierce faces. Badboy and Shithead came smiling out the bush. "We've got some good hands and feet," said Badboy, holding up his machete red with blood.

I gave him a high five as we left the wailing village and moved back into the bush to meet Bilole. They'd paid well for their wrong and my spirit was happy.

Chapter 34

We eat an amazing lunch of roast chicken with roast potatoes, cabbage, orange pumpkin and fresh green beans with lots and lots of spicy chicken gravy. I've never had such a dinner and it makes my whole body feel good. After that we've a Christmas pudding which has raisins and cherries in it and a big scoop of vanilla ice cream on top. The cool ice cream slides down my throat and I can't stop grinning. To end we're given bags of colored boiled sweets. My stomach is so full I think that it'll explode. I lean back in my chair and place my two hands on my round belly. Tula's sat opposite me the whole lunch. She's smiled a lot and I think maybe she really does like me. I look under my eyelids at her. She's eating her pudding with small spoonfuls and looks so pretty.

"That was too good," says Richard, patting his stomach. "Now I'm a fat pig."

"Yes, you are," I joke. "It's your fault for eating two platefuls."

"You also had two. We are two fat pigs."

"No, three." I laugh. "Look at Trigger. His cheeks are still fat with food. He's number one pig."

Tula's voice breaks through our laughter. "Do you want to walk down by the river later, Modetse?" she asks.

"Ah…yes," I stammer.

Richard and Trigger go quiet and smirk at me. Trigger gives a big wink but I ignore him.

"A group of us are going down. Richard, you and Trigger must also come."

My heart sinks. I thought she was asking only me. I see Richard and Trigger grin. Richard looks at me and raises his eyebrows. I pull a face.

"Okay, come," I say.

"Race you to the river, Modetse," says Trigger, jumping up.

I jump up to follow him but Tula stops us.

"We need to change first silly." She laughs. "Go get your old shorts and I'll see you all at the river just now."

"Okay," we chant.

I feel stupid that I hadn't thought about it. How could we swim in our Christmas clothes?

We run back to the hut and change into our old shorts. I take out my wallet and have another deep sniff of the rich leather. I put it carefully inside my pillowcase so no one can find it. I'll sleep on it tonight and dream of the future. I stop suddenly at myself. Maybe it is better not to be L.R.A. Maybe it's better to be a businessman with lots of money. My mind pictures me as the big businessman with Tula as my wife and Thandi back with us and going to the school. A warm feeling moves across my chest and I breathe deeply.

"Hey, Modetse, come on. What you doing?" shouts Richard.

I jerk back from my dream and grab my towel. "Here, take this," I say, throwing it at Richard. "Where's Trigger? I want to go."

"We're waiting for you. Come don't you want to see Tula in her costume?" asks Trigger with a jackal smile. "Come I'll race you down."

"No, I don't," I say with hot cheeks as I follow him out and we race down to the river.

We reach the bank panting and out of breath. The sun is hot on my back and the brown water feels good as we splash into it. I hit the surface hard with my flat hand so that it springs up in Trigger's face and into his eyes.

"Aeei," he shouts, grabbing me and trying to force me under the water but I clutch his head at the back and push him into the water. "Give up," I shout, and he comes up spluttering and coughing.

But he grabs me again and pushes me down. "I won that one," he shouts, throwing his fist high in the air.

"Not for long," I say, and push him under again.

I look sideways to see if Tula's watching. I hear a laugh and turn to see her smiling at us from the bank. I move towards the water's edge and splash some of it up towards the bank so that it hits her legs.

"Oh," she squeals, but smiles. "It feels good."

"It is," I shout. "Come in."

"Okay."

Tula takes off her towel. She's wearing a bright orange costume underneath and looks too good. I try not to look with man eyes as she comes to the water.

"I brought some towels and refreshments," shouts a voice from behind her.

I look up to see Bengu standing at the edge of the forest. Why does he have to come and spoil it? He holds a basket, which looks full of cokes. Three of the small children are with him.

"Come in, Bengu. The water's lovely," calls Tula wading in.

"We will," shouts Bengu, and my stomach clenches. He takes off his shirt and stands tall in his blue swim shorts. His arm and chest muscles are strong. He's very good looking that one. He even looks a bit like Tula and my heart jumps with the fear that she'll like him more than me. How can I compete with a boy like this?

Bengu takes the hands of Lily and Zinzi and splashes into the water. The little ones shriek and hit the water with their small hands. Then Lily grabs up at his chest with her uplifted arms and he picks her up and throws her high in the air so that she lands laughing back into the water with a big splash. He pulls her up before she can go under and she hugs him and shouts, "More!"

I give Tula a small smile.

"My turn," shrieks Zinzi.

"Come, Modetse, you throw Zinzi." Tula laughs. "Bengu can look after Patrick."

I go over and pick up the excited Zinzi and throw her high in the air. She squeals with the happiness and she splashes down, and then I grab her and pick her up again. She puts her arms and feet around me like a frog and hugs me. It is like I'm holding Thandi again and before I can stop it tears fill my eyes. I blink and turn my head.

"You okay?" asks Tula.

There's kindness in her voice. I keep my head away and try and stop the tears.

"There's just water in my eyes," I say, wiping them with my free hand. Tula stares at me.

"A lot of boys have a hard time. You can talk to me if you want."

"I'm fine," I grunt, and then Zinzi squirms from my arms and splashes over to Bengu and he begins to throw both girls and Patrick into the air one by one.

"You sure?" asks Tula.

I'm quiet for a bit but don't want to lie to her and she knows it wasn't water in my eyes.

"I had a small sister," I say. "The little girls make me remember."

Tula puts her arms around my shoulders and gives me a small hug, which makes my legs weak.

"I'm sorry," she says. "That must be hard. Come let's go sit on the bank for a while."

I nod and follow her up to the bank. We sit in the shade of a big lala palm on the soft sand. I look at Tula and smile as she settles down close to me.

"Do you like staying here?" I ask. I think she wants me to talk more about Thandi but I'm scared it will make me cry again.

She shrugs in answer, and says, "Sometimes. I miss the city and my friends."

"Did you go to school in Kinshasa?"

"Hmm." She nods. There's a sad look in her eyes. "I was at Boarding School but then Mama says I have to come with them."

"Oh. Maybe she was missing you?" I say.

"She's too traditional. I want to go to school in England."

My heart sinks and I look down. She's a modern girl with big plans. She'll never be happy with someone like me.

She sees my distress and smiles. "I don't always feel like that. Sometimes I'm glad to be here. There're some good things," she says, and gives me a big smile.

I'm not sure what she means and mumble, "Maybe when you're older you can go."

"Maybe. I want to go to university first. Do you want to go?"

The question takes me by surprise. "Yes," I say. "If I can get the money."

"Do you want to study business?"

"Yes, I want to make lots of money." I see her look impressed and am relieved. It was the right choice. My plans had been to be Commander but now I don't know. I don't want any more blood. I don't want to be that boy again. Her words have made my stomach flutter with excitement and deep inside I hope they can be true but I don't think this can be possible. I give a shrug. "These are silly dreams. How can I go to university?"

"There're organizations that'll pay for you to go to university," says Tula.

"Really?" I ask with a frown.

She laughs. "My dad says you've great potential. He says you'd make a fine doctor. He really likes you."

"Really? Does he?"

"Yes really." She laughs again.

"Why does he think I'll make the good doctor?"

"You're good at Science and Maths aren't you?"

"I like them," I say, and warm inside. I'm surprised. I thought the doctor was just doing his job and that he didn't care for us. If he thinks I can be a good doctor then maybe he's right.

"You're also good at looking after people, Modetse. I feel good when I talk to you," says Tula with a small smile.

"Do you?" I ask with wide eyes.

Tula laughs. "You calm me when I feel frustrated. I don't mind being here when I'm with you."

"Oh, that's nice," I say, and my voice breaks. My cheeks grow hot. I think she really does like me. My stomach feels funny inside. She is so confident this girl. She is not like the other girls who are shy and quiet. Ay, this is some girl!

We sit quietly for a while and then Tula turns and looks at me with deep eyes.

"What's past, is gone, Modetse," she says. "It's over."

"You don't know what I have done?" I say looking down at the ground and biting my bottom lip.

"I don't need to know. It can happen to any of us. It could've been me if I'd been caught," says Tula, looking close at me. "They're the evil ones, not you."

I look up in shock. She's right. She would've been a Pineapple girl if she'd been caught. The horror of how we treated the girls pricks me and I sit silent and stare at the brown water while she speaks. I know she means the L.R.A. and how they can change the people. The faces of Mobuto, Bilole and the General walk into my mind. I see Mobuto shouting at us, "We are the God Army. You must kill the enemy. Fill the graves. The graves are not yet full. Drink their blood! Kill! Kill!" He is so full with hate. Doctor Zuma and Mama Zuma are so different.

I breathe deep. There is no hate here. They tell us that the L.R.A. is evil and serves the devil and his works. They want to help the child soldiers and chase the devil away. They don't hate me for what I've done. That say it's not my fault.

Can that be true? If the L.R.A. has lied then I've killed people who did not deserve it. I've cut off hundreds of hands so that they couldn't work for the enemy. But if they were good hands then I've done a terrible crime. My heart's black and evil. Fear rises up from my belly that maybe this is really true but then suddenly there are dark shadows around me. They surround me and I go dizzy. Inside my mind I hear myself saying, "No, I was right to kill; I was right. Dr. Zuma is lying. He doesn't know. The L.R.A. was right. They are right."

But deep inside my spirit is fighting my words and crying, "No, you are wrong. You are wrong. Jesus is right. Turn to Jesus."

"I need to be...alone..." I say and my voice breaks. I can feel hot tears pricking behind my eyes. Tula is staring hard at me. I grow hot. She has been watching me while this fight is going on in my spirit. She must see the evil in me or think me weak. I can't cry in front of her again. I don't know what to do now or who I am. I don't want to be a killer anymore but how do I take the blackness from my heart? How do I stop these voices inside my head?

Tula looks at me and squeezes my arm. "Okay. I'm going to dive back into the water," she says. She gives me a small smile and runs back into the cool water.

I nod and put my head down on my knees trying to chase away these thoughts and stop this confusion. I take in a gulp of air and lean back against the sharp bark of the lala palm enjoying its prick against my skin, which takes my mind away from my own thoughts.

Suddenly the high call of "Boo–o-o-o-o, boo, boo" hits my ears. I turn and look up into the branches of the big guava tree behind me. Big bunches of pale orange fruit fill the spaces between the leaves and I can just make out a brightly colored rainbird behind some of them. I stare at its beauty and watch as it jumps onto another branch and lets out its clear "Boo-o-o-o boo, boo" call again.

My mind jumps to the broken bodies of the ambush and the red blood, which stained the tattered jungle. So much red but not like the red of Christmas. That's good red and not bad like the blood. I don't want the bad blood anymore. I don't want this darkness. But how do I escape it?

My stomach feels sick. I lean forward with my head back on my knees. My stomach climbs to my mouth while thoughts run through my head like mad people. "Kill," shouts Mobuto. "Don't kill," shouts Dr. Zuma. Blood ghosts rise up and shout at me with bloody stumps. "Don't kill, Modetse, don't kill. Listen to Dr. Zuma. Listen to Jesus."

My head explodes. "Yes," I scream. "I want to listen. I don't want to kill anymore. Help me please. Help me."

Then Thandi is there standing on the dump. I reach out for her but she moves away into the mist; far, far away like she is dead. I reach forward but she is gone. I cry out and fear eats my heart.

Maybe this is true? Maybe the spirits are showing me she is no more? Who would have looked after her on the dump? Sipho was gone. Enoch was gone. The big boys and glue sellers wouldn't help her. She would've been all alone. Where would she get the food?

The pain of these thoughts is too deep and I grip my head with my hands. Where can I go if I leave here? I can't go back and live on the rubbish without Thandi. If she is dead then all I can do is go back to the L.R.A. But my spirit whispers, "No, maybe she's not dead, don't give up hope, don't." My head spins. I must try and believe that. I must still hope. Maybe Dr. Zuma can help me to look for her.

The thought clears my head but then the blackness comes over me again. No, what's past is over. I've changed too much. I can never be that boy again. I am no more Thandi's brother. She will hate me if she sees me now and learns what I have done.

For I long time I just sit and my mind runs round and round. I look at them in the river. They are laughing, playing. I see Bengu pick up Zinzi and throw her in the air and they both laugh as she lands back in the water. She looks up at him with happy eyes. I was like that once with Thandi. I was a good boy. How did I change like this? What happened to me?

The Rambo movies, the training, Mobuto, Bilole, Nkunda, the

General, all rise up again and march through my head. I can see them clear this time. I am standing back from them while they're shouting and screaming; telling me to kill; to cut off hands; to hate.

I shake my head. I don't know what to think. I don't know what to believe. But deep inside I know I don't want to be a killer anymore. I can see now the L.R.A., they are evil. Why did I listen to them? Why did I hate? I shake my head at that boy and my mouth fills with water. My body grows numb. What have I done? What am I? My body shivers and my head spins. I am a devil child. Will the magic blood of Jesus still help me? I want it even though it will make me weak.

The sound of splashing breaks my thoughts. I sit up straight and tense. If it is Bengu I will hit him but Tula's swims over smiling and comes back up to me. My body relaxes.

"You coming back in?"

"Maybe," I stutter turning red. I curse myself inside for sounding so stupid.

"Can I sit?"

"Of course," I say, wiping a patch of earth next to me.

She goes over to fetch a blue towel from the side and wraps it around her waist. I stare at the top of her orange swimsuit, which clings to her body. She comes over and smells cool and sweet, and sits so close by that my heart goes funny.

"I just wanted to see if you're okay."

I nod. "I'm okay."

We sit while my cheeks grow hot. Tula clears her throat.

"I help at a mission once a week where there're victims of the L.R.A. Do you want to come?"

Her question makes me freeze. I stare at her with wide eyes and an open mouth.

"I know it's hard," she says. "But it might help and perhaps you could have a taste of what it would mean to be a doctor."

My mouth opens and closes and I fiddle with my swim

shorts. "Maybe," I mumble.

That's where she must go in the F20 truck when I see her and Bengu. "Does Bengu help, too?"

Tula nods. "Yes, he drives me and helps sometimes."

I put my lips tight together and stare at the muddy ground. I can't let him be the smart one. I must not look weak next to him. "Okay, I'll think about it."

"Good," says Tula, leaning over to give me a hug. My body goes weak and my cheeks grow hotter as I feel her wet swimsuit against my chest. "They're playing football this afternoon. You should play."

"Yes," I say, and my voice sounds like a squeak, which turns my cheeks to fire.

"Let's go," I say, getting up to hide my hot cheeks. I can play the good football. I will show Tula I am number one. I must not let her see my dark thoughts

* * *

The field is hot and dry but there's a cool breeze, which dries the sweat on my body. I tie the long black laces of my white football boots, which the charity has given me. They're Adidas and look nearly new with a smart blue stripe. Richard and Trigger are in my team and Bengu's goalie for the other team.

"May the best team win," says Dr. Zuma. He gives us the big smile as we get ready for kick off.

Trigger kicks first. The ball shoots like a bullet across the field. He is too good.

"Go, Richard," I shout as the ball heads towards him through the air.

Richard runs and head butts it to me with his scarecrow hair. I catch it with the side of my foot and dribble it from side to side towards the goal. Richard runs behind on his thin legs and cheers. Bengu bends forward, arms out like a crab, eyes fixed on me and the jumping ball.

I play evil with him. I dribble the ball with clever feet from side to side causing him to move in time to its music. Then all of a sudden I give a hard kick. The ball slices high to the side and over Bengu's head. He frowns. Richard, Trigger and I high-five and shout our victory.

"Ace, Modetse," says Richard with a big grin.

"Good one, my brother," says Trigger, shaking his square head and giving me the big hug. "Ay, we will win easy now."

I stand stiff but then hug him back. His words make me warm inside. I look to the side of the field and see Tula clapping. My heart smiles. She's glad I beat Bengu. That's very good news and it makes me play even better as the game goes on. I go on to score another goal and we win 2:0.

My whole body is happy like the sun as Doctor and Mama Zuma call us back for mince pies and juice. That night we sit around a big campfire and sing a song about shepherds watching sheep when the angels visit and tell about baby Jesus while Dr. Zuma plays on the guitar.

My eyes look deep at the orange flames of the fire. I don't want the bad fire of the darkness. I don't want the devil's fire like the one that burned Sipho. My heart beats fast as I remember the witchdoctor. He was from the devil. I look up at the dark sky, which is fat with shining stars. "Please let your light come on me and keep me from this devil," I say in my mind. It speaks over the darkness, which hides inside.

The fire burns high and bright. Across from it I see Dr. Zuma looking at me. I look into his eyes and he smiles and gives me a thumbs up which makes me feel warm inside. Maybe he can show me the way to chase the dark spirits away for good.

It is late when we go back to our huts. I check under my pillow as I get into bed and smell the rich leather of my wallet. It is a good smell. I hope my silver coin will bring me luck and that I'll dream of being rich. But the dark spirits mock my thoughts for as soon as I close my eyes, the hands come back to haunt me and take away the goodness of the day. The devil has not yet let me go.

Chapter 35

"Modetse, Modetse."

I saw David running from the far side of the camp.

"Where's Mobuto? Where's the General?"

"What's wrong?" I frowned. Why was there such a look of fright on David's face?

Suddenly there was a loud bang and the thud of "Thowka, Thowka, Thowka," came loud from the bush. Helicopter gunships rose up from the dark acacia trees on the horizon like a swarm of giant mosquitos and flew fast towards us; orange rays of bullets sprayed out from their feet.

My breath stopped! They were enemy gunships! How did they get here?

"I don't know how they found us," panted David with bulging eyes. "It's a major attack. Where's the General and Mobuto? We need them now! "

"I don't know," I shouted, my stomach tight. "I think these want revenge for the ambush. We must get the RPGs. Quick!" I commanded as David stood frozen and the forward noise of the "Chuga, Chuga, Chuga," drowned ours ears. The helicopters were too close! They were too many! My body dripped with sweat and my heart raced as I looked up at their mosquito eyes coming, coming towards us.

"Hurry," shouted David, waking and grabbing my arm and pointing me towards the weapons store. I could see the fear on his forehead. His fear ate into mine and made my heart run too fast.

"Call your squadron, Modetse. I'll run to the RPG Hut."

I jerked my head and shouted, "You!" as Bongi and Joshua ran towards me with wide frightened eyes. "Fire at those helicopters you fucking idiots. You! Joshua! Go get the RPG from David and Fire! You others – shoot with your AKs. Now! Shoot!"

The boys obeyed and start shooting wildly into the air with wide white eyes. Badboy and Trigger ran past me screaming and firing into the sky. Everywhere our soldiers were running and shooting in all directions. I marched my eyes fast across the sky, my heart beating so fast I could hardly breathe. The helicopters, they were still coming.

"Mobuto? Bilole?" I screamed but I couldn't see them anywhere. Where the fuck were they? Where was the fucking General? He should be leading us! "Shoot, you fools," I shouted hard at the soldiers around me who looked like the ghosts, but inside my spirit too was dead from the fear.

"This's madness, Modetse," shouted David, above the noise. "I don't know how they've taken us by surprise. Everyone's panicking."

His face was white and his hands were wet. I'd never seen him so afraid. My whole body was tense and I stared back panting and frozen. Where were the dark spirits? How could they let this happen? Then the ground exploded in front and my mind jumped back. The evil was in me. I would kill these pigs. I would kill them all!

"Get the mortars," I screamed. "Get the fucking mortars! Fire! Fire!"

The noise of the booming guns and the chugging of the helicopters was so loud it made my head feel like it would explode. There was burning black smoke and roaring everywhere and I coughed and spluttered with running eyes.

"Hotshot – fire!" screamed Bloodneverdry, running around like a mad buffalo with his squadron and firing up in the sky.

I hoisted my AK onto my shoulder and started shooting as we ran along. I fired up at the bushes and the sky hoping to hit the enemy bastards. I could see the RPGs going off in front and hear the boom of the mortar fire. My stomach relaxed. At last Mobuto was leading a counter-attack. I would join him with more mortars and RPGs.

The grey helicopters with their double blades hovered down so low now that I could see the rebels and their guns. I ran zigzag to escape their bullets. We reached the RPG Hut and I grabbed one and threw one to David. My hands were so wet that the RPG nearly slipped from my hand.

"Quick, David."

"They're killing us," shouted David. "We are finished."

"No," I screamed. "We must fight. Go!"

David ran outside with the RPG and I followed. We held them on our shoulders. I watched as one of the helicopter came, "Thowka, Thowka," towards me. I narrowed my eyes and pointed up at the sky. I pressed the trigger. A line of fire sprang from the weapon, but the helicopter was too clever and moved fast to the side so my grenade missed. My body tensed and I screamed "Pig!" as I knelt down to reload.

Suddenly another helicopter swooped over and then another and another. Thousands of bullets burst out from their bellies. I fired more grenades. There were now so many helicopters I didn't know where to aim.

Fear took hold of my mind and my hands were so slippery I couldn't hold the weapon. I wiped them on my uniform, stiffened my body and clenched my jaw, but my stomach twisted with the fright. There were too many of them. Where did they all come from? How had they found us? Why had we not got news of the attack? How could our intelligence have failed? Why did David only hear when it was too late?

Suddenly a second swarm of big gun helicopters rose up from the trees. They came fast towards the camp in a flying formation. Many bullets spat out as they came. "Takka, Takka, Takka!" The loud noise of their spinning blades made my ears go like the deaf man. My body was numb with the fear. I'd never seen so many enemy. 'Boom!' Fierce shells dropped across the camp. They made the giant holes in the ground. Soldiers' bodies with broken arms and legs flew up in the air. Badboy did a mad dance against the sky, his braids flying around his face like the beaded curtain; then he fell to the earth like he was broken. My nose burned from the black smoke and blazing fire.

"Modetse, move! We're outnumbered. We must take cover," shouted David. I ran fast behind him towards the side of the ammo hut.

"Aiee," I screamed as a shell has dropped right near us. The hot red earth sprayed onto my face and into my eyes. I tripped and fell down hard. My eyes cried from the black smoke. My legs went weak and my head wanted to grow black. No, I must not be weak. I must not die. I must not let them kill me. I must get back for Thandi! I must.

"Get away from the ammo hut, Modetse," shouted David. "They'll try and hit it. Go, run to the other side."

I nodded and pushed myself up from the ground. I stumbled forward. I was wet with fear and my head was spinning. I was not in control anymore. I needed David to help. The spirits had failed me. The noise hurt my ears. I ran, holding the RPG with one hand and shot my AK with my other hand, but it was no good. The helicopters were too fast and too clever. I couldn't aim properly while I was running.

The boys ran around in circles screaming. They were and too scared by the noise and smoke. I saw some were from my squadron.

"Shoot, you stupid boys. Shoot," I screamed. I couldn't let them see my fear. "There's no time to be scared. Shoot your AKs, you fools. Kill the enemy pigs."

"Take cover, Modetse," shouted David from behind me. "Watch out for that helicopter."

I looked up. There was a helicopter gun coming right towards me. I could see the face of the enemy hanging out of the window. He was trying to shoot me. David fired at him. I stopped and fired a burst of AK bullets. The helicopter darted to the side. We'd missed. It turned its bug eyes on me and bullets spat from its mouth. The ground burst open behind me. The sky cracked with their thunder. Red soil splattered into the air. My ears rang from the noise. I wanted to be sick. I realized that I was standing frozen in the open again, like the fool.

"Modetse!" screamed David. He turned back and grabbed my arm.

We reached the ammo hut and I fell to my knees and crawled under the wooden floor of the barracks. David followed in a rapid leopard crawl.

"At least they can't see us here," I said peering out from the underside of the hut. The sky in front was black with the enemy's gunships. Pockets of fire and smoke were everywhere in the camp. Shells burst over our earth. They shattered the air. Bodies cracked. Blood splattered around us.

"The enemy's too strong, David. They've too many killed." I stared with wide eyes at our soldiers' bodies scattered across the ground of camp. Some of them were still twitching. Others were blown in pieces. I'd gone numb.

"I don't know what to do," whispered David, shaking.

"You're Mr. Cleverboy, David. You must think!" I spluttered. I needed David to help. My mind was like the mad boy's. I didn't know what had happened to me. I felt like a small boy again. I wanted to be back with Umama and Thandi. I couldn't do anything against this big enemy. Where was the fucking General? Where was fucking Mobuto and Bilole? Why were they not taking control?

David turned to me and smiled. His eyes were sad and my stomach dropped. I was very worried. David couldn't do anything either. We were dead boys!

"Boom!" A shell exploded near the barracks. A cloud of stinking black smoke filled with splinters of angry wood spat out at us.

"We can't stay here, Modetse," said David. "Crawl out at the back and run to the huts behind which are near the bush. We'll try and escape from there."

I wiped the dirt from my eyes. I couldn't see my way through the choking black smoke which clutched and squeezed at my throat. I let David go first so I could follow close behind. We coughed and coughed as the black smoke attacked our lungs.

"Modetse. C-c-come on this side."

David turned around to fire his AK at the enemy pigs. I ran, turning around with streaming eyes and firing wildly up at the sky. My boots thudded across the hard ground. I was nearly at the bushes.

"Keep running, David," I screamed, hearing his footsteps behind me.

Suddenly David overtook me and pushed me hard to the side so that I stumbled. I stared up at an approaching gunship. David had stopped to fire up at it and I watched the orange fire burst forward from his AK.

There was a loud "Rat-a-tat-tat," and the crack of the enemy's bullets burst down around us numbing my ears. David jumped up in the air; his head and arms were thrown back and a terrible scream came from deep inside him. Dark red blood sprayed from his chest and my body vibrated. I blinked and stared at him. My brother was shot and his blood was flowing out onto the ground making a dark red puddle.

I rubbed my eyes and shook my head as David fell broken back onto the hard ground. I collapsed on my knees. I shook my head. No, it couldn't be true. David had taken the bullets for me. No! Why had I let him cover for me? Why? I was Lieutenant Hotshot; I should have been the leader, not him.

"David, David. Wake up, wake up, please, my brother, please..." I said as I crawled over sobbing to shake his body.

"Hotshot, get cover."

It was Mobuto. He was panting and sweating, holding two RPGs in his hands. His eyes were big and white with fear.

"Mobuto, they've killed David. They've killed my brother."

"They have killed too many, you stupid boy. Nkunda's dead and you'll be too if you don't take cover. Now Move! Get to those far huts." He strode over and yanked me by the arm dragging me behind him. I stumbled along. I was numb with shock and horror. I turned to look at our camp. Flaming tongues of fire ate our buildings and huge plumes of blackened smoke bellowed up from every corner. I shook my head in disbelief. Then I ran behind Mobuto with wet eyes.

"Where's the General?" shouted Mobuto to Bilole, who appeared from the side of one of the burning huts.

"We've radioed him, sah. He was at Ngema camp but's on the way," panted Bilole, his fat chest heaving up and down and his body wet with sweat.

"If he's not quick we'll be finished. We need RPGs. Shoot you fools. Aim your AKs at the fucking helicopters. Now!" commanded Mobuto as we reached the back row of huts. He fell to his knees and spurted out a hail of bullets at the approaching helicopters.

The anger rose up inside me and I screamed "Fuck you" up at the sky as I too fired up at them. They'd killed my brother and everywhere lay the mangled bodies and blood of our soldiers. They must die! They must die!

Chapter 36

I try and keep my eyes open so that I can't see the battle blood which still comes back to my dreams, until they fall closed by themselves. I fall into a light sleep and toss and turn from the blood dreams until the pink morning sun has just peeped out from behind the hills.

I get up and creep out into the cool morning air. I breathe deep from its peace, walk far into the veld, and sit alone in its tall yellow grass in thick silence for a long time. I close my eyes and when I wake the sun is hot on my head. I squint up at its bright light. It is already a quarter way across the sky so it must be about nine o'clock and the others will all be up and getting ready for breakfast. I've no appetite, and don't want to see anyone. I just want to sit here alone in the heat and wish it would burn me all up and take away my nightmares.

I stare out at the brown humped hills with their clumps of acacia trees in the distance. I can't see the people with no hands at Tula's mission. They're real and it'll make me sick. I don't want to see anyone now, not even Tula. I'm empty inside. She's made me look inside my soul and made me worse.

I feel someone behind me and turn around. I'm about to swear when I see it's Mama Zuma. She's come through the thick grass like a leopard and I didn't even feel it move. Good thing she's not a soldier or I would be dead meat.

"May I sit?" she asks, looking at me with wise eyes.

I shrug with a tight throat. She takes my silence for a yes and settles her big round body next to me. She looks right in my eyes and smiles.

"You are in the valley now, Modetse, but one day you'll come out on the mountain."

I say nothing. Inside I don't think that's possible. How can I climb the mountain when I don't know how?

"You must learn to forgive and love yourself again."

"I've been too evil," I say, and put my head down on my bent knees and cover my head with my hands. Hot tears prick behind my eyes and I fight them back down.

"Everyone deserves a second chance, Modetse. You must forgive yourself. God has forgiven you already. Don't you remember what Dr. Zuma said in the church?"

I turn and look at her. Her wise eyes smile back at me like they're certain. I can see she really believes that this Jesus and his blood is true.

She puts her arms around me and squeezes me. The hug makes a sob rise up from deep inside me and I shudder against her.

"Here this is a card which shows some forgiveness verses in the Bible. I want you to go read them. Will you do that? I know you can; you've have learned well how to read."

I take the card and look at all the listings. I nod, keeping my head down so that she won't see the tears which have now crept into my eyes. The pain in my belly is too deep to stop them.

"Good boy," she says. "As you read them and ask for forgiveness the power of Jesus will come over you." She gives me a smile and heaves up her big body, scattering the red and black pattern of her dress so that it swirls in front of my eyes. I can smell the sweet smell of her rose perfume and soap as she stands over me.

"I'll go and make breakfast. Go call Tula for me just now. She must come help."

I nod and watch as she wades her way back through the tall yellow grass. I look down at the verses and trace my fingers around the letters. I can make out the words of the chapters and I know how to find them. I stare for a long time at the word forgiveness. I hope its power is real and it won't make me weak. My mind is confused about this Jesus. If he is so powerful why does all this darkness happen? Why has he let the L.R.A. take me away from Thandi? How can his power be more than theirs?

I look back down at these verses. I can feel the darkness fighting inside, pulling me down. I can't answer these questions but I know deep down that I need this forgiveness from his blood.

I stare out across the yellow veld while my mind whirls and my stomach feels sick. Mama Zuma and her kind eyes stand tall in my mind. She believes in this power. Dr. Zuma believes in this power. Then suddenly I jerk. I'm supposed to call Tula for Mama Zuma.

I get up, brush the grass and dust from my khaki shorts, and run to the Games hut where Tula normally is in the morning. I try to make my mind blank. I cannot let these thoughts run mad through me. I will look weak when she sees me. I pat down my hair and push back my shoulders as I bend to enter the cool of the thatched mud hut.

"Modetse, hi," says Tula giving me a big smile. She's sitting on a round straw mat with Zinzi and Lily in the middle of the hut. They're doing a wooden puzzle and its rounded pieces are spread out across the mat. They all look too happy and I wish my mind was like theirs.

"Hey, Modetse," shouts Zinzi. Lily gives me a big grin and waves.

"Hey, girls," I say, and smile at them. "You making a good puzzle?"

They nod and Zinzi grabs a piece and pushes it into place.

"See how clever I am?" she says.

"You are too clever. Both of you," I say, and laugh.

"Why don't you join us?" asks Tula.

"I can't. Your mother sent me to find you. She says you must go help her cook the breakfast."

Tula pulls a face. "I hate cooking."

I smile. "That's why you're so slim," I say, looking at her long brown legs crossed over in front of her bright orange and red sarong.

"Yes, if my mother had her way I'd be fat like all the tradi-tional girls."

This makes Lily and Zinzi giggle.

"You'd better go help her," I say with hot cheeks.

"I know," sighs Tula. She pushes away the wooden puzzle. "Girls, you try and do some more of this and I'll come back and look just now. Do you want to walk with me, Modetse?"

"Of course," I say. My cheeks are hot. They grow worse as we walk in silence towards the kitchens. I'm trying hard to think of something clever to say but can't and the air around me feels heavy and thick. I open my mouth to say how hot it is when Tula suddenly asks, "Are you coming to the mission?"

I look down and clear my throat. This wasn't the talk I wanted. I don't think I've the courage to go there, but how can I tell her that?

"I understand if you have second thoughts about it," she says.

She must take my silence for a "No" and I don't know what to say. I don't want to look like a coward and be too scared to go.

I scuff the ground with my foot and look at her. "Do you really think it'll help?" I ask. My muscles tense. I don't want to see these people. Maybe I will still hate them and the dark spirits will triumph and make me want to kill? I don't want to look into my soul. My body tenses and my jaw clenches up and down.

Tula stares at me with deep eyes. "It could. Sometimes if we do something practical it helps our mind and you have the magic touch inside to help people. I can see it in you. Just think about it," she says, and touches my arm.

I shiver and nod. "Okay," I say in a small voice. She sounds like her mother now. My mind is confused. They have some power these people. Maybe this Jesus doesn't make you weak. I just don't know if it would be enough for me.

"Well, I'd better go make the stupid porridge. Are you playing football again later? You were very good yesterday," says Tula as the air between us thickens.

My body warms at her praise and my shoulders relax. "Maybe that'll be good. I'll beat Bengu again."

Tula throws back her head and gives a happy laugh. "Yes, he was cross about that. He'll probably try hard to beat you today."

"He won't beat me," I proclaim with a straight back.

"Good." Tula laughs. "See you later." She turns and waves as she goes into the kitchen and I wave back but then stand and stare after her with a good feeling. She's glad I beat Bengu which must mean she does like me. I smile to myself and then hear Mama Zuma's voice giving her commands. I bet she won't like that.

I walk back to the field, my mind a mixture of happy and sad. Talking to Tula has opened my wounds again and inside I am very fearful of the mission. Already they are making me feel weak. I walk around the edge of the flat field with its short yellow grass. It reminds me of the camp and the training but that is all a long time ago now. I never want to go back to that. I think about all the people I have met here. Mama Zuma, Doctor Zuma, Tula, even the irritating Nurse Sophie. They are all too good to me. They want to help me. They show me love and there is some strange power in that love.

Deep inside I want to cry out my pain. I want to say I'm sorry and to beg the people to forgive me. Commander Mobuto's face drifts into my mind. I see his gold crocodile tooth glinting in an evil smile and hear his voice shouting commands to "kill, kill, and kill!" I stare down at the letters L.R.A. cut deep in my arm. Nurse Sophie is right. They've tried to poison me. I see Nkunda laughing as we shoot at the villagers. I can smell again Sipho's burning body so strong in my nose that I retch.

I shake my head and my body prickles with horror at all the pictures of blood and broken bodies which fly into it. War is not good. Why did I think it was?

Suddenly the truth of what I've done hits me like an RPG grenade in my belly. I retch as the smell of blood is strong in my nose. I look down at my blood hands. How did I do these things? I begin to shake all over. I have taken mothers from their children. I have let the children be killed. My darkness is too great. How can I be forgiven? How?

I turn away from the field. It reminds me now of the bush. It's making all these blood memories come back so strong I can smell them and hear the screams in my ears. I turn and run back to my hut. I go in panting with my heart beating in my ears. My body is wet and silent tears fall from my eyes. I take out the card that Mama Zuma gave me and wipe my eyes as I pick up my brown leather Bible and search fast for the verses.

I find the first verse with shaking hands and trace my fingers along the words. "Everyone has been bad compared to the glory of God." I say the words out loud so that they ring in my ears. Dr. Zuma's words come back to me. Everyone needs God to save them he says; we are all the same in God's eyes he told me. I frown. That's not true. He was never bad like me. Tula is not bad. These people don't understand badness. They don't understand. My spirit feels heavy as I look at the next verse. I want to believe their truth but I don't think I can. "All are new creatures in Christ Jesus," reads the next verse. I don't know what it means. I shrug and search for the next one, "Forgive so your Father in Heaven can forgive you." I'm not sure who I must forgive. Everyone else needs to forgive me. I'm the one who's been bad. I'm there for a long time and read the verses again and again. Maybe if there really is a God he'll forgive me too? But what happens then? I will be a nobody. I can never escape my past. Everyone will know I am just a weak boy who was evil and is now pretending to be good. It will not take away the blood or give the people back their hands. It will be better for me to feel my pain and live with it. That way I will be punished. This forgiveness is for the weak people. Not for me.

But the thoughts of forgiveness stay with me all day and that night again I can't sleep. All is quiet as I get up from my bed and creep out of the dark hut being careful not to wake the snoring Richard and Trigger.

I step into the warm, night air and look up at the sky with its millions of fat shining stars. The moon is strong and my eyes can see the trees and long grass of the bush in the distance. I move towards them and feel the soft brush of the night breeze on my face. I breathe deep and the rich smell of the bush hits my nose. It is so quiet here; it feels so good. There're no guards here. It is not like the camp. If I want to escape I can. I'm strong now. No one will stop me. I am free to go.

I walk and walk until I reach the long thick grass deep in the bush, which tickles my bare legs as I push through it. There're many dark acacia trees dotted around and I can see the outline of their long thorns in the moonlight. The grass is up to my waist now and dark shapes rustle through it. They're reedbuck I think. There are no lions here but there could maybe be leopard. I stand still and listen. The thick night air buzzes in my ears. I see the mound of an ant heap to the side before the tree line. I go over and brush the soil with my hand. The mound stays still and nothing moves across it. Good there'll be no ants to bite me. I sit down on the hump and stare up at the shimmering sky.

The clear chirrup, chirrup of the night cricket suddenly breaks through the silence. I draw in a deep breath and let the sweet smell of the African bush calm my spirit. The verses I've read from the Bible walk through my mind and from deep in my belly I feel a deep peace rise up inside. It is so real and has come so quickly that I shiver. There is a strong spirit here by me. It tingles through my body and makes me afraid. I bend my head down and silently ask the God of the Bible to forgive me for what I've done. I don't understand the verses and I don't know if it's true but there is power here and I don't want to run from it anymore. I want it to forgive me even if it leaves me weak. The thoughts push out hot tears of shame and they fall from my eyes and slide down my cheeks. Mama Zuma has said that God's grace is so big anyone can be forgiven. She says that all I must do is accept it. Dr. Zuma says that too.

I think again about the verses. Dr. Zuma says that the Bible is a magic book. It has great power and tells the truth. I bow my head and speak to the God of the Bible.

"I'm sorry," I whisper. "I'm sorry for all the bad blood...the cut hands...the killer bullets. Please God I am so sorry."

My deep sorrow makes David...Thandi...Sipho... Enoch...even Jabu run through my head and my chest heaves with sobs for them. I think of Richard and Trigger...they're not bad boys. Trigger he is different now. He has no bad dreams; his eyes shine when he talks; he smiles and walks tall, like he's clean inside. The power of Jesus has set him free.

I want that too. Trigger was a killer before. I want what he's got. I too have goodness inside. I'm not just an evil killer. I don't want the evil spirits inside anymore. I don't want the darkness to win. I want to be clean.

"Please, Jesus, forgive me," I whisper to the silent night. "I need your magic blood which can take away my bad blood and defeat the dark spirits. Please help me! I believe you can help me. If you don't help me I am lost." I look up at the glittering sky with all its stars. All around is a deep quiet. My body prickles. That spirit is stronger. I can feel it around me so fierce that it covers me, pressing down on my body and washing through me so that my heart beats hard in my ears and my chest heaves up and down. But this time it is not from fear. My mind is still and the silver light of the moon and stars shine softly down on me. This spirit is not from the darkness. It brings peace.

I drop my head and pray loud, "Please come to me, Jesus; make me clean."

My words hang in the air like the bees and buzz in my ears. God is talking back to me deep in my belly. I feel the big sadness rise up from there; it shudders through my whole body. God is taking out the darkness. I feel it go from my shoulders. New power rises up through me and my body shivers. The power grows bigger and shoots out of my head like the lightning. It throws me forward into the deep yellow grass.

My heart races and my eyes blur. My whole body tingles and sobs shake through me as I lie in the grass with the tears pouring like the river from my eyes. I cry and cry until all the pain is out and my head is light. When I lift up my face the wet ground has stuck to my cheeks and a faint pink glow is coming in the sky.

I sit up and my body shudders with another big sob, then stops. I feel strange inside, like I'm clean. I know that the God of the Bible and his blood has come inside me and chased away the evil of the past. I am empty inside but I am also full. Everywhere there is strange quiet. Even in my head and my belly there is this deep quiet like I've never known before. Ay, this Jesus spirit has great power. Dr. Zuma is right. His power is too much for the darkness to stand. My head buzzes. I think the dark spirits inside have really left. I bow my head down and whisper to this Jesus, "Thank you, Jesus. Thank you. Please stay with me."

Chapter 37

The clean feeling stays with me as the morning sun climbs out and I feel good even though I've slept very little. Maybe it is time now to visit the mission. Maybe?

"You've a faraway look in your eyes, my brother. You look different," says Richard. "I bet your mind's full of Tula."

I smile and shrug. Yes, she's on my mind but it's more than that. I can't speak to Richard of last night. "She helps to chase away the bad thoughts sometimes," I say.

Richard's got a strange expression on his face when I say this. "Are you still having bad dreams?" I ask.

Richard nods. "They've come back to me. There're too many bodies in my dreams. I'm frightened I'll die."

"You must talk to the doctor, Richard."

I don't know what to say to him. He might laugh at me if I tell him about last night. He must find his own way.

Richard looks at the ground. "I can't forget," he whispers.

We're both silent and embarrassed.

"It's hard," I say after a while. "But you must ask Jesus to forgive you."

"I don't know if I can," says Richard. He holds his head in his hands. "The pictures keep coming. I think I've been too bad."

"I know," I say. "Talk to Mama Zuma, she'll give you something to help you."

"What?" asks Richard. "Did she give you something? Is that why you are suddenly better?"

"Yes. Go see her," I say, and get up to leave. I'm not ready to talk about myself. "I need to find Tula."

"Yes, you love that Tula." Richard laughs. "But there's only one problem for you, Modetse.

"What's that?" I say with a cross face.

"Bengu."

233

I turn quickly and glare at him. The last person I want to think about is him. Richard's right. Bengu's always coming to interrupt Tula and me and watching me.

"Maybe I should kill him?" I spit and then I frown at myself, shocked at how easily the old feelings of hate come back. I thought the evil spirits had gone. I must be careful not to let them back in.

"You can't do that," says Richard.

"What must I do then?" I shout. "I can't let him steal Tula."

"How can he steal her? She must choose. You must just pray she loves you."

"What do you think?" I ask. Richard looks in my eyes. I hold my breath.

"I think she loves you. You must ask her out quickly."

My heart smiles at his answer. He's right. I've been a coward and wasted too much time. I'll do it today before we visit that mission. "I'm going to find her now and ask her."

"Go." Richard laughs and gives me a high five.

I run like the cheetah towards the schoolyard. My heart is excited and my hands feel wet. I make for the Art hut. I hope she'll be there then I'm going to take her for a walk down to the river and ask her to be my girlfriend. After that Bengu will have to keep away. I turn the corner and race over the red soil.

I bend down in the cool entrance of the hut and stop. Bengu's sitting with Tula and they're both laughing. My body jerks. I watch her put her hand on his shoulder and give him a kiss on the cheek. He puts his arm around her and pats her. My breath sticks in my throat. I turn and run away before they see me with my heart beating in my ears.

I run and run and run. The hard red ground pounds in my ears...why was I so stupid? You idiot, Modetse...you idiot. I want to hide in the dark green forest. I'll go back to the L.R.A. I'll never come back... She doesn't like me... I'm a killer... I'm evil... She was just being kind...she doesn't like me. I've made myself look a fool. I hate Bengu. I'll kill him. I hate him. I hate them both. My body bristles with hate and I can't think of anything else. Why was I so stupid? Why did I think she could love me? Why did I think I'm forgiven? She has chosen the good city boy. The aid worker who is just like her! I tear through the forest straight into Dr. Zuma whose coming back with Zinzi and Lily.

"Modetse! What's happened?"

I stare at them with red eyes and mumble, "Nothing; it's okay."

Lily and Zinzi look at me with open mouths. "Go back and find Mama Zuma, girls."

They nod and look at me with wide eyes before running off.

"Is it the mission tomorrow?" asks Dr. Zuma.

"Yes," I murmur, glad he's given me an excuse. My shoulders sag and I stand there panting, fighting to keep back the tears.

"You'll be okay," he says putting his arm around my shoulders. "You're a tough one. I know you'll come through."

My mind's whirling and I don't know what to do. I want to go to the mission to pay for my wrong but I don't want to be with Bengu and Tula now. I can't talk to them. I don't want to even see them. I clench my fists and squeeze my eyes tight to push back angry tears. Where is Jesus? Why has he left already and let darkness come back?

"It's okay, son," whispers Dr. Zuma. "You can do it. God will give you strength."

I look up at him. Why does God let me suffer? I want to ask but I cannot. He won't understand. I give a small smile as he stands looking at me with sad eyes even though my heart is crying.

"Come sit with me in my office for a while, Modetse, until you feel better."

I frown but walk next to him to his office. I try and push Tula from my mind. I've been stupid. I'm not an aid worker. I haven't done lots of school and have money. I should've known I couldn't have Tula. I must leave now and make my own life. I can't stay here anymore but I don't want the darkness back. I must pray to Jesus again and ask him to come back and help me to stay clean where I go. Maybe Dr. Zuma can help me with that before I go.

We walk into the cool of the office and he shows me to sit in the blue armchair.

"Here, it's going to be a hot day," he says, handing me a coke.

I take the bottle and have a big sip of the sweet drink. It gurgles down my throat. Inside I'm so tired. My whole body is heavy and I wish I could just sleep forever.

"Mama Zuma tells me she gave you some verses. Have you read them?"

I nod and look at the floor. My mind's going round and round. I was so happy, so clean and now I'm full again with anger and hate. How could Jesus leave me so soon?

"It takes time, Modetse," says Dr. Zuma, leaning forward with his elbows on his knees and looking close at me. "Don't worry if things don't all happen at once; if your emotions go up and down. It's a battle of your spirit. It will go back and forward. God and the devil are fighting over you. When people go to Jesus the devil tries hard to get them back. Just remember Jesus is the stronger one. Keep your eyes on him and he will win in the end."

I look up with a frown. It's as if he can see into my mind. As if he knew that I was clean and that now the dirt is trying to cover me again. I feel a shiver down my back. My body tingles as Dr. Zuma puts his hand on my head.

"Help Modetse," he prays, "in the name of Jesus. Modetse, I pray peace upon you and strength. Protect him from the darkness in Jesus' name."

A deep quiet falls onto the hut and I feel again the strong spirit of Jesus over me. My body shivers and tears prick behind my eyes. Jesus has not left me. He is fighting the darkness from my soul.

"Once Jesus has come he'll never let you go," says Dr. Zuma. "Always remember that."

"Now," he says sitting back in his chair. "Tula has told me that you have a young sister back in Kampala is that right?"

My heart races. "Yes," I say. "I need to find her."

Dr. Zuma leans back and puts his fingers together. "We have a charity which operates there and works with street children," he says. "If you can give me details then I will see what we can do. I promise well do our best to find her and then we must discuss your future. The UN organization has a program which will help you to study further. Would you like that?"

I stare up at Dr. Zuma with wet eyes. He is such a good one this man. I try to say "Yes..." but the sob in my throat won't let me so I just nod.

"Right. Now do you think you could draw a picture of your sister? How old is she?"

I frown as Thandi stands in my mind. "She was five years when I left," I say. "I don't know now. I don't know."

"It's okay," says Dr. Zuma. "Just take your time. You were in the camp over two years, I think from what you and also Richard have said, and you've been here for nearly six months. She must be over seven I would think."

I lift my eyebrows. That is hard to think she could be that old. "I hope she is still there," I say. "I don't know how she will have lived without me."

Dr. Zuma goes silent. "I hope so too," he says. "But whatever the outcome well make sure you're okay, Modetse. You must keep going forward and I promise well give you all the help we can. I can see a bright future for you if you choose it. You're very good with people you know. It's helped Richard to have you here; my naughty daughter too is calmer with you here."

I flinch at the sound of Tula but look up and ask, "Really?"

"Really," says Dr. Zuma, and smiles. "Now, go well," he says, and offers me his hand.

I take it and give him the double handshake. I walk back out into the hot sun feeling better inside. He has given me hope but maybe it is foolish. All this time I have always thought of finding Thandi but the time is so long. How will she still be there? Where did the years go?

Chapter 38

"You scared?"

I keep my eyes down and shrug my shoulders.

"I'm glad you're coming," says Tula. "It won't be as bad as you think. They're good people."

"I'm fine," I grunt. "Let's just go!" I tense my body, clench my jaw and keep my eyes down. I don't want to talk to her now that I know she likes Bengu.

"Tula, Modetse, the truck's waiting."

Dr. Zuma's smiles at me and walks over to take my hand. "Go well, Modetse. This will be a good cleansing for you. Be strong."

"I'll try, Doctor," I say and shake his hand.

I follow Tula into the cab of the throbbing F20 ignoring Bengu who jumps into the driver's seat. At least I'm not sitting next to him. I stare out through the side window so I don't have to look at them. It's been a long time since I've been in a truck and the whirr of the engine brings back many memories. This is going to be a hard day and I'll have to hold fast to my mind, but I must do it. I must give back for my wrong.

We bump over the dust road throwing up a red curtain behind us in thick silence. I see Tula look at me under her eyelashes. She thinks my mood's from fear. I'm so angry with her. Why does she treat me like a friend if all she wants is Bengu? The thorn and acacia trees blur as we race past and I imagine beating his face in with my fists and then stop myself. No, I must not let the darkness win. I must not think of him. I must not lose the magic of the blood.

"The mission's just around this bend," says Tula, after we've been travelling about twenty minutes.

I stare out in front and see the square whitewashed buildings appear. I catch my breath. Tula pats my leg and I have to tense my arm not to hit her hand away. I look to the side and count ten round thatched huts sitting between shrub and acacia trees. Lots of people are standing around and I wish I could just run away. Bengu stops the truck and jumps out to push back the rusty iron gates. A high wire fence with a foot of barbed wire on top surrounds the property.

"You okay?" asks Tula.

I nod. My stomach's tense and full of knots and my whole body's prickly with fear. I can feel the beads of sweat on my forehead and wipe them away with my arm.

"Relax. It'll be all right," says Tula. She squeezes my hand and I pull it away and glare at Bengu as he jumps back in. Seconds later we roar through the gate and a small herd boy runs towards us to close it behind us.

"The doctor's name here is Dr. Jabula," says Tula. "He's really nice and is grateful that we come to help. The more helpers they get to assist the nurses here the better. He'll tell us what he needs us to do."

Her voice and words sound false and I know she's trying to keep me calm. I hold my face tense but my heart's pounding so hard I fear Tula must be able to hear it. As we get nearer the buildings my breath grows shorter and sharper and more sweat breaks out across my forehead. I wipe it away with a hard swipe of my arm. I feel my cheeks grow hot.

"He was a soldier himself many years ago. He understands," says Bengu.

I glare at him. What does he know?

"Most of them have been soldiers in Africa," says Tula. "It's really brave of you to come, Modetse."

I give her a hard sideways look. What game's she playing? She's one of those who likes to have all the boys after her just because she's pretty. She's lucky she wasn't a Pineapple girl. She knows nothing!

The truck grinds to a stop and the doctor comes over to us straightaway. He's a big man with shiny black skin and kind brown eyes. He's many scars on his face and I see a big one on his arm which looks like an old bullet wound and I feel better.

"Tula, Bengu, welcome," he says with a big smile. "And who's our new helper?"

"This's Modetse," says Tula with a smile.

"You're very welcome, Modetse," says Dr. Jabula, giving me a strong double handshake.

His words warm my heart and I grip his hand and murmur, "Good to meet you, sah."

"Right, now I think if you guys bring in the supplies and then we separate them that can be the first job. We've some cooking to do and then well give the patients some lunch."

"Have you got new prosthetics?" asks Tula as we start to unload the boxes from the truck.

"Yes, we've had a whole box of adult ones. We're hoping to get some for the children by the end of the month. They're harder to come by unfortunately, and of course need constant changing as they grow, but the ones who've already got them are doing really well. They never stop smiling."

"That's good," I say, but my voice breaks and comes out gruff. The doctor turns and smiles at me.

"Yes it is. They're quite content. You'll be amazed at how easily humans adapt to things you know, Modetse. We teach here that you must just go forward and count your blessings. No point in brooding on what's past."

I nod and pick up one of the heavy cardboard boxes and follow the doctor into the cool dark interior of one of the whitewashed buildings. The floors are painted green and the doctor takes out a set of keys to open a high steel gate to the storage room.

"We keep this locked so as to not tempt people," he says. "We've a good amount of supplies but we still have to be careful with them. Times are hard and although we do grow as much as we can we're still dependent on aid for many staples."

I put the heavy box on the floor and we begin to tear open its sides. I take the tins of milk, packets of flour and sugar and tins of strawberry jam and put them on the shelf next to the tinned apples and pears where the doctor shows me. I'm glad there're some sweet treats for them.

"Doctor, where do you want the medicines?" asks Bengu.

"If you'll take them around to the surgery and give them to Nurse Rani that would be great Bengu."

I'm glad Bengu's not staying here with me. I don't want to see the surgery and the people without hands. I'd rather hide here in the cool dark of the food house and help with the cooking.

I think Dr. Jabula knows this because he smiles and says, "Tula, you and Modetse can help to serve the stew first."

"Okay. Come, Modetse."

I keep my eyes down and follow her into the large back kitchen. Three women are standing in front of big gas hobs stirring huge black pots full of delicious smelling stew. The smell of the rich beef makes my mouth water.

"Hello, Tula," says one of the women, turning around to smile at us. I bite my tongue so that I do not gasp as my eyes rest on her false arm. The plastic hand is holding the long wooden spoon and stirring the stew. I can't look her in the eyes and keep mine to the floor. What if she knows me? Does she know I was L.R.A.? All of a sudden I want to run away. My whole body is wet with the sweat and my heart beats so hard I can hardly breathe. Tula takes my hand and pushes me towards the woman.

"This's Mama Paida," she says. "She's the most wonderful cook in the whole world."

"Hello. It's nice to meet you," says Mama Paida.

She's a big woman with a wide bosom and fat hips. I look up into her round brown face. She gives me a big smile showing good white teeth and kind eyes. She doesn't hate me. My breath sighs out and I fight to keep back the tears, which want to run out of my eyes.

"The stew's nearly ready. We'll take it out to feed all the hungry tummies. Tula, I think you and your friend will feed those in the East Hut. Patience and Stephen are helping in the West Hut."

"Shall we take out the plates?" asks Tula.

"Good idea."

We grab piles of white plastic plates and silver steel spoons and I follow Tula to a big hut with long wooden tables. We place the plates along the length of each side.

"They're coming in now," says Tula. "Once they're seated we'll spoon the stew onto the plates."

"Okay," I mumble. People start to shuffle into the hut and I hold my breath. All of them are missing hands and one's hopping on wooden crutches because he's also missing a foot. White bandages with stains of red and brown are wrapped around their stumps. Bitter water floods my mouth and my stomach jerks.

Tula squeezes my hand and whispers, "Breathe through your nose, Modetse."

I do as she says and I feel the water die down in my mouth. My whole body churns inside. I want to fall to my knees and beg them for forgiveness.

"Now, Modetse, you look after Sebo," says Tula, sounding like a nurse. She gives me a smile and pushes me over to an old man in the corner.

He's wizened with wise eyes, which watch me like the leopard. My body prickles as I take one of the big pots and walk over to him. The eyes follow my every movement as I place the silver steel spoon into the rich dark tomato and beef stew and put it on his plate. I try and spoon up as much meat as I can. I know men like meat. I swallow hard and bring the spoon up to his open mouth. It doesn't feel right to feed an old man. The eyes stare hard at me but he grunts with satisfaction as he swallows the mouthful. He doesn't talk and my hand starts to shake as I take another spoon to his open mouth. I tense my body to stop myself running away. I wish I hadn't come.

"Thank you," he murmurs as I scrape the last of the stew from the plate.

I bow in reply. I don't trust myself to talk and walk away with a tight chest.

I look around and see that some in the room have false hands and are able to feed themselves. Tula's feeding a lady at the far end of the long room with a big smile on her face. She's got nothing to fear. I look to the other side and suddenly catch the eye of one man. His eyes are hard and full of hate and I feel my stomach jump. Does he remember me? He looks straight at me and I see him clench his jaw. He's two plastic arms and looks like he's one of the helpers. Maybe he does know me? Maybe it was me who took his hands? I start to shake. I can't stay here. I'm going to be sick. I turn and run from the room onto the porch and sit down hard on the step with my head down between my knees taking in big gulps of air.

"Modetse."

I turn to see Bengu standing there. I groan. This is too much! I put my head back down and clasp it with my arms. I feel his hand on my back and shrug him away.

"Leave me!"

"You're doing well," he says.

I lash out at him. "What do you know? Why don't you just go get Tula? I'm not like you two. I can never have a girl like her."

Bengu stands still and gazes deep into my eyes. "I know you like her, Modetse. She likes you too."

I jerk my head up and demand, "What you mean?"

"What I said. She likes you."

"No, she likes you," I say, and spit on the ground. "You're the city boy who has never cut off the hands and feet. I can never be like you."

Bengu gives me a funny look and then smiles. "She's my

cousin."

"What?"

"We're cousins."

I stare at him with my mouth opening and closing like the stupid fish. "Oh," I say and then go quiet. I don't know what else to say. Now I understand why they look like each other. I feel like a stupid.

"Can I sit?" asks Bengu.

I shuffle over to make room for him. "I'm sorry. I thought you were together."

"It's okay. I'm like her big brother. I just wanted to be sure you really liked her."

"I do," I mumble. "I really like her. I will be good to her if she likes me too."

"Well, ask her later. I've a feeling she'll say yes." Bengu smiles.

"I'm sorry," I say, and then the guilt takes over again. "I must help these people and not think of myself."

Bengu nods. "You are. Just remember some people lose their souls too. It's not your fault."

I nod and say nothing but the memories fly back in my mind like the bees. I don't know what to feel or think inside. How can it not be my fault? I laughed when I cut off the hands! I wanted to see the blood.

"Modetse, you okay?" asks Tula coming over to me with big eyes full of worry. I look up through half eyes. She must think I'm a fool and a coward. "I think the one man might know me," I whisper. My voice croaks like the frog and I feel my cheeks grow hot.

"Oh, I'm sorry. Did he say something?"

I shake my head. "He looked with hate."

Tula nods and bites her lip. "You must just ignore some of them. We'll need to help fit prosthetics now. Okay?"

"Yes, of course," I say.

I don't want her to think I'm weak. I must not be surprised that the people will hate me. It is good for them to do that. If I was them I would also hate. I must help so that I can give back. That is all I can do.

Chapter 39

I follow Tula across the dry red ground to the rectangular white painted building with the word Hospital written in black above the door. The windows are covered with mosquito netting and the veranda in front is painted with the grass green paint. It looks cool and clean. We go up the small clay step and walk through the wide wooden door. There're many rows of black iron beds with little mounds of white in them. Silver poles with bags of blood and what looks like water stand next to each bed. I stop and my heart jumps to my mouth. The bodies here are small ones. I keep my eyes to the front so I don't have to look too hard. I think if I see they're missing hands I'll be sick. I tense my body as a nurse in a white uniform turns from one of the beds and smiles at us.

"Oh, hello, Tula. I'm glad you're here. We've four new hands to fit today. You two will be helpful."

"This is Nurse Rani," says Tula pushing me forward. "This's my friend Modetse."

"Welcome, Modetse. I'm pleased to have you help," says Nurse Rani, shaking my hand.

She's got warm smile and it helps to take away the memory of the hate of the dining hall. I try to smile back and give her a firm shake. A look of sadness flickers through her eyes before she shows for us to come.

"Right, follow me through to the store. The patients' wounds in Ward Two have healed enough for us to fit them."

We follow her to the end of the ward and through a set of double doors. I give a sigh of relief as we leave the children behind. She unlocks the door to a small room packed with boxes.

"Tula, if you'd be so kind as to open those white boxes over there. They're the ones with the prosthetics. Put gloves on first. They're all sterilized and if you just lay them out as labelled the doctor can fit them later. Labels are here."

Nurse Rani opens a drawer and hands me a plastic packet with neatly typed labels. I stare at the names, Mohammed, Rasha, Jacob, Beauty. The guilt washes over me again and my body grows heavy. Fake hands for the real people. Aiee, what did we do?

"They're very excited," says Nurse Rani as if she can read my thoughts. "Once they get the hang of it they don't even know they're prosthetics." She gives me a big smile and leaves the room.

I stand silent with hot cheeks while Tula goes over to the boxes.

"Right." She smiles and grabs the white taped boxes stacked in the corner of the storeroom. "Here, Modetse, cut through the box tape and open them for me."

She hands me a letter opener and I run it quickly down the center of the box. I push back the lids and pull away the white sponge covers. Neat rows of brown plastic hands stare up at me. I touch one and draw back from its coldness. I feel sick. They are dead hands, which will never be warm. How can the people forget with these hands? They will always cry for the real ones.

Tula looks at me and pulls on some white plastic gloves.

"It's okay," she whispers, and then lifts out some of the hands.

"This is the wire base," she says. "They've got a soft cushion on the end with straps and a harness to go on the patient's shoulder. The people say they're really comfy when they're on."

I don't answer and just stare at the dead hands as I try to hold fast to my mind. It wants to jump back to my nightmares. I cry deep inside and wish I could go back and give these hands life but I can't. Tula turns to look in my eyes.

"You sure you're okay with this?" she whispers.

I nod and hold my body tense. It's good that I must suffer. I must feel my guilt. Tula gives me some gloves and I put them on and pick up a pair of the dead hands. I can feel their cold through the gloves.

"There're some labels to match each pair. If you can stick them on it'll help."

"Okay," I murmur trying to read carefully which matches which.

Tula glances over and shows me her thumb. I place the hands gently on the counter with the harness laid out at the top.

"You wish you hadn't come?"

"No, I'm glad I've come."

Tula comes over to me and puts her arm around my shoulders. My heart quickens and I catch my breath and look down. "I'm also glad you've come."

I look up and see her smiling deep into my eyes. She gives my arm a little squeeze.

"Thanks," I whisper. I look away to hide the excitement in my eyes. This is such a strange day. Inside I've so much guilt and sadness but there's also the hope that God gave me with his forgiveness and maybe Tula really does like me. My mind jumps to pictures of us together and I feel bad that I've been so horrible to Bengu. He was just looking after her like a brother, just like I did for Thandi. He's a good one and maybe now we'll be friends.

"Well done, you two. That'll help," says Nurse Rani, bustling back in. "Why don't you go outside for a while and get some fresh air. You can unpack medical supplies a bit later."

"If you're sure," says Tula.

"Of course. Off you go get some fresh air before the storm hits."

I lift my eyebrows at the distant thunder. She's right. It sounds like a big African storm is coming for us.

We step outside into the hot wet air. I look up and see the black clouds growing fast on the far sky. All of a sudden a fork of white light shoots through the air and a loud crack of thunder rumbles around us and makes me jump.

"I think it'll be a brief bit of air." Tula laughs. "Come, let's walk down there. I'll quickly show you the river."

"Okay." I smile and hurry behind her. I've only gone a few steps when a loud voice suddenly screams behind me,

"Fuck you! Fuck you!"

I turn around with wide eyes. Fear shoots through my body. My heart races. I see Tula pull a face and show for me to keep moving but I can't. I stare back up the buildings. There's a man standing outside the dining hall and he's screaming at me, pointing his plastic hand at me. I don't recognize him but he knows me.

"That's him. He's the one," he shouts to the man next to him. He's the devil who cut my hands."

I stand frozen as the man starts to come towards me then I see Bengu run from the hut and grab his shoulder to pull him back. The man fights back, his face is full of the fierce hate.

"I'll kill you!" he screams at me. "You've taken away my manhood. How can I feed my family with no hands? How? I hate you! I hate you! Give me back my manhood! Give me back my hands, you bastard devil child!"

I'm frozen to the spot with shame so big I can't think. My fear has come to life. The man is still struggling with Bengu and I'm afraid any second now he will fly at me and rip me apart. His friend shakes his plastic hand at me and takes a step towards me.

"Bastard," he shouts. "What're you doing here? Go away. We don't want you here. Fuck off."

People come out of the huts. They stare at me with big accusing eyes. I see Sebo from the dining Hall. I just want to die. I'm so full of guilt but I refuse to run. I did wrong I know but I've told God I'm sorry. I'm here to help and give back. I can't do more than that! Let them hate me. It is their right.

"It's okay," I whisper to Tula, who's standing gripping my arm and looking with angry eyes at the man. "Let them have their say."

"You're brave, Modetse." Tula smiles. "Come let's go down to the river and we can make it back up on the other side away from these people."

She takes my arm and guides me down.

"Yes, fuck off," shouts the man. "Fuck off, you devil, and never come back."

Tula pulls me harder and we walk down to the soft river sand.

"Let me sit a bit, Tula. You go inside."

"You sure, Modetse?"

I nod. The tears are pricking my eyes. Tula puts her hand on my shoulder and gives me a squeeze. "It's okay," she whispers. "Remember it's not your fault. Come up back past those trees when you're ready."

I nod and look at the trees she's pointing at. I watch her walk back up to the huts and a sob jumps in my throat. I squat down on my haunches and put my head on my knees. The hot tears fall from my eyes and run down my cheeks. The thunder cracks and fat drops of rain begin to fall. I feel them hit into to me and wish they would just come harder and harder until they carry me away.

Then I feel something on my shoulder and freeze. The man has come to kill me. I turn my head to the side so my eyes can just look out. There is a cold hand on me. I lift my head and stare at it. It is small...

I stare up into the brown eyes of a young girl. Aiee, I know these eyes, this face. The sky and ground start to spin around my head. The girl lifts her plastic hand and touches my cheek.

"Thandi...is it you?" I whisper.

Chapter 40

All my dreams of finding Thandi are running through my head as we bump our way back to the camp in the F20. She sits squashed between Tula and me and turns to look up at me with big eyes. I touch her shoulder to make sure she's really there and that I'm not dreaming. My stomach jumps as she puts her plastic hand on my leg. I feel its coldness and shiver. I turn my eyes away from it and look out of the window. The yellow grass blurs in front of my eyes. I tense my muscles, turn back to Thandi and give her a smile.

"God is good," whispers Thandi.

A sob catches in my throat as I reply, "Yes, he is."

"Dr. Jabula's phoned back to tell them the great news," says Tula.

"We'll have a big party for you, Thandi," says Bengu, leaning across and giving Thandi a smile. He looks at me with serious eyes like he can read the pot of happiness and sadness in my heart. God has answered my prayers but he has also punished me. I should've known I would pay more for my evil but I never thought Thandi could lose her hands.

I look sideways at her. Her eyes look old like she's seen too many bad things. Horrors run through my mind. Maybe they beat her on the dump? Maybe the L.R.A. took her and made her like the Pineapple girls? Maybe she walked into the bush to look for me and then found the village where they took her hands? I've failed her. I let them catch me and now she has lost her hands. I shake my head. I must not let these thoughts live – they will make me sick.

"This is where I'm staying," I whisper as we pull up to the wire gates.

"I feel like I'm in the good dream," says Thandi.

"Me too," I say, and then jump out to open the gates for

Bengu.

I climb back in and we drive to the dining hall where Mama Zuma comes running out with Dr. Zuma close behind.

"What wonderful news," she shouts pulling open the door. "I'm Mama Zuma, little one. Come let me give you a big hug."

I jump out and lift Thandi out. Mama Zuma puts her arms around her like the big mama lion and squeezes her tight. Her hug makes Thandi sob. Mama Zuma holds her close and whispers, "It's okay. You're safe now. You're safe and back with your brother. He's prayed hard to find you and we're very lucky. God has brought you back. It's going to be okay."

Her words warm my heart. I feel Dr. Zuma's hand on my shoulder. He gives me a squeeze and I look up him. He looks at Thandi's hands and then looks deep in my eyes and gives a small nod. I nod back but my eyes blur with the tears. It is not the end I have prayed for. This is not how it should be.

"Right, time for a party," says Dr. Zuma. "Welcome, Thandi, we're so happy to have found you."

Mama Zuma pulls back from Thandi and Dr. Zuma goes over to give her a hug. Mama Zuma takes my arm and we go into the dining hut.

"We'll eat now and make a big fire we can sit around later and perhaps sing some songs. I don't think we want to press Thandi about what's happened since you disappeared. She's had a lot to take in today. Is that okay?"

"Yes," I say. My shoulders relax. I don't want to hear about how she lost her hands tonight. I don't want to hear it ever.

That night Dr. Zuma cooks spicy sausages on the fire and we eat them with put and tomato onion gravy. I watch Thandi closely. She is quiet but eats all the food, lifting it with her plastic hands. Above us the dark sky is filled with millions of fat stars. I look up and imagine that Umama is looking down on us, happy that we are together again. Thandi looks up from her eating and we meet eyes. I smile at her and she smiles back. She doesn't look like the Thandi I remember on the dump. Her spirit has grown old. Guilt gnaws at my bones.

I see Dr. Zuma staring at me. He gives me a wink and turns to Thandi. "You okay there, Thandi?"

Thandi looks up from her eating and nods.

"Where were you staying before the hospital?" says Richard through a big mouthful of sausage, and I flinch inside. We were not going to ask her anything tonight. I frown at him to try and shut him up, but Thandi answers, "In Koboga region; with Auntie Goko."

Richard turns to me, "Is she your aunt?"

I glare at him and shake my head.

Thandi shrugs and says in a small voice, "She was a lady who found me in the city when the soldiers took Modetse." She looks up at me. "I was crying and crying for you and the people were shouting at me, but then she comes and helps me. She came from the farm in Koboga so we went back there."

"That was good," I say. "I wish I could say thank you to her. I worried too much that you were alone on the dump."

"I was lucky. Auntie Goko found me the same day. She knew that the devil soldiers came to catch the boys in the city. She helped many of them. My heart cried that she did not find us sooner. Then maybe they would not have caught you."

"Ay, maybe," I say as I stare at the fire with its strong flames. Inside my heart cries but it is no good. I cannot go back to that day. "At least she found you, Thandi. It is too bad I can't say thank you to her."

"The devil soldiers killed her after they cut my hands," says Thandi. Her face grows tight and her voice breaks as she says these words. I see hate in her eyes.

"I'm sorry," I whisper, and I swallow back the bitterness that has come into my throat. I push my food away and wish the flames could burn the guilt from my soul.

"Let's sing a song," says Tula in a loud voice.

"Good idea," says Dr. Zuma. "I don't think Thandi wants anymore questions tonight, Richard. Go get your guitar, Bengu."

Bengu nods and jumps up to go to the hut.

"You like singing, Thandi?" says Tula as the air around us becomes thick with silence.

Thandi nods and looks down at her food. As soon as Bengu's back we start singing "Shine Jesus shine" and I say a silent thanks to see Thandi begin to smile again.

"Thandi, can sleep in your dorm tonight, Modetse. Richard and Trigger are going to sleep in the new quarters aren't you boys," says Dr. Zuma.

"Yes. We've moved some things already," says Trigger giving me a smile.

"You are lucky to find each other," says Richard.

"Yes, we are very lucky," I say as Thandi and me look at each other.

Dr. Zuma takes me to one side by the fire before we go back to the hut.

"Dr. Jabula phoned me as soon as you left," he says. "He told me that Auntie Goko was well known as a person who tried to help kids hurt by the L.R.A. Thandi was well looked after until the soldiers came. But then she saw terrible horror, just like you, Modetse. Give her time. Pray for her. She will eventually heal and so will you."

He looked deep into my eyes and I nodded. I know that what he is saying is true and I am happy for Aunty Goko; but it does not take away the pain of her plastic hands. I will have to pray hard to God to do that.

The next day I wake early, lie in the half-light and stare up at the thatch ceiling. I must talk to Thandi today and tell her the truth of how I also cut off the hands of people. She must know a bit already from the shouting man. I cannot live a lie with her. She is my sister. I will need to take whatever comes from her. I close my eyes and pray, "Please, Jesus, help me tell her the right way. I don't know what to say."

I turn and look at Thandi. Her breathing is deep with a good rhythm. My mind calms. She would not breathe like that if she was paining too much inside. I look at her for a long time until the sky turns pink and the roosters wake.

"Modetse," whispers Thandi.

"I'm here," I say. "It's okay. It's still early, Thandi. You can sleep longer."

She mumbles, closes her eyes and falls back into sleep.

We get up when the sun is fully awake. I help Thandi put on her plastic hands with a firm face. I push the plastic with its foam inside over her stumps and then tie the leather straps tight. Inside I feel sick. She is quiet while I do it and the air in the hut grows hot. I don't know what thoughts are going through her head.

I put my arm around her shoulders as we walk to the dining hut. Mama Zuma's inside already and has the table laid for us with a red and white tablecloth.

"You must show Thandi the mission today, Modetse," says Mama Zuma as we sit down. "We'll leave school for today I think so you can show Thandi around but perhaps you'd like to do some crafts with her later. Richard and Trigger are there already."

"Would you like that, Thandi? We could maybe make the clay pots?"

Thandi nods but my stomach drops. Can she make pots with those hands? I stare at them and then jerk away as Mama Zuma gives us two bowls of steaming maize porridge with yellow butter. We sit silently and eat.

"Good morning, you two," says Tula as she comes into the hut. "You sleep okay, Thandi?"

"Yes," says Thandi, and gives Tula a small smile.

Modetse's going to show Thandi around and do some pot making later," says Mama Zuma.

"Good idea," says Tula giving me a smile, which does not match her worried eyes. "You've got a lot of catching up to do."

"Take it slowly," says Mama Zuma. "You've got a lifetime to catch up."

I nod. Everyone is sounding so strange. We are all trying hard to sound like everything is okay, but Tula and Mama Zuma must know that deep inside I'm scared. Will Thandi want to go back to Dr Jabula when she learns the truth of me as a devil soldier? Will she hate me? I breathe deep and keep my face firm.

"Come, Thandi, I will show you the forest and then well go to the river."

"Yes, it's too hot today. The river will be nice for you," says Mama Zuma.

"You want more porridge, Thandi?"

Thandi shakes her head and then gets up to take her bowl to the sink.

"It's okay. Tula will wash up says Mama Zuma.

Tula pulls a face, but Mama Zuma frowns at her.

"Let's go then," I say, putting my arm around Thandi's shoulders. We walk in silence towards the forest. "It is like the big green cave," I say with a smile as we push the palm fronds aside and go deep inside it. The air is rich and sweet. "Look there's wild honeysuckle Thandi. You can eat if you want."

"It is pretty," says Thandi, bending down and trying to pick the orange flower with her plastic hand. I quickly kneel down and pick three for her. "Here taste," I say.

She puts out her pink tongue and then chews on it. "It's sweet," she says. "Like the sugar."

"It is sugar for the bees," I say, and laugh. "Come I will take you to the river now. Maybe we can paddle our feet."

"Okay," says Thandi. She lets me guide her from the forest and soon we hear the sound of the water and smell its foaming water. I put my arm around Thandi as she walks next to me. I cannot bring myself to hold that cold hand. The sun is even hotter now but a cool breeze has come which dries the sweat on my arms.

Soon our feet touch the soft river sand. "The river's full today from the rain," I say as we come near the coffee-brown rushing water. "It's too dangerous to swim today but we can sit here and watch if you want?"

"It makes me think of the river in Kampala," says Thandi.

I nod. "Yes it's got that nice water smell but at least no stinky fish or rubbish like Kampala."

She goes quiet and stares out across the brown moving water at the hills like the camel humps in the distance.

I stare out with her at them. "Please, God; help me to talk to her. Please don't let her hate me when she learns that I cut hands off," I pray in my head.

We sit with only the river sound around us, but then Thandi turns and looks at me with slit eyes. "Did they treat you bad?" she says. "Were they like the jackal thief?"

I swallow and give a nod. "They were bad men. They stole my mind like the jackal stole the butter."

"Did they make you bad?"

"Yes," I mumble, drawing my knees up in front of me and hugging them with my arms. I look down and whisper, "I did many bad things. I've had to ask God to forgive me my past."

Thandi says nothing and my heart jumps.

"I'm sorry, Thandi," I whisper. "I'm so sorry. I've told God I'm sorry."

Thandi shrugs and the air grows thick between us. Then she asks in a small voice, "Did you take the hands of people? Was that why the man was shouting at you?"

I drop my head down on my knees.

When I look up she is staring hard at me and biting her lip.

"Auntie Goko was like Mama Zuma," she says after a while. "I would lie often with her fat body and she would look after me and tell me God will help us. The soldiers cut off her hands and then she died."

Ants gnaw at my stomach. "I didn't know, Thandi. I'm so sorry."

"We were just getting the sticks for the fire – then the devil soldiers come from the bush. One runs after us while we're getting the sticks and…" Her voice breaks and the tears fall from her eyes.

Shame like an elephant sits on me and I can't talk. I can't read what she thinks in her eyes. Is she thinking I too am a devil? Does she hate me?

"I see that soldier in my dreams," whispers Thandi. "Always he comes with his big head and his machete. He grabs my legs and pulls me down and then chops and chops, and the blood it runs from my heart and from Auntie Goko. Then the hospital people came to help at the village. They stopped the blood from my arms but Auntie Goko's spirit was already gone. They told me I was very lucky."

She wipes the tears from her cheeks with the top of her arm.

"I'm sorry, Thandi. It was very lucky that they found you. I thank God for that, Thandi. I do." I try and shut out the pictures of broken hands which jump in front of my eyes.

"Why did the soldiers cut the hands, Modetse? Why?"

Her eyes are fierce now and I turn away.

"I am sorry, Thandi. The L.R.A. told us the government soldiers were evil. They were the enemy pigs who were killing our family. They showed us many pictures with the government killing the people. I saw them killing the girls like you, Thandi. They said the villagers must lose their hands because they were helping the government. I did not think they were your friends. I did not know of people like Auntie Goko."

Thandi looks at me in silence.

"They killed my friend David. They shot him from the helicopter until his blood sprayed all over the camp. He was a good one, Thandi. He was my friend and they killed him. The government soldiers they killed many boys that day. They also did bad things, Thandi."

Thandi turns away and looks down at the sand. She makes circles in the soft sand with her plastic fingers as I try and defend myself but she says nothing. The silence grows heavy between us. I bite my bottom lip. She is too young and has seen too much. She will not be able to understand my side.

"What village did you stay at?" I ask through the heavy silence.

"Nigiri," says Thandi, and draws more circles.

The name echoes in my head. I've heard that name before…Nigiri. Where is Nigiri village? Then I hear again Mobuto's voice. He was sending me to Nigiri…is this the same one? I stiffen and stare hard at Thandi.

"Was it Nigiri village in Koboga region?" I say, and my voice breaks.

Thandi keeps drawing her circles and nods.

The air closes in on me. It is the same Nigiri…please let the time not be right. I frown and try and count back in my head…how many months have I been with Dr. Zuma…when was Nigiri…how long before the attack did we go there…how long? I stare at Thandi's hands as I try and count the months.

"Have you had the plastic hands long Thandi?" I say, and my voice breaks.

Thandi shrugs and mumbles, "I think it is maybe eight months. I don't know. It's not so long. My stumps they can still hurt." Her mouth grows tight and she draws harder in the sand with the stick.

My head is spinning and bitterness has risen into my mouth. The fat woman…the sticks…the soldier with a big head…the words run through my head like a witchdoctor's curse and the pictures come to life. I see the fat woman coming out the hut with the young girl behind her…them bending over getting the sticks…me giving orders…

I retch and scream inside my mind, "Aiee, please, God, no...
Please let it not be true," but Thandi's words ringing in my head
tell me it is. I see Shithead...he is running fast after the girl...I am
shouting at him to do it...he is grabbing her legs...his machete is
coming down...cutting deep into her hands...they are jumping
off...her blood is running into the red ground..." Oh God...help
me, Jesus," I groan and hold my head in my hands. What have I
done? Thandi is right. We were devils with no good in us. I feel
her eyes staring into me and I look up with fear eyes.

"Do you know Nigiri?" she asks with narrow eyes.

I swallow and say nothing but she keeps staring at me. My
heart is a drum in my ears and my breath grows loud.

"What's wrong, Modetse? Tell me. What's wrong?"

Her face is cross and she is still staring hard at me. I look
away and keep my head down. "I'm sorry, Thandi. Yes, I know
Nigiri."

"Did you know the soldiers?"

I nod.

"Did you go with them?" says Thandi. Her voice is angry and
I feel her eyes fierce on me. "Tell me, Modetse."

I lift my head and look at her but I cannot speak.

"Tell me," demands Thandi.

"They were my soldiers," I whisper. "I'm sorry, Thandi. I'm
sorry."

Thandi's head jerks back like she has been slapped. Her eyes
grow wide and fierce. Her mouth drops. She sits stuck looking
deep at me with those hate eyes. The air around me grows thick.
This is the end. She can never have me for a brother again. Now
she looks deep into my spirit and sees the evil that was there.
Every time she looks at her dead hands she will hate me. She will
see me for the robber who has taken from her the gift of work.

"I'm sorry, Thandi. Please go inside. Go and see Mama Zuma
and Tula. They will help you. Dr. Zuma will see that you go to
the school and are all right. I'm sorry, Thandi. Please go. Go now.

I must be alone. Stay well with God, Thandi. Stay well."

Thandi does not move. She looks like a nyala frozen in the lights. Her mouth is closed now but in her eyes I see great pain questions. Then she pushes herself up and runs back up to the huts.

I sit still like the stone. I am finished. I have lost her again. She will never want me now. It will be better for her if I am dead. She will not want to look at me and remember her pain. I was a fool to think that I would not pay for my evil. I must die to pay for it. Yes, I must die so she can mourn her brother and move on. That way she will cry for a brother she has lost and time will heal her hurt. She will not have to live with one she hates.

I get up before the fear can stop me and run back down to the river. I will take stones from the side and drown myself in its strong water. I will dive down with my stones and stay under until the breath is gone from my lungs. There is no other way to help her.

I reach the edge of the riverbank and look around with fierce eyes for stones. I need big stones: hard and sharp and grey. The stones here are small and smooth. I turn back to the forest and push away the leaves and monkey vines until I find some jagged pieces of granite by a small rock face. Some of the middle stones are a little loose. I dig away, panting until the way is clear to lift one of them. My knees bend as I stagger with it back to the river. I take off my shirt and tear it in two with my teeth. I tie the broken pieces together to make a rope and then loop it tight around the granite leaving some free that I will tie around my arm so the stone can drag me down under the water. The river is deep and fast flowing. It should take me quickly.

I test the loop around the stone. It's holding well. I put it down and make another loop and pull it tight around my wrist. I pick up the stone and walk like a slow frog to the rushing water. Its coldness closes over my feet and I shudder. It will not be long now. I will be gone and then Thandi will learn to live again.

Mama Zuma will help her. She is wise. She will know what to do. I walk deeper into the brown water and feel it hard tug at my legs. It wants to pull me in. I stop and check that the loop around the rock is still tight. I must not let the strong water push it away. The cloth bites hard into the sharp edges. Good, it should hold but even if it comes off I will hold hard to the stone until it drags me down. I go deeper into the water. The soft mud sucks at my feet like the big fish. The water climbs up to my waist and holds me tight. I sway against the strong pull of the river. Two more steps and it will take me. I close my eyes and pull my foot from the sucking mud as the stone burns heavy in my arms. My ears fill with the roar of the rushing water. "Forgive me, Thandi," I whisper to the empty sky.

"No, Modetse, please, no."

Her cry breaks through the water noise. I stop and open my eyes. The river rushes around me with strong brown waves and I try and turn and look back up the bank but the current tugs hard at my legs. Then I see Thandi. She is running with big steps over the wet sand towards me. I try and pull my foot from the mud and stagger sideways against the strong brown water.

"Modetse, wait," she shouts. Her arms and their plastic hands are stretched out in front. I stare with my open mouth as she splashes into the brown water. It goes quick by her waist as she comes for me. The strong current begins to pull her downstream. She falls to the side and nearly goes under the water.

"Modetse..." she calls as the fierce water bubbles around her head.

I tear at the loop around my arm with fierce teeth as the water rushes around me. What have I done? Thandi is going to drown in this river. She cannot swim. I scream through my teeth and then I hear the cloth rip. I drop the heavy stone and splash with fierce arms through the thundering water towards her. The water is nearly covering her now. She is standing with her head back on the top of the water and her plastic arms reached out to the sky.

Her eyes are filled with great fear.

"Help me, Modetse...help me!"

"I am coming, Thandi. It's okay. I am coming," I shout as I fight the water with mad arms and legs towards her. Now her head is going under. Aiee, the river will take her. No...please Jesus, no... I dive forward and feel my hands touch the top of her arm. I push her up so that her head comes out of the water. She opens her mouth and eats from the air like a fish. I grab her around the waist with my other arm and pull her towards me. She drinks more air and coughs. I hold her tight and she clings to me with her plastic hands.

"Thandi, why did you come in this water? You should not have done that. I'm so sorry, Thandi. I'm so sorry."

"You must not leave me again," sobs Thandi as the river rushes hard around us.

"We must get out before the river pulls us under, Thandi. Don't worry. I will hold you tight. I will never let you go."

I put both my arms hard around her and push against the strong river so she is in front of me. I pull each foot forward from the soft sucking mud and push against the fighting river with a grunt. The current still pulls at us like a crocodile, wanting to draw us down, down, deeper until we are no more but I will not let it. I grit my teeth and move through the sucking mud, keeping Thandi tight in front. If I can just take a few more steps we will be safe; if I can just get us to the shallow water. I narrow my eyes and clench my teeth as I pull my foot forward again and stagger. Thandi whimpers.

"It's okay, Thandi. It's okay. I've got you."

I lean forward and fight against the river as I take another step and then another. The mud lets me go and I give one final push against the fierce current.

"Put down your feet, Thandi. It is not so deep now."

Thandi obeys and pushes her feet into the soft river mud. She pushes through the water towards the bank. Soon we are in the shallow edges. I put my hand on her back and help her out onto the muddy bank as the river rushes on behind us. We sit panting in the soft sand with sore chests. Thandi drops her head on my shoulder. I feel the cold plastic of her hands against my flesh as she puts her arms around me and shiver.

I put my arms tight around her. She shudders, smiles, and closes her eyes. I look down at the top of her head and rest my chin on it. Thanks to God that she still wants me more than hate. I must go forward and be her hands. I look out at the camel hills. They are like the hills of my life. I was fallen in the dark valley but now I am coming out on the mountain. I am a lucky one. I have survived. *Mungu ni pamoja na mimi.* God is with me!

**LODESTONE
BOOKS**

Lodestone Books is a new imprint, which offers a broad spectrum of subjects in YA/NA literature. Compelling reading, the Teen/Young/New Adult reader is sure to find something edgy, enticing and innovative. From dystopian societies, through a whole range of fantasy, horror, science fiction and paranormal fiction, all the way to the other end of the sphere, historical drama, steam-punk adventure, and everything in between. You'll find stories of crime, coming of age and contemporary romance. Whatever your preference you will discover it here.